PROLOGUE

'Rose, I have your wife and son.'

The words keep playing through my head while one of the most powerful men in the country continues to talk at me. I'm not listening to him any more.

Who is this person speaking to me in my earpiece? Is this a sick joke? It can't be, can it?

We're live on telly. Millions of people are watching. My heart feels like it's going to explode.

The voice speaks calmly and slowly again in my ear.

'Rose, if you want Rory and Kate to come home, you are going to have to do as I say. Nod if you understand.'

Whoever this is, he has Rory and Kate. I can't deal with this. I need to leave. I need to get to my family right now.

But I can't, can I? The voice said to do as he says.

I feel a scream build inside of me. I can't let it out.

I need to stay calm. I can't stay calm.

He has my son.

I have no choice.

I slowly nod my head.

And then the voice speaks again.

'Rose, I am in control now.'

DEAD LINE

Steph McGovern

DEAD LINE

MACMILLAN

First published 2025 by Macmillan
an imprint of Pan Macmillan
The Smithson, 6 Briset Street, London EC1M 5NR
EU representative: Macmillan Publishers Ireland Ltd, 1st Floor,
The Liffey Trust Centre, 117–126 Sheriff Street Upper,
Dublin 1 D01 YC43
Associated companies throughout the world

ISBN 978-1-0350-3523-6 HB
ISBN 978-1-0350-3524-3 TPB

Copyright © Steph McGovern 2025

The right of Steph McGovern to be identified as the
author of this work has been asserted in accordance
with the Copyright, Designs and Patents Act 1988.

1 3 5 7 9 8 6 4 2

A CIP catalogue record for this book is available from the British Library.

Typeset by Palimpsest Book Production Ltd, Falkirk, Stirlingshire
Printed and bound by CPI Group (UK) Ltd, Croydon, CR0 4YY

Visit **www.panmacmillan.com** to read more about
all our books and to buy them.

For the McRocks of my life

PART ONE

ROSE

The day before the hijack

t's always a relief when it's a hairnet or hard-hat day. No faffing about. Quick wash of my pits and bits in the sink, throw on some brightly coloured clothes and off I go. I won't even bother brushing my hair. No one will see it.

I have five minutes before I need to leave. I glance out of the bedroom window and check that my driver Tom is there. I can see him shivering as he leans against the car door. He takes a slow drag on his cigarette. No matter what the weather, he never misses the chance to smoke before a long drive.

I creep downstairs, missing the second step from the top because it always creaks. Then I carefully pick up my phone, handbag, suitcase and keys. I have mastered the art of leaving the house with minimal noise. My wife Kate calls me the night ninja.

I say wife, but we're not married. We've actually only been together four years, but we've packed a lot in. Buying a house, having a baby. All the big stuff. I just knew when I met her she was the one and didn't see the point of wasting any time.

Kate has sacrificed a lot for me. Taking the gas off her high-flying science career to look after our son, Rory, while I disappear off around the country at all hours. She has a lot to put up with, not least the fact that she never knows when I'll be home or even when I'll call. My job is so bloody unpredictable. It's a nightmare for my family, but I haven't got time to worry about that this week. Not with what I've got coming up.

Tom opens the car door for me. I keep telling him not to bother with these daft formalities, but I think he quite enjoys it, even after all these years.

As I climb inside, the smell smacks me in the face. Not the smoke clinging to Tom's ill-fitting suit, which the taxi company make him wear – I don't mind that. It's the bloody air freshener. Even the slightest whiff of that car-shaped bit of cardboard doused in some overbearing citrus punch and I retch. Ever since my bout of pregnancy sickness there are certain smells that instantly make me gag.

Suppressing the urge to throw up, I put my seat belt on.

Tom always waits until we are both safely in the car with the doors closed before he speaks. No matter how quietly we think we're whispering, we've learned the hard way that my neighbours do not appreciate our 3 a.m. greetings in the street.

'Morning, love, how are we?'

Tom's gruff Manchester accent is a welcome start to the day.

He's been my regular driver for six years. Picking me up in the middle of the night to whisk me off to my broadcast locations and always having to listen to the dramas of my life unfold in the back of his car.

Tom's blacked-out Audi is my safe space. The hours I spend travelling in it are some of my most intimate.

And he sees it all. The adrenaline rush I get from broadcasting, the grumpy exhaustion I feel from travel. The rows I have on the phone with my producer, the bollockings I get from my boss. The baby voice I put on when I video-call my son and then the laughs, and tears, I share with my partner over something cute he has done that I have missed.

Tom sees first-hand the emotional highs and lows of my job.

Thank God he's not a blabber. He never has been and I'm pretty sure he never will be.

It's a funny old relationship. We're not mates as such, because we only ever really spend time together in the car – in fact, I can tell you more about the back of his head than the front.

But I trust him. And that is rare for me, especially these days.

No one tells you, when you do a job like mine, that you can't have a normal life. Since choosing to barge my way into the homes of millions of people every morning – because that is basically what happens when you join the biggest news show in the country – everything has changed.

But the adrenaline that comes with this job is so addictive. I can't give that up. Especially not now, when I have one of the biggest broadcast interviews of my career coming up.

I need to make sure I am at the top of my game.

Tom and I are on our way to Alfreton in Derbyshire, roughly a two-hour journey through the Peak District. Not the easiest drive, but nevertheless, I am grateful to have stayed at home last night and not in some crappy hotel.

The last time I went to Alfreton I'd been reporting from a farm. It was there I discovered that pigs quite like northern lasses' pasty legs. One bit me live on air. It was one of those moments, quite early on in my career, when I wasn't entirely sure what to do. *I can't kick a pig on national TV*, I thought, as I hopped about with this animal clamped to my leg.

Its teeth had broken through my welly and into my skin. The farmer tried to reassure me that the pigs were just curious and didn't mean any harm, but I knew what this was really about: the pig's revenge for all the bacon sandwiches I'd eaten.

Along with a few bruises on my leg, I'd also ended up as a

viral sensation that day. Some smartarse had speeded up the footage of me being chased by the pigs, added the Benny Hill theme music and then put it on YouTube, where it has since had 1.2 million views.

Tom laughs when I remind him.

There is nothing exceptional about this morning's drive. After a bit of a chat, I try to get my head down for an hour. Tom always keeps a spare pillow in the car, though I don't like to think about all the other people who have dribbled on it, like I am about to do now.

The gentle motion of the car on the motorway and the low hum of its hybrid engine quickly puts me to sleep. I work such crazy hours that I have to get naps in whenever and wherever I can. I reckon I could actually nod off standing up if I needed to.

About an hour away from our destination I wake up and see a missed call from my cameraman Jonesy. I can't be bothered to listen to the voicemail he's left; it won't be anything important, plus we'll have plenty of time to catch up when I get to the broadcast location.

I put my make-up on instead.

I am a pro at doing a full face on the move, whether it's in the back of a car, like today, or on a bumpy train journey. So far I've managed not to blind myself with my eyeliner, despite those around me anxiously expecting it every time there's a swerve or jerk.

It's 5 a.m. when we arrive, pulling up to a makeshift gate with a small cabin next to it. Neither looks very secure against the wind that's howling around now.

Inside the cabin I can see a fella with a high-vis jacket on. Without so much as a nod, he lifts the railings and we drive in.

'He's cheerful,' says Tom sarcastically, but we're used to it. We're on a building site on a chilly morning in late October. I'm pretty sure we'd all much rather be in bed.

Sixty minutes until I'm live on air. Time to get a wriggle on.

I leave Tom to park up and have his arrival ciggie. He normally sleeps in the car until I'm done, unless of course we're at a food factory, in which case he'll hang around like a yappy seagull waiting for some freebies to be thrown his way.

It doesn't look like there's going to be any free scran this morning, though. Thankfully, I've packed a bag of Wotsits and a can of Coke Zero to keep me going.

Life on the road is far from healthy.

I use the torch on my phone to help me find the broadcast truck. It's normally easy to spot because of the huge satellite dish on its roof, although I got caught out by that once at Grimsby fish market when I approached what I thought was a sat truck and it turned out to be a motor home with a massive Sky dish on top. Inside, they were running a knocking shop for all the local sailors coming in and out of the docks. You can imagine the reception I got at 5 a.m. when I turned up looking for 'my crew' with a full face of TV make-up.

I'm not expecting to be mistaken for a prostitute today, but you never know. It happens quite a lot.

I locate the truck and see the satellite slowly moving. They obviously haven't found a signal yet. The wind won't be helping.

In the old days, when the network had money, we would recce each site ahead of time. There's no chance of that now, not with all the budget cuts we've had over the years. We just turn up an hour before the broadcast and hope for the best. And that means everything is touch and go when we're trying to get on air.

We've got skeleton staff these days too. Just the four of us on location: the camera operator, the broadcast engineer, the producer and me.

'Here she is. Morning, treacle!' Jonesy shouts as I approach the truck.

'Ah, look, it's my favourite – sorry, I mean least favourite – cameraman,' I say with a grin.

'You never answer your friggin' phone.'

'Not to you, Jonesy, no.'

I bloody love working with Jonesy. He's a brilliant cameraman, and he gets me. We work hard, but we have a giggle too. And a sense of humour is crucial in this job. Although Jonesy doesn't know when to stop, which can be a bit of a nightmare at times. Especially when he overdoes the innuendo.

I'll never forget when we went to interview a woman at her house for a story about interest rates and in the middle of her living room she had a large ornate trunk. Jonesy must have cracked about ten inappropriate chest gags before we left.

'Haven't you heard of the MeToo movement, bellend?' I said as we got back in the van to leave.

'Ah, I was only having a laugh, she didn't mind,' Jonesy had replied in a sulk.

'That's not the point,' I countered. 'One day you're going to end up in a load of shit because of one of your dodgy gags – which are about thirty years out of date, by the way.'

Anyway, that was a while ago now, and I noticed the other day that he'd managed to stop himself from making a very predictable joke when one of the new producers had asked for his number for the call sheet. Maybe he is learning. Plus Jonesy isn't a sex pest, unlike some of the blokes I work with. He's just a shit comedian.

I pop my head into the truck and see our engineer, Sandy, looking frantic. That's not unusual when you're struggling to get a satellite signal and have less than an hour to go before you're broadcasting live to the nation.

To me it looks like she is just randomly pressing buttons, but Sandy is one of the best in the business, so I'm not worried. I try not to interrupt her. The tech team don't appreciate it when a presenter rocks up asking annoying questions about stuff they don't understand.

The team behind the scenes are the real stars of the broadcast operation, working in all conditions, often with out-of-date or broken kit, and under incredible time pressures. And yet somehow they always seem to make it happen. They're the magicians of the TV world.

Everyone thinks telly is dead glam, but news broadcasting really isn't. Yes, of course we get to cover amazing stories, visit fascinating locations and meet some incredible people, but we do all that on a tiny budget.

And we love to moan about it.

'Hello, it's Rose, isn't it?' I hear a voice say behind me.

I turn to see two men standing in hard hats, high-vis jackets and safety goggles. One of them is holding a clipboard and a pen.

With them is my producer, Zoya, also kitted out in full PPE.

'I'm Bob, the national site manager, and this is Alan, our health and safety director,' says the shorter one of the two, who looks like he can't be far off retirement.

I meet blokes like Bob and Alan all the time in my job as a roving reporter. Every company seems to have them. One is usually an overzealous safety officer and the other some type of boss. The problem is, after over a decade in this job, they've all morphed into one in my head.

I am ashamed to say this, but I'm unlikely to remember their faces once I leave here today. However, in this moment, they are the most important people in my life. They are the difference between this being a brilliant broadcast and a shit one.

There is also a chance I might have met them before, so I greet them in the same way I greet everyone these days.

'Ah, it's so lovely to see you both, what a fabulous site you have here. It's so kind of you to let us in to broadcast. I know you'll both have been working hard to make it all possible, so thank you. And thanks again for getting up so early too,' I say, mustering up as much energy as is humanly possible for five in the morning.

Their wide smiles suggest my love-bombing has worked.

'Dan on security didn't give you any problems getting in, did he?' the taller man – Alan, I think he is called – asks.

'The bloke on the gate? Ah, no, he let us straight through.'

'Ah, right, after he checked your ID, I'm assuming?'

'Erm . . .' I try to buy myself a smidge of time. I have no idea what to say. It sounds like the security checks should have been tighter, but I don't want the hassle of having to do them now.

Fortunately Bob interrupts before I say anything else.

'He's a good lad is Dan, a grafter, but he's had a really tough time. We're all trying to keep an eye on him and, you know, support him through it, like.'

'Aw right, the poor fella.' I have no idea what else to say to what feels like a bit of an overshare on Bob's part. But it looks like we've got out of doing any more security stuff, which is a relief.

'Right, time for the safety briefing then. Take it away, Alan.' Bob's tone makes it sound as though this is the most important thing he has ever said.

I listen to the briefing and nod enthusiastically. I've heard these safety talks at nearly every business I've ever been to. *Wear your safety gear at all times. Don't look at your phone while you're walking. Hold the handrail when going up and down stairs. Always report any incidents you have, no matter how minor you think they are, even a paper cut.* Blah blah blah.

I know they're important, but my God they're dull. Plus they take bloody ages.

Thirty minutes now until I'm live on air.

After the briefing, I put my safety gear on as I talk to my

producer, Zoya. She has spoken to the team back at base to find out when I'm on air and how long I'll have for each segment I'm doing across the three-hour show. We call the segments 'hits'. I usually get six hits on every show, not including the headlines.

We don't have long to talk. My MO is to get on air for the first headline and then worry about what's happening on the rest of the show after that.

Today is a big one in the news calendar: Budget Day. The chancellor will be announcing the government's fiscal plans in Parliament at lunchtime. In other words, what they'll be spending money on and how much they'll tax us for stuff.

It's a dry topic so I'm trying to liven it up by being out on location. I know from the government leaks that there's going to be more money for construction, so it seemed like an obvious choice. Not least because the viewers love it when I'm in a hard hat and high-vis. So much so that someone set up a 'Rose in safety gear' fetish website, which was basically a load of photos of me in PPE at various businesses. It was an interesting one to explain to my mam after her friend told her about it.

So, the more safety gear I have on, the happier the audience.

Jonesy, however, hates it.

JONESY

3 a.m.

The day before the hijack

'Oh, it's an effing hard-hat day. Bollocks – loads of faffing about,' Jonesy mutters to himself as he heads down-stairs.

His call sheet for the morning has just arrived, giving him all the details of his job today:

STORY: Pre-Budget OB analysis at a construction site
LOCATION: Unit 7–15, King Street, DE55 7AG
CORRESPONDENT: Rose Steedman
CREW: Engineer: Sandy Wearn, Producer: Zoya Aflani,
    Camera Operator: Liam Jones
RISK ASSESMENT: Attached – completed by Pete F.

He isn't really complaining. It's a job, and ever since he went freelance he's been grateful for any scraps of work thrown his way.

As he reaches the bottom of the stairs, his dog Murphy appears, holding his lead in his mouth.

'We're off to Derbyshire, Murph,' Jonesy whispers. 'We haven't got time for a walk, but I'm taking you with me. It's Rose today. We love her, don't we, Murph?'

Jonesy doesn't like leaving Murphy alone in the house all day, so he takes him to work when he can. Plus he enjoys the company.

They get in the van and head off. The satnav is saying roughly two hours from Jonesy's house in North Wales. He treats it like a personal challenge to beat the estimated arrival time.

When Jonesy hits the motorway, he calls Rose for a natter. It goes to voicemail, as usual, so he switches on the radio and puts his foot down.

He gives a little whoop when he parks up next to the broadcast truck at 4.50 a.m.

'That's gotta be a record, that, Murph. And with a wee stop. Nice one.'

He gets his kit out of the van and gives his dog a quick pat on the head.

'Right, Murph, I'll be back for you just after seven.'

With a camera over one shoulder and a tripod on the other, he heads to the truck.

As he approaches, the door bursts open and Sandy appears.

Jonesy is delighted to see her.

'We're on a double bubble this week, me and you,' Jonesy announces to Sandy, who looks unimpressed and doesn't answer.

'Bit early for you, treacle?' Jonesy jokes.

'Some bastard has broken into the truck again!' she cries, pulling open the back door and nearly hitting Jonesy in the face with it.

'Oh, you're kidding – what have they nicked this time?'

'A load of microphones and our talkback packs. Oh, and the bloody Jaffa Cakes.'

'The Jaffa Cakes – shit, man.'

They're used to the kit being nicked. The satellite on top of the truck is a dead giveaway to the fact that there will be expensive gear inside, so it's always getting broken into when it's parked up overnight.

It hits the team particularly hard when the thieves take the snacks too.

Jonesy has worked with Sandy for a long time; in fact, he was the first person to hug her when she found out her husband was shagging some lass from the golf club. Darren obviously didn't realize the hot-tub selfie he took with golf caddy Lauren on his new iPhone would automatically upload to the family iCloud account. The photo popped up on Sandy's phone just as she was showing Jonesy a picture of her daughter's new dogs. Of course, Jonesy cracked an inappropriate gag about which puppies he preferred and then offered to get 'Dickhead Darren's cock chopped off', as he put it.

That typical Jonesy reaction didn't stop Sandy feeling gut-wrenchingly sick, but it did prevent her from having a full-on meltdown in the middle of the Kit Kat factory where they were filming that day.

Still, Jonesy's early-morning enthusiasm is doing her head in right now and she needs to crack on.

They have about an hour to get the equipment sorted and the satellite connected and, with a load of kit missing, they're in for a tricky morning. That said, it's nothing new. These days they're lucky if the kit is working at all.

ROSE

The day before the hijack

Five minutes until I will be live on telly. I quickly check my phone. No word from Kate yet. A good sign, I think. Hopefully Rory slept through. I'm regretting not nipping in to give him a quick kiss before I left. Imagine if I'd woken him, though. That would have been a nightmare for Kate, especially now she's back at work full time.

'Right, we're all connected,' Jonesy says as he hands me the microphone I need to clip to my jacket.

I am standing in front of a half-built house. It's still pitch black, so Jonesy and Sandy have managed to light it up with a strategically placed torch, a house brick and my empty Coke can. Once my microphone is on, I need to sort out my talkback. It's the bit of equipment that connects me, in an audio sense, to the presenters in the studio and also to the team in the gallery, which is the control room of the TV show.

My talkback looks a bit like a walkie-talkie, but with a wire coming from it that is attached to my personalized earpiece. There are two knobs on it. One that controls the volume and the other that controls which radio frequency – or what we call channel – I need to be on.

'What channel today, Jonesy?' I ask while fiddling with my talkback box.

'Channel 5, chicken.'

I turn the knob on the top until it's on 5. I have no idea what the different channels do, I just know that I need to be on the one that connects me to my team.

I hear a crackle in my left ear, where my earpiece is, and then a voice booms into it.

'Rose, it's Jess here, directing. Three minutes until the headlines. You're after the missing penguins.'

That brief statement tells me everything I need to know about how newsworthy the programme team think my story is today. Not very. If I'm after a headline about penguins, I must be pretty low down the running order. Unless, of course, the president of the United States has something to do with the penguins going missing. Or the king, maybe. Now I'm thinking about all the potential iterations of why the missing penguins story might be much more important than I'm giving it credit for.

There's another crackle in my left ear.

Jess speaks again.

'You all right to come with us for a rehearsal?' she screeches, making me wince.

My talkback is far too loud.

'Yep, good to go,' I reply, turning down the volume of the audio coming into my earpiece.

There's no time for chit-chat when you're about to go live. As the director, Jess is the person in charge of the show from a technical point of view, making sure what's going out on air looks and sounds good. She does this with a team of tech experts behind the scenes, but ultimately the buck stops with her.

I am just one of many people Jess will be checking in with before the show starts.

Everything is right up to the wire.

We rehearse the top of the show in the final minutes before we go live. I've already planned what I'm going to say; now it's just a case of making sure I nail it on air.

The programme title music starts. I always get a buzz from hearing it. The adrenaline of being on live TV kicks in. Off we go. I'll be talking to the nation any second now, just need to wait for my cue.

'How long until we're on?' Jonesy asks while trying to fix his hard hat, which is sitting at a jaunty angle after being knocked out of place by the camera on his shoulder.

'Have you not got talkback?' I quickly ask, knowing the programme will be coming to me live any second now.

'Nope. Mine got nicked out of the van last night.'

This means Jonesy can't hear anything that's going on back at base; he can't even hear Sandy in the satellite truck. So he has to rely on me for all his prompts. This is not ideal. Still, it's not the first time; I'm used to this kind of carry-on.

'Ten, nine, eight . . .' comes the countdown from the second voice to pop into my ear. It's a softly spoken woman. I think it's Carol or maybe Belinda, they sound so alike. Whoever it is, I know from what she's saying that she is the one in the gallery in charge of timings for today's show – what's called a PA in TV land.

Jonesy is oblivious to what is being said to me and carries on talking.

'They nicked the fucking Jaffa Cakes too,' he shouts, which comes at the same time I hear the presenters in the studio finishing the headline about missing penguins, which is then interrupted by director Jess shouting.

'CUE ROSE.'

I am now talking live to the nation.

'Hello from this multimillion-pound building site in Derbyshire. Today we'll learn what's in the chancellor's red box. We're expecting a billion-pound boost for construction, so I'm here to find out what difference it could make.'

I carry on smiling after I've said everything I need to, just in case the camera is still live on us. I've been caught out by that before – thinking you're not on air any more when really you are. It's the stuff nightmares are made of.

'And we're off you.'

That's the confirmation I needed from the gallery to tell me it's safe to speak normally again.

'Back with you in twenty minutes, Rose, and you'll do a hand to the regions.' That's the third voice I've heard in my ear so far this morning. A bloke this time, possibly Sharif; it sounds like him. He must be today's person in the gallery in charge of connecting the outside broadcasts to the studio via the gallery.

You hear lots of different voices in your ear when you're on an outside broadcast. And the team back at base work three days on, three days off, so I'm never quite sure who'll be on shift. You often don't get to see them either; you just hear them through the earpiece.

People always ask me if I find it distracting, having all these voices in my ear, but I don't. I'd be more worried if I couldn't hear anything. The way I describe it, it's a bit like when you're in a restaurant and you're chatting to whoever you're with, but you're also half listening to the table next to you. If you tune yourself in, you can follow their conversation and the one you're having. I guess not everyone can do this, but I think years of being a nosy bugger mean that I'm pretty good at it. And now I'm paid to do it every morning.

Just before I take my earpiece out, I hear Sandy, who is talking to me from the truck. She wants me to tell Jonesy to turn his camera off. I keep forgetting he can't hear her.

'They're off us,' I explain to Jonesy, who is poised as if we're still live.

'Phew, that was close.' He breathes a sigh of relief as he puts down the camera.

'You're telling me, you muppet. You nearly announced to the nation that some fucker had nicked your Jaffa Cakes.'

'Ah, sorry, babe, it's a bugger not having talkback. Although, if McVitie's had heard us there'd have been a lifetime supply of Jaffas coming our way.'

He's right. Once on a live broadcast, some eagle-eyed marketing executive at a well-known bread manufacturer spotted a piece of toast peeking out of my pocket on the telly. Within an hour, they'd delivered a load of their baked goods to my team at the studio and, more impressively, turned up at my broadcast location with a giant, branded comedy toaster, which they parked right in the back of my shot for all to see.

That's the power of telly, I guess. What I do or say on it can have a huge impact. For good or for bad.

I can see Alan and Bob heading over to us. They're buzzing.

'We watched you on my phone! I can't believe it just happens like that,' Alan says in amazement. 'I thought there'd be loads of you and it'd be a big rig set-up.'

'Nope, not these days. There isn't the money,' I explain.

'So you just rock up, whack up a satellite and then next thing you're live to the nation. Wow!' says Bob, who is clearly a fan of our show. You can spot them a mile off. I can guarantee at some point he'll mention my height. They always do.

'Is there not even a time delay or anything?' asks Alan.

'Nah, people think that, but no, as soon as I say it, it goes out on the telly. So no swearing, Bob, when I'm interviewing you in a bit.'

We all laugh, although admittedly mine is a bit forced. That's the thing with this job; we're always cracking the same gags. I also get a lot of the same jokes said to me – my favourite being 'I wake up with you every morning, Rose'. Every time someone says it, I give the same hearty laugh as if it's the first time I've heard it.

'You're welcome to use the security hut if you need to. It's just Dan in there at the moment,' says Bob, gesturing to a dimly lit Portakabin.

Normally in between hits I'll look for different spots to broadcast from, to give the audience a bit of variety, but there's no point yet. It's still dark, the building work can't start until 8 a.m. and I'm freezing.

Zoya is outside the cabin in a small sheltered area that I assume is a designated smoking spot. She is stubbing out a cigarette with her foot while lighting another and also talking at speed on the phone.

The smell of menthol smoke wafting towards me makes me feel a bit nauseous, so I disappear inside the cabin.

There's not much to it; a little kitchen area in one corner then a few plastic tables and chairs scattered about the place.

There's a whiteboard on one of the walls with the words 'ON-SITE INCIDENTS' written at the top in capital letters. It's been underlined three times. I am sure the safety officer, Alan, prides himself on the fact that there's nothing listed beneath it yet.

I still haven't had a proper chance to speak to Zoya, but that's often the way. She'll be going through the running order with the team at base. It's a movable feast when you're on air.

Her job is a stressful one too. As well as keeping across the editorial content, she'll be organizing guest transport and working out what we need for social media. The boss of the programme is always after 'behind the scenes' videos that have the potential to go viral. That's one of the big things we're measured on these days. The 'reach' outside of the show is what they call it.

I'm a reluctant contributor to the programme's online world these days, though.

I have a tricky relationship with social media. I used to love it and was one of those prolific posters, detailing every aspect of my life for the world to see. Service station selfies, crew boomerangs, 'life on the road' reels and so on. I got a buzz from 'likes' and became one of the media's great oversharers.

That all changed when the details I was putting out there became life-threatening. Still, that was years ago and everything is calm on the social media front now. But I hate it.

I unplug my earpiece from my talkback unit so that we can all listen to the programme sound coming out through its built-in speaker. It's a bit like when you disconnect your AirPods from your phone and everyone can hear what you're playing.

The whole point of this talkback device is that it allows me to hear what's going out on the telly and it gives the team in the gallery a way to communicate with me while we're live on air too.

I wear the bulky unit clipped to the back of my jeans. Next to it is another box connected to my microphone. Sometimes I'll wear an extra mic pack as backup, but not today. My jeans are relieved. It's less work for them trying to hold everything up.

I settle down in one of the cold plastic chairs and scroll through my phone. I should probably be looking at work stuff, but I'm too distracted by cute videos of Rory. I can see so many of Kate's mannerisms in him now. It makes me feel all warm and fuzzy inside, though not quite enough to stop me shivering.

Alan is watching Zoya out of the window and tutting.

'She really needs to stay in the smoking area.'

I ignore him, but he continues.

'Why can't she just stand still?'

I get up and head over to the window. Zoya is pacing up and down, the wind blowing her about as she walks, talks and smokes. She's got her hood up, which she is wearing under her high-vis jacket. Aside from a bit of light from the cabin window, she's in darkness. It's hard to see her face until every so often the orange glow intensifies as she takes another drag.

Alan raps his knuckles on the window and furiously points at the smoking area. Zoya nods and takes a seat on the bench.

Jonesy has joined us by the window now, desperate not to miss anything.

'She's a bugger for the ciggies, isn't she? Like me when I was her age. Anyway, come and park yourself down here, Rose,' he says as he pulls out a chair and gestures for me to sit in it. I know what's coming.

For the next ten minutes, I stare aimlessly at Jonesy's phone as he shows me countless photos of his new girlfriend, including one of her topless, which he quickly swipes past and mutters something about art. We then move on to the latest pics of his grandkids. After five minutes of telling him I think they're all gorgeous, I try to move things on again.

'Where's Murphy?'

'The van. I'll let him out shortly.'

'Who or what is Murphy?' Alan asks.

'My dog,' Jonesy replies enthusiastically.

Alan storms out of the cabin. No doubt he'll be going to find an extra form that we'll now have to fill in.

I hope it doesn't cause us any stress. Jonesy's been told off before for bringing his dog on broadcasts. I don't want him getting us in trouble again.

'What kind of dog is he?' This time the question comes from the other corner of the room, where another PPE-clad bloke is sitting. I hadn't even noticed him until this point.

'He's a Springer–German Pointer cross. Are you a dog fan?' Jonesy says as he turns to answer.

'Yeah, we've got an Alsatian.'

'Ah, nice. Well, come and meet my Murphy in a bit, if you like.'

'Didn't your parents ever warn you about strangers and dogs?' Sandy interjects sarcastically.

The bloke in the corner doesn't react to the gag.

'It's my son's dog, really. I got him before . . .' His voice starts to drift off.

It dawns on me that this is the security guard who was meant to check our IDs on the way in. The bloke that Bob had been going on about. I wonder what happened to him. Something to do with his son, by the sounds of things. Whatever it is, the pain is etched deep on his face.

A shiver runs down my spine. I can't think of anything worse than something bad happening to my son.

'What's your dog's name?' Jonesy asks, interrupting my dark thoughts.

'Muffin, she's called.'

Jonesy, who obviously hasn't clocked the sensitivity of the situation, jumps straight in.

'Muffin the Alsatian? Jesus Christ, who came up with—'

'GALLERY TO ROSE.'

The voice of Sharif back at base bursts out of the talkback box, punctuating the programme sound we had been listening to and coincidentally saving us all from an inappropriate muff gag from Jonesy that must have been on its way.

'GALLERY TO ROSE! WE'VE LOST A GUEST!'

This is not unusual. The guest planned for this time slot probably hasn't turned up or the team are having problems connecting them from wherever they're doing the interview. Either way, it means they want me to fill a gap.

We rush out to our broadcast positions.

'Bring Bob over,' I shout to Zoya.

Just as we're all in position, I hear Sharif's voice again in my earpiece.

'False alarm, Rose. We got the guest. We'll be with you in another five minutes.'

And breathe out.

This happens a lot too. One minute they need you on air straight away and the next minute they don't. None of it fazes me any more.

Given that Bob is quite red in the face now, I wonder if it might have been a disaster interviewing him at this point anyway. At least he's got a few minutes to get his breath back.

'You'll have two minutes for the next hit, Rose,' Zoya tells me, having just come off the phone again.

That's less time than I thought I was going to get, but I'm not surprised. All that carry-on with the missing guest will have meant the presenters doing a bit of filling and that's now eaten into the time I was meant to be getting. Typical.

'CUE ROSE,' shouts Jess in my earpiece.

We're back on air. I leap into action, chatting to camera about where I am and why, while also making my way towards Bob.

He looks nervous. I need to put him at ease. I ask my first question slowly and with a big, warm smile. I want to give him the best chance to show off what he does and what he knows. The opposite of what I'll need to do on tomorrow's broadcast. The person I'm interviewing then will need to be held to account. In other words, I'll need to grill them. But there is no time to think about that now, even if it is constantly playing on my mind.

Bob waffles through his first answer. He is starting to relax, though, so I'm sure his next response will be a lot better.

Then a voice speaks in my ear.

'Wrap it up now, Rose.'

Oh, for fuck's sake. I keep this profanity in my head.

Poor Bob. But I've got to listen to what they say. I thank him and hand back to the studio. That's that hit done.

'Is that it?' asks Bob angrily when he realizes that we're not on air any more.

'I'm afraid so. That's the nature of live news,' I say apologetically.

He walks off in a huff, furiously typing on his phone. I'm pretty sure he'll be replying to lots of messages from his family and friends asking why he was only on telly for about forty-five seconds.

'We'll get him on again. There's time in the last hour,' says Zoya, who has just reappeared next to me. 'Plus he was telling me he's part of the steering group that's been regularly meeting with cabinet ministers. So we should ask him about that.'

'Is he? I didn't know that. Why wasn't that in the brief?' I ask.

'I dunno,' Zoya replies, shrugging her shoulders. 'I'll feed back to Pete who was setting up yesterday.'

It's does my head in when there are mistakes or things missing from the briefs. Pete, who is another one of my producers, has been working with me for years, so he should know better. It's definitely not Zoya's fault, but that doesn't stop me being passive-aggressive towards her. I'm a bugger for doing that.

Zoya is quiet by nature, which is unusual for a telly person, but she is very good. And she's always one step ahead of me, which is crucial. I particularly like the fact that she isn't one of the industry clones obsessed with trying to get in front of the camera. She has a fascinating background and a fire in her belly when it comes to news. Also, she actually listens to people. She is a proper journalist. A truth-seeker. Someone who wants to expose injustice and make the world a better place.

Although, I'll be honest, we're not exactly doing Pulitzer Prize-winning journalism this morning, but that's also why she's good. She's a grafter and just cracks on with whatever job she's been given. Right now that means working out how we're going to make the next live hit – which is still coming from an empty building site in the dark – look good on camera.

Alan and Bob watch on. It's pretty obvious they think we're an amateur operation. I'm not surprised. That's exactly what we look like. Not a national broadcaster revered across the world. 'Gaffer Tape Productions' is what we often refer to ourselves as.

Zoya, once again, has played a blinder. She's using her car lights now to make this area of the construction site look like it's been professionally lit. Alan and Bob seem surprised that she's managed to pull this off.

For all Zoya's obvious talent, she has to deal with being stereotyped. The headscarf she wears makes people frequently underestimate her. A bit like how my regional accent seems to make some people assume I'm thick. What a load of bollocks.

I've said to Zoya that their ignorance gives us power. It doesn't take much to floor them, and that's very useful if you're a journalist. She knows that, though; in fact, she knows that more than most.

We're set up and back on air.

The next hit is very much like the first one, except this time it's me on my own and I have a hard count. That means I have to stop talking when I'm told to, otherwise the gallery will just cut me off. I love this challenge of trying to fit what I'm going to say into the exact amount of time I've been given.

Time is such a funny thing in telly land. And it's my job to make sure every single second of it counts.

Tomorrow, that's going to be more important than ever.

JONESY

The team have got at least twenty minutes until they're back on air. Rose has wandered off and Alan has arrived with a cuppa for everyone. Dan's not far behind with biscuits.

'It's quite a bit of kit you've got there. Can I have a look?' Alan asks as he hands Sandy a mug and sticks his head around the door of the satellite truck.

'Aye, come on,' Sandy says, gesturing for Alan to use the steps to climb in.

'It looks a bit like a spaceship in here.'

'A spaceship that's falling apart, though.'

'Not helped by the fact that we keep getting stuff nicked,' Jonesy chips in.

'Really? Well, I suppose it would be worth a few bob in the right hands. Dan, come and have a look.'

The security guard, who hasn't said much up to this point, follows behind Alan. He does look genuinely interested, which Alan is delighted about. He is hoping the buzz of the TV crew will help distract Dan for a bit.

The lads squash themselves into the truck and are pretty much bollock to bollock. Not that they seem to mind; they're transfixed by all the screens and buttons in front of them.

Rose's voice booms through the truck's speakers even though she is nowhere to be seen. She obviously hasn't realized that she's left her microphone on. It's not uncommon. Sandy has accidentally heard all sorts over the years, including the prime minister having a wee. It still makes her chuckle whenever she sees him on the telly.

No one seems to be taking any notice of what Rose is saying, which sounds like a bit of a tense conversation about childcare arrangements and whatnot. Sandy turns off the speaker just in case. She knows that Rose doesn't want people knowing her business. Not after what happened a few years back.

The young reporter who Sandy had first met over a decade ago used to lap up the public's obsession with her, annoyingly so at times. Back then it felt like there wasn't a single bit of Rose's life that the world didn't know about. It's not like that now, though.

'Come on, let's have a photo of us all, to put up on the office wall. It's not every day you have a famous TV crew in,' Alan says as he gets out his phone.

'I'll take it,' says Sandy, who hates being in pictures.

They gather around for the photo and, for the first time in what Alan thinks must be a long time, Dan smiles.

'Didn't you always want to work in this kind of field, Dan?' Alan asks.

'Erm, I've done a bit of pirate radio as a lad, but nowt like this.'

'I reckon you could learn this, no problem,' Alan continues.

Sandy tries not to take offence at the assumption that her job is easy.

'Don't be daft, man – I wouldn't have a clue,' Dan says dismissively.

Alan is desperate to help Dan.

Mental health is a big problem in the construction industry and the stats around it scare Alan. As the safety boss, he's always trying to think of ways to raise awareness.

He gets a bit of stick from the lads sometimes, like when he got everyone to stick a feather to their hard hats. He was trying to make the point that your helmet is used to protect your head from physical damage, but we shouldn't forget the importance of our feather-like mental health. To be honest, Alan knew his 'feather in your cap' idea was shit when he started it. He just got carried away with the metaphor, plus he'd spent over £100 on getting posters made to put up around the site.

It didn't stop him trying and he knew the lads appreciated it, even if they never said so.

'How did you end up in your jobs then?' Alan asks, wanting to keep Dan's interest piqued.

As a man who loves any opportunity to talk about himself, Jonesy is first off the blocks to answer. He tells them all about his life in the army, fighting on the front line, his near-death experience when he was shot at by the Taliban, and also the thrilling tale of surviving for a whole month on Digestives, although it is unclear whether this was in the army or not.

Dan, who has been listening intently, gets to the question now on everyone's mind: 'But I don't get how all that got you into becoming a cameraman?'

Jonesy's face lights up. 'Right, so for me it was all about taking snaps.'

During his time in the forces, Jonesy had picked up a love of photography. His dad had bought him a digital camera, long before everyone had them on their phones, and he took it with him on all his missions.

He explains to them how he used photography to document his trips with a focus on finding beauty in the chaos and destruction. Never one to miss an opportunity to show people his pictures,

Jonesy whips out his phone, which they pass around enthusiastically.

'So, like I said, I loved photography,' Jonesy explains. 'And when I left the military I applied for funding to retrain. They didn't want me going loopy, so they paid me to do a week's camera course at a college down south.'

'A week? Is that all you did?' Alan is once again shocked by how little preparation goes into a job he'd always thought would take years to master.

'Ah, yeah, it doesn't take long. To be honest, I reckon you can pick up the basics on YouTube these days and then it's just a case of learning on the job. I started filming local football games for the news and went from there.'

'Which team?' Dan asks.

'Wrexham. You know, I think it was me who made the club something worth investing in. When the Hollywood stars heard a top cameraman like me was filming the team, they knew they were on to something good.'

Everyone laughs and again Alan is made up at how much enjoyment Dan is getting from this chat. He is also surprised by how normal these TV folk seem. Not up their arses at all, which is what he thought they would be like.

'Telly, radio, it's all the same, you know. I'm sure you could pick it up if you fancied giving it a go, Dan,' says Jonesy encouragingly.

'You're welcome to come back and sit in the truck when we're live on air so you can see what happens behind the scenes,' Sandy adds.

But Dan's face changes, as though he suddenly feels guilty for finding some enjoyment in life.

'Ah, no, I'm a bit past all that now.'

'Ah, don't be daft. Look at me, ex-squaddie with no qualifications. I didn't think I'd ever make it into something like this.

And I'm a granddad. A young, good-looking one, obviously. Plus we're not splitting the atom here. I'm basically just pointing a bit of glass and plastic at things.'

'See, Dan, I bet they do apprenticeships or traineeships too,' enquires Alan hopefully.

'An apprenticeship? You trying to get rid of me, boss?'

'Nah, man, don't be daft, just thinking there's—'

Dan cuts in to finish Alan's sentence:

'There's life after my lad's death?'

ROSE

The day before the hijack

'Rose, I need to tell you about my new sideline,' says Jonesy as Murphy jumps out the back of the van.

'Please don't tell me you've been making more gin – that last batch was minging.'

'No, no, nothing like that. It's dog photography.'

'What, you teach dogs how to take photos?' I joke.

'No, you idiot. I take nice photos of people's dogs.'

'Right, well, whatever floats your boat.'

I have never understood people's obsession with pets, but then I've never really been an animal person, not least because I'm allergic to quite a few of them. I don't have the heart to tell Jonesy that I have to take antihistamines every time I work with him.

Murphy arrives back by Jonesy's side covered in brick dust.

A voice booms through my talkback.

'Rose, we're going to have to drop you in this hour, I'm afraid. Zoya will fill you in,' says Sharif in my earpiece.

I see Zoya making her way towards me. The smell of her latest cigarette arrives before she does.

'So, go on, what's knocked us off air this time? Let me guess
. . . the missing penguin has been found in bed with the prime
minister?' I joke.

'I thought he liked pigs?' laughed Jonesy.

Zoya doesn't laugh. 'Abdul Khalid is being released from
prison.'

Jonesy's face drops. He definitely doesn't see any humour in
this news.

'Whoa – wasn't he the fella that tried to blow up Wembley?'
asks Sandy.

'How is he out already? That's what I wanna know,' Jonesy
responds angrily. 'We're soft in this country, fucking soft!' he
adds, kicking up some of the dirt on the ground in front of them.

I'm not surprised by his reaction. Jonesy's time on the front
line has no doubt influenced his views on terrorists and how we
deal with them.

I get the sense that this is bad news for Zoya too. Every Jihadi
terrorist story that ends up in the press tends to lead to a load
of Muslim-bashing in the media. I imagine that must be hard for
Zoya and her family, especially given her job.

All three of my team look pissed off. I need to get them back
on form. No matter what's going on in the world, you cannot
let yourself get distracted. There's no room for slip-ups in our
line of work. 'You have to park your problems,' my boss always
says to me. Emotion is not allowed.

We've got some spare time on our hands, so I suggest filming
something for social media. The team know I hate it, so there's
no chance they're going to miss this opportunity. And I am right.

'What about doing something daft with Murphy?' suggests
Zoya, who seems to welcome the diversion. 'Let's put a hard hat
on him and get him running behind you.'

We spend twenty minutes faffing about, strapping a helmet
on a dog and choreographing a route for him to follow using a

trail of biscuits, all while trying to stay in the designated 'crew safety zone'. After seven attempts, we finally get a thirty-second clip we can use.

This is why I prefer live TV. Everything happens there and then; there's no chance for retakes. No matter what.

I'm back on soon to do a headline.

It's much brighter on the site now and the builders have turned up to start their shift, which means there's a lot more to show on the telly. It's warmed up too, so everyone is feeling a bit more energized.

We have just over an hour left before the programme finishes and we're done for the day. Well, kind of. You're never really 'done' when you work in news.

'We've had a thousand likes already,' says Zoya.

In the past, I would have loved hearing that; not now. I won't go on social media unless I have to. I bet Rory would enjoy seeing the video, though. He loves dogs. I'll have to get Kate to show him it. She sounded stressed on the phone earlier, so I'll wait a bit before I message her. She can show him after nursery. I hope she gets him there OK; the roadworks around ours are a nightmare at the moment and Kate hates driving. I wish I was there to help. She's been juggling so much and all I do is abandon her.

In my ear, through my talkback, I can hear more details about the terrorist who is being released from prison. They're obviously dedicating a lot of the rest of the programme to covering it.

Then, just as the presenters start explaining why he's been released, director Jess's voice cuts over the top.

'Missing penguins has been dropped. You're now after a Khalid headline from Wandsworth Prison.'

'Okey-dokey,' I reply, relieved it's the penguins ditched from the show and not me.

The programme team only have three broadcast trucks at their disposal, so they must have decided to move the one at London

Zoo over to Wandsworth Prison. Makes sense. The Khalid story is huge, although I still want to know what happened to the penguins – and I suspect the audience will too. That's another thing about news programmes like ours – it's a constant balancing act working out what we should be doing and what we can deliver with the resources we have. We don't always get it right, and the viewers are never shy to tell us that.

I do my 8 a.m. headline and then check my phone. My face lights up. Kate has sent me the most adorable picture of Rory dressed as a pumpkin. I look up to the sky and thank the supermarket gods for saving my arse last night when I was reminded that I'd offered to get an outfit for his nursery Halloween party today. Oh, look at him. He is so cute. And, more importantly, I've swerved another parenting fail. For now.

I head over to Jonesy, who is chatting to the security guy again.

'Sorry to interrupt, lads. Jonesy, we need to work out the choreography for the last two hits. I want to talk to some of the builders on the site this time. Plus we've got Bob and an economist too,' I explain.

'No sweat, treacle, let's get on it. See you a bit later on then, Dan. I should be with you about lunchtime.'

'What's all that about?' I ask Jonesy as we walk away.

'I've just offered to take some nice pictures of the security bloke's dog for him. I thought it might cheer him up.'

'Ah, you're a softie deep down, aren't you?'

'Well, it's no skin off my nose. I've got some time to kill before I head up to Geordieland for tomorrow's gig.'

'It's not Newcastle, it's Teesside,' I snap. 'They're Smoggies, not Geordies.'

'Whatever. Either way, I've got nowt to do, so I may as well do something nice. Try to carve out that place for myself in heaven.'

'There's bollocks all chance of you getting through the pearly gates, Jonesy,' quips Sandy, who is on her way over to readjust some cables on the back of the camera.

The building site is now heaving. The diggers and cement mixers are all whirling into action. Zoya is walking towards me with Aoife Hamill, an economist from one of the big banks who we've shipped up from London. You don't get paid for appearing on a show like ours, so I'm very grateful she's turned up.

'Hey, Aoife, cheers for coming to do this for us.' I greet her as a mate.

'Don't be daft, you know me, any chance to wear safety gear,' Aoife laughs.

Aoife does actually look ridiculous. She is wearing a tailored navy skirt suit – Hugo Boss, by my guess – and then a hard hat, high-vis jacket and big boots. She doesn't care, though. That's why I like having her on. She's a lot more down to earth than the usual City types. She has a lovely Dublin accent too.

'So the plan is I'll chat to a couple of the builders about how the Budget could help them, then I'll go to Bob about the extra money for construction and then I'll come to you for the wider economic picture. Is that OK?'

'Yeah, grand. Whatever you want, Rose,' Aoife replies.

A voice breaks through the general hubbub of the programme sounds in my ear.

'Gallery to Rose, gallery to Rose. Four minutes until you're on. We're giving you some extra time too; you'll have just over five minutes,' explains Sharif with some urgency to his voice.

I imagine there is a lot happening in the gallery with all the news stories moving around. Good news for me, though – five minutes is loads of time to play with.

While I'm getting everyone into position, I overhear one of the builders trying to convince one of the other lads to get some song lyrics into an answer. I hope he manages it.

I am obviously covering serious news, but I do like to jazz it up when I can. Otherwise people who aren't into the business stuff might turn over to watch *Frasier* repeats instead.

'One minute to you, Rose – you're straight after the weather,' shouts Jess.

Our weather presenter is by far the best-loved person on the show. In fact, I'm surprised Bob hasn't asked me about her. Most people either fancy her or want to be her. It's always a great comfort hearing her voice in my earpiece just before I'm about to start.

It's going to be quite a stormy day by the sounds of things, which inevitably means loads of predictable weather metaphors will be used in the coverage of the Budget today.

As the weather update finishes, the presenters in the studio start reading the introduction to my segment. I know exactly what they're going to say because it's the script I wrote.

'Today is the day the chancellor will announce what is in his red box as he reveals the government's Budget. It's expected that there will be a significant investment in construction, so Rose is at a building site in Derbyshire to find out what difference it could make. Morning, Rose.'

'CUE ROSE,' shouts Jess.

'Good morning, everyone. Yes, this is a multimillion-pound development in Alfreton, building affordable housing for key workers . . .'

'Five minutes, Rose,' I hear in my earpiece as I'm walking and talking.

'. . . It comes at a time when a key report from the Housing Federation says that there is a shortfall of a million affordable houses in England. This is one of many sites hoping to plug that gap. As you can see, the builders have just started for the day. There are around a hundred people working on this site. And I'm pleased to say we can chat to a couple of them now. Phil, Barry and Karl, morning.'

'Morning,' they reply awkwardly, two of them looking straight down the lens and one of them at the floor.

Oh, man, it looks like their nerves have got the better of them.

'Phil, you've been in the industry a while. What are you hoping to hear from the chancellor today?' I ask, while trying to discreetly gesture for him to look at me and not the camera.

'Well, I think more money will be a good thing. We need the investment. We've struggled since the recession and now this is a chance to get things moving again. Oh, and a cut in fuel duty would be good. Petrol prices are shocking.'

That was a good answer. Let's hope the next two can deliver the same.

'Barry, what about you?'

'Yeah, what Phil said really. But also, for me, I just want to see more opportunities for the young'uns. I worry about my kids and what chance they've got.'

'Is that what you think as well, Karl?' I say as I turn to the third builder, who is grinning from ear to ear. I know what's coming.

'I believe the children are our future. Teach them well and let them lead the way,' Karl says in a deadpan tone.

And there we have it. The lyrics.

'I think Whitney might have thought that as well, Karl. Do you want to sing the rest?' I laugh as I speak.

I can hear the gallery chuckling in my ear, too – that is until it is punctuated by a deep voice with a much more serious tone.

'Move on, Rose. Get to the—'

The voice is cut off by Carol or Belinda – I still haven't worked out which of them it is doing timings this morning.

'Four minutes,' she says.

That's the other problem with talkback; you can end up with different people talking over each other at the same time. I think the serious voice is the programme editor of the show: the boss, Gary.

'Well, thanks, lads. Let's chat now to site manager Bob Sewell. Bob, give us your thoughts on how important this investment from the government would be.'

After he gives his answer I spend another minute with Bob, asking about his role on the steering group. I estimate that I have about two minutes left, which will give me just enough time to wrap things up with Bob and get to Aoife.

'Two minutes!' I hear in my earpiece again. I knew it.

'Thanks, Bob. Well, I'm also joined by leading economist Aoife Hamill. Morning, Aoife. Just explain the economic backdrop the chancellor is delivering this Budget in.'

Aoife is in full flow when I hear another timing in my ear.

'One minute.'

This is just enough time to get some quick thoughts from Aoife on fiscal policy and then a hand-back to the studio from me.

I am about to wrap things up when I get another instruction.

'Keep talking, Rose, we're waiting for live pictures from Wandsworth,' someone shouts from the gallery.

I ask Aoife another question, which once again she answers with ease.

Surely we must be coming to the end now, I think.

'Keep talking,' says the voice again.

As Aoife is speaking, I quickly plan what I might do next while keeping half an ear on what she's saying. Jonesy doesn't know that I've got to carry on filling, but I'm confident he'll just follow me, whatever I do.

Time for a bit of freestyling.

'Aoife, lovely to chat to you, as ever.'

I turn to the camera to speak directly to the audience down the lens. 'Well, I can't let you go until I've shown you around the site a bit more. Let's have a little look about.'

I set off, not knowing what the hell I'm going to show, but that's half the fun of live TV. In fact, the unpredictability is what

I love the most. Trying to stay in control when there is total chaos all around you. In many ways I live for those days.

'The team started work here this morning at 8 a.m. They reckon they'll have built fifty new houses on this site by the end of the month, ranging from two-bed semis to three-bed terrace houses.' I am filling big time now.

Then I spot two lads at ground level doing some bricklaying. In the corner of my eye I can see Alan looking frantic. I am very close to the edge of the safety cordon he has set out for us. But stuff it, I'm live on telly with time to fill – there's nothing he can do about it.

'As you can see, there's all kinds of work going on here . . .' I say, crossing the designated line and walking over to them now.

'WRAP. We need to get to Wandsworth now,' Jess shouts in my ear.

I carry on speaking down the lens to quickly wrap things up.

'. . . and hopefully I'll show you more of it later on. I might even do a bit of bricklaying if they let me, but that's it from me, for now.'

The presenters in the studio pick up off the back of what I have just said and make a gag about me being game for anything. I carry on smiling and nodding down the camera lens until I hear Sharif in my ear.

'We're off you. Thanks, Rose.'

I take a deep breath and give Jonesy a little shoulder squeeze to acknowledge that we're not on telly any more.

'Bloody hell, that was a long one, my arm is absolutely killing me.' I'm not surprised – he's been holding the camera for about fifteen minutes.

'How the hell did you do that?' says Aoife, who looks a bit shell-shocked by the whole thing.

'Ah, I'm a professional waffler. Although, if it had gone on for much longer, I would have had to start asking you about your views on *Married at First Sight*.'

'Oh God, I love that show. I could talk for hours about that. Do you watch the UK version or the Australian one?'

I laugh. This is another reason I rate Aoife. Despite having such a big job, she doesn't take herself too seriously.

Our chat is interrupted by Bob, who is practically skipping towards us. He must have had some nice messages about his stint on the telly. And he definitely hasn't looked at the social media cesspit yet. Very rarely are people on social media nice about the pundits and experts we have on.

Alan, also heading towards us, looks a lot less happy.

'You are absolutely not doing any bricklaying!' he bellows at me. His face has turned red and there is a headteacher-like tone to his voice.

'Ah, yeah, I was just filling time, Alan. It's fine, honestly,' I reassure him. 'We won't be back on again now.'

'But you just said it on the telly,' he says, looking confused. 'I just don't get this TV malarkey. All seems like a lot of mucking about.'

'Mucking about' is probably a good description of my career to date.

'That's a wrap, guys. The boss says our stuff was excellent, so thank you,' announces Zoya, who has just been on the phone to the producers back at base.

It's at this point that people often feel the need to clap. Bob and Alan lead the way and then others awkwardly join in, including me.

Then Bob finally says it. What I've been expecting all morning.

'You know, Rose, I hope you don't mind me saying, but you're a lot shorter in real life, aren't you?'

I smile. I hear this from viewers everywhere I go.

After thanking everyone, we pack up the kit and get ready

to leave. We don't like to hang around unless they're offering bacon butties. And they're not.

I hand my talkback and microphone to Jonesy, who is going to keep hold of them overnight. We can't risk them being nicked out of the van ahead of tomorrow's broadcast. Not given how important it is.

Zoya is sorting out Aoife's taxi to the train station, so I make my getaway. We've agreed we'll meet later at the hotel we're staying at tonight. Everyone has got their own stuff to do first.

My priority is to get to our next destination in enough time to watch the Budget coming out at lunchtime.

As I walk towards the car, Alan comes over. I'm assuming it's to give us a safety debrief of some description.

'There's a friend of yours waiting in the Portakabin,' Alan says. 'I'm afraid I can't let him in any further because of health and safety.'

'Eh, a friend?' I can't think of anyone I know who would be here. I'd better go see who it is.

I walk into the cabin. In the middle of the room stands a tall, pale man with dark-rimmed glasses.

He smiles.

A wave of fear travels through my whole body.

He's back.

ROSE

Five years before the hijack

'd had a busy morning on air with various bits of breaking news. Another big retailer had gone bust so I was outside one of their shops in Altrincham High Street.

I was desperate to get home, but Tom wasn't due to pick me up for another twenty minutes.

There had been a few people hanging around to watch what we were doing, which is quite common when you're out and about. It's a novelty having a TV crew on your high street. Plus some of them were clearly desperate to get into the back of our shots so they could tell their mates they'd been on telly.

One man, in the huddle of bystanders, kept smiling at me. That's not unexpected in this job, but he had a familiarity about him, so I wondered if I'd interviewed him before.

I pretended to look busy on my phone so that he wouldn't come and talk to me, but it didn't work. He had managed to strike up a conversation with my producer, Pete, and now they were heading towards me.

'Hello, Rose, lovely to see you,' said the man with a soft voice.

I was hoping Pete would introduce him so I could at least hear what his name was. He didn't.

'Hello, lovely to see you too. How are you?' I replied, giving nothing away about whether I knew him or not.

Pete made his excuses and left while this random bloke asked me how my morning had been and what I was up to for the rest of the day. He was talking to me like he knew me. That happens a lot, people thinking they know me because they see me on the telly.

After ten minutes of chit-chat, Tom pulled up in the car beside me, which allowed me to make my excuses and leave. The man said he would see me again soon, which was also something I heard a lot, because if they watch the show then technically they will see me again soon.

In the car on the way home I scrolled through my social media to see how the audience had reacted to my broadcast. I'd done various behind-the-scenes videos too, including one with me doing my make-up in the back of Tom's car. The first thing I did was look at how many likes it had. Three thousand. I was disappointed. I needed to do something else to try to get more.

I was constantly being told by the people I worked with that I had to share more of my life with the public, to show that I am relatable, but I wasn't really sure I was any more. My world had changed so much since becoming a TV presenter. Still, telling everyone what I was up to seemed to be the only way to get ahead in this game now.

Plus I was now obsessed with it. Constantly refreshing to see how many 'likes' I had and spending hours poring over the comments people had left on my posts. It wasn't good for me, but I couldn't stop myself. It was like picking a scab.

Today was no different. Underneath my posts from the morning were hundreds of messages. Quite a few commenting on what I looked and sounded like. Some nice, some horrible. Then there were the angry people accusing me of being a government mouthpiece, alongside those suggesting I was clearly supporting the opposition.

I was in the middle of replying to the people who were asking where my coat was from when I noticed a comment from someone called Big B. The message read:

@Big__B It was so lovely to spend time with you on location today. I am looking forward to getting to know you more.

Weird. A bit creepy even. I assumed it must have been from one of the people who had gathered in the crowd to watch. Maybe they'd never seen me before on telly and that's what they meant about getting to know me more. I had no idea. Either way, I always tried to respond to the nice messages, so I sent a generic reply.

@ReporterRose So lovely to see you too. Best wishes R x

And I didn't think anything more of it.

Two days later, I was back out on the road, this time reporting from Manchester airport. It was the beginning of the school holidays so I was doing the annual great British getaway story.

'Ah, there's your friend,' said producer Pete, pointing towards a crowd of people.

'What you on about?' I replied, bemused.

'It's your friend who gave you a lift home from the high street OB the other day.'

I was even more confused. I was driven home by Tom from the outside broadcast – what we call an OB – like I normally am. I had no idea what Pete was on about.

'I'll go and get him for you,' offered Pete.

Before I could make sense of what was happening, Pete had approached a man in the crowd and was directing him to where we were on the other side of the security cordon.

Then I realized it was the bloke Pete had brought over to me at Altrincham High Street.

But why did he think the guy had driven me home? It was all a bit strange.

'Ah, nice to see you again,' I lied.

Pete's phone rang and he wandered off to answer it.

'I'll leave you and Billy to catch up.'

Once again, I was left with this man I didn't know.

He was very pleasant, but there was just something starting to creep me out. It was all a bit overfamiliar. And I couldn't get away from him. Not without appearing rude.

When Pete came back, he suggested we all go for breakfast in one of the airport restaurants after the broadcast had finished.

I couldn't believe what was happening. Pete was clueless. A lovely lad, with a bag full of qualifications, but no street smarts.

For the rest of the morning, I was stuck with Billy hovering by me. It was doing my head in, but I couldn't say or do anything about it without looking like a total bitch. And that's the thing in the TV game: you have to be nice to everyone at all times.

I considered discreetly texting Pete to tell him that I didn't know who this man Billy was, but I could see that Pete had his phone set up in a way that meant his messages appeared in full on his home screen. Billy might see it.

Instead I messaged Tom, asking him to pick me up early. There was no way I was staying for breakfast.

As we wrapped up the broadcast, I told the crew I was leaving. And that's when Billy said it:

'Shall I give you a lift home again, darling?'

Eh? What the hell's going on?

He spoke again before I could respond. 'I've got your favourite snacks, like last time.'

What had I missed? This wasn't making any sense.

I just wanted to get away from him.

'Erm, I'm fine thanks, Billy. My driver is here.'

Tom laughed when I told him about it on the journey home. I suppose it did sound ridiculous when I said it out loud. We agreed that I was tired and had probably misheard him.

I needed sugar. The brain fog had set in and I still had a long day ahead of me. We stopped at a petrol station. I picked up a bag of Haribo and some strawberry laces and stood in the queue to pay. And then I saw him. Billy was filling up his car outside on the forecourt. Surely it was just a coincidence, but we were miles away from the broadcast location now. Had he followed us?

Tom had spotted him too.

'Do you reckon he's after my job?' he said, laughing, as I got back in the car. I didn't respond.

'He can have it – to be honest, these hours are killing me,' Tom continued.

'Just take me home, Tom,' I said with sigh. I wasn't in the mood to joke.

In the silence of the drive home I scrolled through social media again. There was another message from Big B.

@Big__B Another wonderful morning spent by your side. Thank you. X

I stared at it for a while. It was clearly this fella Billy who had been hanging around me. I clicked on his profile picture to see if it was him, but it was just a photo of a big dog. Probably his, I assumed.

I couldn't decide what to do. Should I reply or not? I concluded that I was probably overthinking it. He hadn't actually done anything wrong and it was still important to be nice. I had my reputation to think of.

Plus some people saw it as a badge of honour having a fan as obsessed as Billy was with me. Yep, as daft as it sounds, having a stalker is seen as a sign of success as a presenter.

I should have been chuffed.

Similar to how you're meant to feel when you receive human poo through the post.

I remember getting mine during a morning meeting with a crowd of other reporters. I was opening the mail I had just collected from my locker while I was listening to our boss dishing out our assignments for the day. As I opened one particular envelope, the smell hit me. As soon as I realized what it was, I threw it on the floor in horror. At that point, several veteran correspondents clapped and said that I had now 'made it'. Apparently, this fella had been sending shit in the post to reporters for years. To this day, they still haven't caught him.

Anyway, having a stalker was different, not least because I was living on my own.

Over the following weeks and months, I received regular tweets from Big B. Nothing controversial or inappropriate, just comments on what I was doing. Then, occasionally, when I was out on location, he would appear. It was annoying, but nothing I couldn't handle, and technically he wasn't doing anything wrong.

On my birthday and at Christmas he sent cards to the office for me. He wasn't the only fan who sent me stuff, so again I told myself it was nothing to worry about.

Then one evening my dad rang.

'What's this about you having a secret boyfriend?' Dad laughed as he said it.

'Eh? What boyfriend?' I laughed too, assuming there was a punchline coming.

'This fella has sent me a letter asking for your hand in marriage,' Dad continued.

'What? Who has? What you on about, Dad?' None of this was making any sense to me and it didn't sound like a joke any more.

'Billy. Says you and him have been dating for yonks and he wants to take it to the next level.'

'Billy?' I replied with utter confusion.

Then it hit me. Billy. Big B.

I tried to stay calm. I didn't want to worry my dad so I pretended that it was one of my mates having a laugh. I'm not sure he bought it, but I really didn't want to scare him.

When I came off the phone, I burst into tears. I suddenly felt very alone. And very scared.

I'd been buzzing about moving into my own flat when I got my job on the telly. But now I wished I was still in the cramped houseshare with my mates.

I called Gary, my boss. I couldn't stop my tears.

He's not great with emotion at the best of times, but he did manage to calm me down a bit.

Turns out that because there are so many security threats in our business, particularly to female broadcasters, there's a team of people dedicated to dealing with psychos like Billy. It was a relief to hear that. Although I was miffed that no one had bothered telling me that I'd probably get a stalker. I might have dealt with things a bit differently if I'd known.

I didn't sleep much that night. It was one thing following me about, I could handle that, but sending letters to my dad, that had freaked me out. I was racking my brain until the early hours, trying to work out how Billy had found my dad's address.

The whole thing was so unsettling. Had I done something wrong? Should I have behaved differently?

The next day someone from the security team called me to explain that they had spoken to Billy. He'd told them that he was my boyfriend. I was dumbfounded.

Billy had described in great detail how we had been messaging each other and meeting up.

According to the security expert, there are some blokes of a certain age who think that social media exchanges are as direct and personal as text messages. They don't understand that the message they've posted will be public, as will any replies they get too. And they don't get that someone like me will often respond to lots of people who watch me on telly.

It also didn't help that I'd been putting kisses on my replies to him. I thought it was a friendly gesture, but apparently that is the equivalent of a full-on snog to these men.

The videos I'd posted of me at home or on my journeys to and from work had also given him a fake closeness to me. He claimed they were messages to him.

Then of course I was regularly posting about where I was going to be each day on my broadcasts. Billy thought I was telling him where to meet me. What a mind melt.

It had to be nipped in the bud.

In that moment, I knew I had to keep my private life private.

I needed to protect myself and my family.

But still he'd turn up. Not all the time. But enough to freak me out.

I was really struggling with it. Constantly looking at my phone to see if he had messaged, followed by sleepless nights wondering when and where he would turn up next. And, even when I did sleep, I would often wake up convinced he was in the flat.

It was psychological torture.

And then one day it just stopped. No more sightings, no more messages. Nothing.

ROSE

'Billy, what are you doing here?' I try to say it calmly.

'I wanted to see you, to say sorry,' he says in a soft, slow voice. He sounds even creepier than I remember.

'Right, well, thank you. Erm, I really need to go now, though.' I am polite but firm.

'Wait, I just want to talk. I need to apologize. I haven't seen you for so long and I just want to explain myself. Please, Rose.'

He starts to walk towards me and puts out his hand as if to touch me. I back away.

'I got caught up in something and, well, I am so sorry to say this, but I ended up having to go away for a while. I am so sorry I left you like that.'

Does he mean prison? Fuck, he means prison. I need to get out of here. I back away further, eventually hitting the cabin wall, which wobbles from the weight of me falling against it.

'Can I take you for breakfast?' he asks.

'I really can't. It's Budget Day, I've got so much prep to do.'

I move my hand slowly along the wall, hoping to reach the door handle, and then suddenly I feel myself falling backwards. I hit the ground hard.

Now Zoya is standing over me.

'Oh God, I am so sorry, Rose. I didn't realize you were leaning against the door,' Zoya says as she helps me up.

I can't speak. My head is all over the shop.

'I just came to tell you that we need you for some more filming for tomorrow.' Zoya takes my arm to walk me away from the cabin.

I don't look back. I have no idea where Billy is now. Is he following me? I'm too scared to look.

As we get further away, Zoya starts to whisper.

'Are you all right?'

I shake my head.

'Don't worry. I'll sort this. I knew something was up when Sandy said you were with a mate. Like you'd invite a mate here?!' Zoya says, guiding me off the site. 'Tom is parked just up here.'

Thank God for Zoya. So often underestimated and yet always knows what to do in a crisis.

'It's him, isn't it, that stalker?'

I nod.

'I'll call the boss and let him know what's going on,' Zoya says reassuringly.

'No, I'll do that myself.'

'OK. What about calling Kate?' Zoya asks.

'Definitely not!' I snap back.

I really don't want my partner to know anything about this. It'll stress her out and she's got enough on her plate. The last thing I want to do is cause her more anxiety.

I just want to get away.

'He's back,' I tell Tom as I climb into the car. I'm still shaking.

'Who? Not that mad fucker Big Bollocks or whatever he's called?'

'Yeah, I think he's been in prison, you know – that's why he went quiet.'

'Shitting hell, do we need to go to the police?'

'No, just get me out of here. I'll call the boss.'

Gary is the person I always ring first in a drama. He's got me out of loads of scrapes over the years, from run-ins with the prime minister to potential exposés about my private life in the press. While I might be able to physically pick myself up from a fall, he is the person who does it for my brain.

'Gary, it's Rose. My stalker is back. He turned up at the end of the OB today.' I rush to tell him everything before he gets a chance to react.

He replies calmly. 'Well, this is not ideal, but, listen, there's no suggestion he wants to hurt you, so don't panic. Let me talk to the security team again.'

'I think he's been in prison,' I blurt out.

'Right, but we don't know that for sure, do we? And if he has, we don't know what for. If he's out already, it can't be anything too bad.'

My mind is running wild.

'Rose, just calm down, I'll sort it.'

I hate it when people tell me to calm down. I'm not trying to be stressed, I just bloody am! Gary can sense that he's not helping. He tries to move the conversation on.

'Listen, there's no way he's going to turn up tomorrow. You'll be at one of the most secure sites in the country. Just focus on getting through the next twenty-four hours and let me deal with it.'

He's right. The location for the broadcast tomorrow is incredibly secure. Plus it's top secret. Only the crew and my partner know where I'm going to be. It's taken months to get the clearance to be allowed in. This is going to be a huge broadcasting first. No one has ever been given access with any kind of camera, let alone one that will be broadcasting live to the nation.

And on top of that, I have one of the biggest interviews of my career to do while I'm there.

What a day for Billy to reappear.

My boss is right. I'm safe, there's no suggestion I'm not, and I need to focus.

Just after I hang up, I see that I have a message from Kate.

How cute is our little pumpkin?! He went into nursery no bother and I got parked OK in the end. Phew. Am at work now. Busy, but all good. Chat in a bit. Love you hot dog. xxx

I smile as I read it. Hot dog. What a ridiculous pet name she's given me. But I love it. I reply and then slip my AirPods in. I must try to rest for a bit. I put Maggie Rogers' latest album on shuffle. Her music always helps to chill me out.

A wave of exhaustion hits me. A few songs in and I nod off.

About an hour later I wake up to see the cooling towers of Ferrybridge Power Station. This tells me we're about an hour away from the hotel I'm staying at tonight.

I have travelled up the A1 countless times over the years and, as a northerner, it's always a comfort to see the landmarks that let me know I'm not far from the place I call home. Although there'll be no time to go home today.

The familiar towers also signal that we're approaching my favourite service station, Wetherby. When you spend your life on the road like I do, you're always going to have your top stops. I struggle to pass Wetherby Services without calling in for a Greggs' Steak Bake. Today I am classing this as a necessity after a stressful morning. Although I'm not sure how I will justify the two sausage rolls I am about to buy as well.

I stock up on various snacks to get me through the rest of the day. I won't have time to get out again. As soon as I arrive at the hotel, I'll need to sit and watch the Budget coverage and prepare for my next broadcast.

Back in the car, I get a call from Chris, one of the production

managers on the show. He talks me through the security proce-
dure for tomorrow. It's unlike any other outside broadcast I've
ever been on.

So far there have been background checks, various forms of
ID sent, several confidentiality clauses signed and at least four
different risk assessments filled in.

Chris says that when we arrive tomorrow we will have to be
searched and scanned. We will also have to hand our phones in
for the duration of our visit.

Then comes the killer line: we will be escorted everywhere,
all morning, including to the loo.

'The loo?' I say, shocked at the thought of trying to wee in
front of someone else.

'Yep, someone will walk you to the toilet and stand outside
the cubicle door while you do your business,' Chris replies.

'Are you kidding? I can't wee under pressure like that.'

'Well, then, you'll have to hold it in until you get out.'

'Jesus Christ! Thanks, Chris. Any other good news for me?'

Chris laughs and says he'll send me the full list of on-site rules
and regulations. Not that I'll bother reading it. Zoya will tell me
if there's anything specific I need to know.

As soon as I end the call, the phone rings again. It's Kate. I
panic. I know it's irrational, but my first thought when I see her
calling is that something bad has happened.

I blame this job. The tough stories I'm exposed to every day
have made me paranoid.

My mate who's a therapist explained it to me once: hearing
traumatic things and then interviewing people about those awful
events can sometimes play on my subconscious and make me
think I'm experiencing them too.

Thankfully, Kate knows I'm a catastrophist and so she brings
the much-needed sanity to our lives. Right now, she is also
unintentionally reminding me why I love her so much. Despite

her having a ton of work to do, she is calling to give me a rundown of Rory's morning – what he had for breakfast, when he had a wee, how he reacted to seeing the pumpkin outfit, that kind of thing. It's exactly the wholesome content I want to hear. She also reminds me it's my mam's birthday at the weekend, which I'd obviously forgotten.

'You couldn't cope without her, could you?' Tom says after I hang up.

'No, Tom.' And he's right; I couldn't.

'You didn't tell her about Billy, though?'

'No, she's got enough on, I don't want to worry her.'

'Yeah, I get that. When does she find out if she's getting that grant from the Chinese university?'

'She finds out tomorrow, hopefully. She's got a big meeting first thing.'

I momentarily study the back of Tom's head. How did he know about Kate's research project? Did I tell him? I must have done. I need to be careful with stuff like that, given how sensitive Kate's work is now. Still, it's only Tom and he won't say anything to anyone.

'She's the one, you know. The only person I've ever seen calm you down when you're having one of your dramas.'

'What you on about, dramas?'

'Rose, are you serious? I feel like I'm living in an episode of *EastEnders* with you sometimes.'

'You cheeky git!' I snap back. Although he's not wrong.

'She keeps you grounded, stops you being a telly twat,' he continues.

'Alright, alright, that's enough with the character assassination!'

Tom is spot on with all of it. Getting with Kate has been the best thing to happen to me. After everything with the stalker and the general madness of my job, she is the one who has brought the love and stability I have desperately craved and needed. And she is an amazing mam to our Rory.

I really don't think I could live without her.

After about two and a half hours of travelling, which included ten minutes of ordering a Moonpig card and chocolates for my mam, we arrive at the hotel.

In front of it are two lads on a bench sharing a bottle of cider. They nudge each other as Tom opens the door to let me out.

'Cheap and cheerful, ey, Rose?' says Tom, laughing.

'Cheap definitely, but this place doesn't look like it's seen any cheer for years,' I reply, getting out.

'Ey-ey, are you a celeb or summat?' says one of the men on the bench, standing up to get a better look at me.

I pretend I haven't heard him. I always feel so awkward when people say stuff like that. What am I meant to reply? I'd sound like a right twat saying yes, but equally I'd look daft saying no, because technically I am a celeb, even though I don't feel it.

Ignoring them doesn't work.

'Are ya filming here?' the other lad shouts now.

'Yeah, *Embarrassing Bodies*. Wanna be in it, lads?' replies Tom, quick as anything.

'Nah, nah, mate, you're all right, like.' The lads sit back down and carry on drinking their cider like nothing has happened.

I laugh. Tom is great in situations like this. It helps that he is in a good mood. Probably because he's getting a lie-in tomorrow.

Tom has been up since the crack of dawn driving me all over the country, so I've told him not to pick me up until after the broadcast. He's staying with his brother, so he'll probably want to have a few pints with him. I can just get a local taxi to the site.

I envy Tom, staying with family. I'd love a nice home-cooked tea at my mam and dad's, but I want to concentrate on work and that would never happen at their house.

Crappy hotel it is then.

I have a basic room with a single bed. I try to make it as homely as possible. I have brought in a fluffy blanket from the car, plus a hot-water bottle, some antibacterial wipes and a photo of Kate and Rory in a frame. I know it sounds a bit naff, but it's the little things like this that make a difference when I'm on the road.

After I wipe down the table, I lay out my snacks. There's something reassuring about snacks.

Then I clean the remote control. I did a story once about hotel cleanliness and was grossed out by the amount of bacteria on the TV remotes.

I turn on the telly. PMQs is on. After this, the Budget will be delivered. There will be the usual run-through of the latest economic statistics from the Office for Budget Responsibility and then will come the announcements.

I settle down with my notebook. I'm still quite old school on that front. I even have a paper diary, which I take everywhere with me. I'm like a teenage girl when it comes to stationery, which includes having one of those pens that you can click between colours so that I can colour-code things, like I did when I was revising for my school exams.

I'm all set by the time the chancellor takes to the dispatch box.

I must listen carefully.

He is one of the most powerful men in the country.

Tomorrow I will be interviewing him live on the telly in front of millions of people.

ZOYA

As soon as Rose is safely in the car and on her way, Zoya runs back to the cabin.

Billy's gone.

By this point, Alan, the safety officer, has come over, looking flustered.

'Is everything all right? Someone just told me they saw Rose fall. I'm going to need to check her over.'

'She's fine and she's gone.'

Alan is clearly miffed by this news. 'Ah, that's not fine. It's an on-site accident, it needs to go on the board. And, as the qualified first aider, I need to assess her.'

Zoya knows she's going to have to handle this carefully. There is information she needs from Alan and she's not going to get it if she pisses him off.

'I'm so sorry, she's gone. It's entirely my fault. But, listen, I can help you fill out the necessary paperwork. It was me who caused the fall.'

Zoya's mea culpa works.

'Ah, right, OK then, that'll have to do. Follow me,' Alan says, letting his anger subside a bit.

Zoya walks with him to the cabin and asks about the man who turned up.

'Rose's mate? Dan will have the details, he signed him in,' Alan explains. 'I know the gentleman said he was a very close friend of hers, but even so I couldn't give him the clearance to access the site.'

For the first time in her journalism career, Zoya is grateful that she is working with a jobsworth.

Alan gets the details from the visitor book.

Name: Billy Rubin
Organization: NA
Date: 30 October
Time: 09:00
Vehicle reg: NA

'There's not much to go on from this. That name sounds made-up for a start. Bilirubin is a product your red blood cells make when they break down,' says Zoya.

Alan looks surprised that Zoya even knows this.

'It's not made-up – I saw his driving licence,' says the security lad, who is also in the cabin.

'What about the vehicle reg?' Zoya asks.

'I dunno, he said he didn't drive here.'

'Did you not see him arrive or leave?'

'No, sorry, I didn't.'

'Do you have security cameras?'

'No. Why you lot so bothered about this fella anyway?'

Zoya doesn't reply. It was obvious to anyone who saw what happened that Billy was a man Rose was scared of. She's not going to confirm that to them, though.

Rose had never talked to Zoya about her stalker. It was her partner Kate who'd let slip once that she'd been freaked out by some bloke who used to turn up everywhere. It didn't take much to work out that must have been him today.

Zoya wants to help. She cares a lot about Rose, and Kate now too.

She takes a photograph of the visitor details and then fills in the obligatory accident form that Alan is waving in her face. She needs to get out of there.

Zoya lights a cigarette as she gets in her car. She knows she needs to quit, but today is definitely not the day for it.

She looks at the notes she'd left on the passenger seat that detail the plans for the next day's broadcast, including the hotel where they are staying tonight. She punches the postcode into her satnav. Two hours and twenty minutes is the estimate. She needs to get a move on if she wants to get there in time.

Zoya tries to start the car. Nothing happens. She realizes she must have killed the battery when she used the headlights for filming. She throws her head against the steering wheel and curses under her breath. All in all, she's having a stressful day.

She picks up her phone to look for help, ignoring the ten missed calls from various family members. She knows exactly what they want to talk about and she doesn't want to deal with any of it at the moment. No matter how much danger she might be in.

ROSE

There's a knock on the door. I'm so deep in concentration it makes me jump.

As I get up I realize that the desk I am sitting at is now covered in various sweet wrappers. I quickly sweep them into the bin so I don't look like a total pig.

There is another knock. A wave of fear hits me. What if it's him?

No, no, I tell myself. *It can't be, he has no idea where I am. Unless he followed me. Oh, shit, what if he followed me? Surely Tom would have noticed? Or maybe not. Oh, man, this is all I need.*

Then I hear Zoya's voice.

'Rose, are you there?' she says through the door.

Phew. Panic over. I open the door and Zoya comes in and plonks herself on the bed. She looks worn out. I want to ask her about what happened with Billy, but she jumps straight into talking about work.

I need to stop thinking about him. He can't hurt me.

Zoya's really good at keeping me focused in times of stress.

My interview tomorrow with the chancellor is a big deal. Zoya knows this. So we crack on.

We work our way through the Budget announcements. We were right about the construction spend, so that's good. He also announced more money for defence; that will annoy some people. Then a raft of spending freezes, including to health and education. This is massive news. People are going to be fuming.

There is so much to cover, and that's before we work out what extra things we might need to ask the minister.

Interviewing politicians is a slippery business. In fact, they are my least favourite people to speak to. Very rarely do you feel you are hearing the truth. But holding politicians to account is an important part of my job, so I have to do it well.

I know I will have six minutes to grill him. The interview needs to be focused, with direct questions that challenge him. He can't be given a free ride to say what he likes.

That means swotting up on the topics we're going to cover, arming myself with relevant stats and working out all the possible things he might say to each question I ask, so I will be prepared to challenge any bullshit.

With a long afternoon of research ahead of me, I send Zoya off to her room to get some rest. She really does look wrecked.

Before she leaves, she uses the loo in my room. Her phone, which is on the table next to me, lights up.

There are fifteen missed calls, including one from my partner Kate.

Zoya and Kate are good mates, a friendship that came about by accident when Zoya was dropping off work stuff at mine. Kate had invited her in for a cuppa and they ended up bonding over some weird science connection to do with Zoya's dad.

I'd never seen Kate so excited. Turns out she'd read one of Zoya's dad's research papers when she was studying for her PhD. Something to do with liver function. That was the only bit I could make out from their very animated and jargon-heavy chat.

It was lovely to see Kate talking so passionately to Zoya about her own science career again. She'd found it hard having to take a backseat on all that when Rory was born and I think it knocked her confidence a bit. Even though we'd agreed that I'd be the one to go back to work, I've always felt guilty about it.

A few nights after Zoya's first visit, I arrived home to find her and half her family in my kitchen, including her dad, who had brought over a chemistry kit for Rory, and her nana, who was dishing out a semolina cake. Since then, Zoya has been a regular at our house, often while I'm away and Kate is on her own with Rory.

The phone lights up again. It's another call, but this time it's showing just a number, not a name.

I have such a bad habit of looking at people's phone screens when they're near me. I like to think it's because of the natural journalist in me; the reality is I'm just nosy.

I wonder what's going on.

I worry about Zoya.

'Old before her years' is how Kate describes her.

She's close to Kate, but I get the vibe that Zoya likes to keep a bit of professional distance with me. There's a hierarchy in our industry that Kate always scoffs at, but it's there and there's not much we can do about it. The 'talent', which is what people on the telly are called, are treated very differently to everyone behind the cameras. It's not fair and can cause tension sometimes, but it's just the way it is. I get the sense that Zoya doesn't want to cross any lines because of it.

Zoya is still in the toilet when her phone lights up again. It's her nana calling her this time. I'm tempted to answer it. But before I have time, Zoya walks back into the room.

'Your nana is calling you,' I announce, to explain why I'm looking at her phone.

'Ah, yeah, I'll call her back in a bit,' Zoya replies as she picks up the phone from the table in front of me and puts it in the pocket of her jeans.

'What if it's an emergency?'

'Honestly, it won't be. She'll just be checking in on me and will have forgotten I'm working,' Zoya replies as she heads out of the door.

Something doesn't sit right with the way Zoya has just said that.

She's lying.

ZOYA

2.15 p.m.

The day before the hijack

t's been fifteen minutes since Zoya left Rose's room. Her phone, which she'd tossed on the bed, keeps ringing. She doesn't want to deal with what's coming, but she knows she has to.

Zoya reluctantly picks up her mobile and calls her grandmother.

'Nana, it's Zoya,' she says hesitantly.

'Where are you?' her nana snaps back.

'I'm at work.'

'Where?'

'I told you last night, Nana, a business up in Teesside.'

'Can you come home?'

'Not yet, no, Nana. Tomorrow afternoon.'

'Zoya, have you spoken to your cousin?'

Zoya takes a deep breath. She was right. This is about him.

'No, and I am not going to either. Sorry,' Zoya responds curtly.

'You need to. All of this, it's very upsetting for the family.' Zoya can hear the emotion in her frail grandmother's voice. She hates to upset her, but she has no choice.

'Nana, I have to go, I'm really busy. I'll call you tomorrow. I love you.'

Zoya cuts the conversation short. She knows that this will

annoy her nana and she doesn't want to do that, but there is just no talking sense to her. Plus it's hard getting her grandmother to understand anything these days.

She calls the next family member on her missed calls list. It's her brother Bilal, who has tried her five times already today. It connects straight away.

'Zee, we've been worried sick, man,' her brother exclaims.

'Sorry, Bee, I'm working, you know what it's like.'

'I know, but it's important you answer your phone.'

'I don't know why everyone is so stressed out.'

'Sis, we need to protect you.'

'I am fine, honestly. I am totally fine.'

'But you realize he's gonna be looking for you, don't you?'

'What you on about?'

'Zee. He knows. We all know.'

Zoya drops the phone to the ground.

ROSE

The *Six O'Clock News* has just finished. They led on health-care, then education, then a round-up of everything else in the Budget. After that came the other big stories of the day: the Wembley terrorist being released; the court case involving the disgraced politician Janet Jacobs; a storm coming from the Atlantic; and the return of the missing penguins.

I didn't hear anything new, but then I wasn't expecting to. Social media, as much as I now hate it, is where you hear everything first, although sometimes it can be hard to differentiate between fact and fiction.

Everyone thinks they're a journo, though I suppose, in a way, they are, given how easy it is to record and publish everything from your phone. But there is a lot of fake news out there, making our job harder and harder, especially with people like Janet Jacobs spouting such bile towards mainstream media.

I've had plenty of run-ins with her over the years. The funniest being when she accused me of putting on a fake regional accent. Apparently I'm dead posh in real life. Me and my schoolmates had a good giggle about that.

Unfortunately, the majority of what she says is much more

dangerous than that. She's toxic and regularly stirs up unnecessary trouble and hate.

I call Gary to check in before tomorrow's big broadcast.

I can't deny the nerves are starting to get to me now. He'll
calm me down.

'Hey, boss, I've just watched the *Six*. I see mad Janet has been
on one again.'

'Oh God, don't start me on that woman. Terry on cameras was
telling me that she was saying some really weird stuff on her
way into court today.'

'Oh, like what?'

'Just stuff about it being time to reclaim the media in whatever
way you can.'

'But she always says stuff like that.'

'Yeah, but Terry said this felt different. As if she was trying
to incite her fans into actually doing something. You know, not
just moaning on social media. I guess it was the phrasing of it
that sounded off.'

'Ooo right. That sounds a bit more sinister. But what can they
actually do? Glue themselves to the satellite truck?'

We both laugh.

'Anyway, boss, I'm assuming you want me to go big on healthcare tomorrow?'

It's normal for me to chat to my editor before a high-profile
interview to discuss our editorial strategy. Tomorrow's interview
is one of the biggest for me.

'Yeah, definitely, there's plenty of meat on the bone to chew
there. But once the Budget stuff is out of the way, quiz him on
the terrorist stuff. You need to push him. Loads of people are
kicking off about it.'

'Yeah, of course.' I try to sound confident, as if I have already
thought this through.

The relevance of this had totally passed me by. Shit! It's obvious that this is a huge story I need to talk about.

'We need you to nail this interview, Rose. No dicking about. Straight, solid questions. The fuckers are finally putting up someone senior to grill and, given everything going on, there's loads to get him on. It's our job – your job – to hold him to account.'

This pep talk has done nothing to calm my nerves. I now feel sick with the pressure of it all.

I am used to interviewing high-profile people, but this feels different. There has been total chaos in politics recently, so all the top ministers have been avoiding the press.

I am going to be the first journalist in ages to be interviewing one of the country's most senior politicians, on the biggest national news network and on a day when loads of stuff is happening. All eyes will be on us.

If I fuck this up, I am fucked too.

'One more thing, Rose. I've got some bad news.'

I suddenly feel a knot in the pit of my stomach. This must be about Billy.

'Oh, shit. Has he found out where I am?'

'No, no. It's Zoya.'

I'm relieved, but also confused.

'What about her? She's here in the hotel with me.'

Then I suddenly remember she was meant to come and watch the *Six O'Clock News* with me and hadn't shown up.

'She's gone home. She's not well.'

'Eh? I saw her earlier. I mean she looked knackered but seemed fine.'

'Yeah, well, she's not, so she's gone home.'

The tone of his voice tells me he does not want any more questions about Zoya. I stay quiet and let him continue.

'I don't have anyone else to send up and, even if I did, I'd never get their security clearance in time, so you won't have a producer tomorrow.'

'Right, I'll just have to cope then.'

'You will.'

I finish the call and slump back on the bed, processing everything that's just been said to me. What the hell has happened to Zoya? It's not like her to phone in sick. Why didn't she say bye, though? Then I suddenly remember about her nana calling her. I hope it's nothing to do with that. And Kate called her too, I recall. Maybe I'll get her to phone Zoya and check she's OK. She's more likely to talk to her than me.

She has left me in a bit of a pickle, though.

Normally I wouldn't be fazed about not having a producer. I spent seven years working behind the scenes in telly before a stroke of serendipity moved me in front of the camera. A bug doing the rounds in the business news office meant that I was the only one there able to explain the latest round of quantitative easing, which had just been announced by the Bank of England. The news editor wanted an item on the bulletins about it, so he shoved me on the telly to do it. I looked rough and probably sounded terrible too, but that baptism of fire gave me the presenter bug — and here we are, ten years later.

So I know what I'm doing as a producer and a presenter, which helps a lot, but on a broadcast as complicated as tomorrow's this is a bit of a nightmare. Couple that with it being the day I have to do one of the biggest interviews of my career. My nerves are wrecked. I feel light-headed.

I need to eat before I carry on with swotting.

I head to the hotel bar to meet Jonesy and Sandy.

'We can afford the steak,' announces Jonesy as I reach the table.

'Are you kidding me?'

Our meal allowance never normally stretches to anything more than a club sandwich.

'It's steak night on a Wednesday so it's £9.99 plus a drink of your choice. I know how you like getting your chops around a big juicy . . .'

'For fuck sake, Jonesy, shut up!' Sandy doesn't even let him get to the punchline this time.

'You're like an old married couple, you two,' I say, laughing.

'He wishes,' Sandy shoots back.

'Where's Murph this eve?' I ask Jonesy.

'Oh, I've dropped him at my mate Al's house. He only lives up the road. I didn't want him cooped up in the van. I dropped him after I'd been round Dan's house.'

'Dan?'

'The security guard from the site this morning. You know.'

I'd forgotten all about him offering to take pictures of his dog. Anyway, it seems to have gone well, so that's good. I mean, I'll be honest, I'm not really listening now as Jonesy waffles on about getting the perfect dog picture. I'm just doing the occasional nod and 'Oh, wow, that's great'. Sandy isn't even bothering to pretend to care.

I finish my food then head back to my room to call Kate. It goes to voicemail.

That's weird. It's past 8 p.m. Surely Rory will be asleep by now, so why isn't she answering? Maybe he's struggling to settle. The guilt hits me again. I should be there. What if he's poorly? No, Kate would have told me. Or would she? She knows it's a big day for me tomorrow, so maybe she's keeping it from me. On the other hand, she could have put him to bed and then fallen asleep. Hang on, of course that's what it is. She's been working so hard on preparing for her research project meeting tomorrow, she's probably nodded off. God, I really hope all this graft pays off for her.

What a week for both of us. My big interview and her big meeting. Such bad timing. But it is what it is.

Time to focus.

I plan everything I can for the interview. What I am going to ask, what I think his reply will be, then what I will say back, and so on and so forth.

At 9.30 p.m., I call the programme output producer. That's the person who will be making the final decision on the timings and running order of the show tomorrow.

It can get very confusing, all these different people in control of the show. To break it down, the technical side is headed up by the director. Then, on the editorial side, you have producers. Setting up the content is the 'day producer' and then running the programme when it's live is the 'output producer'.

Then above all of them is the big boss, the editor of the show, what some people call the showrunner: Gary McGough. The man feared in the news world for his cut-throat attitude and ruthless decisions.

At this point in the day, it's the output producer I need to talk to. I want to make sure I know what else is on the programme that might be relevant to my interview. I'm also going to make a play for some extra time.

I'm relieved to hear that it's Danielle in the hot seat. She's very good, so I know there won't be any messing around. She's not long started her twelve-hour shift so I need to be quick. She sounds flustered as she explains the line-up.

There is a lot of news kicking around, so she's going to have a hell of a job fitting it all in.

Still, that's not my problem. My job is simple: deliver the best interview of my career with one of the most powerful people in the country.

I gulp down my nerves.

I'm prepared in every way I can be.

If only I could have a quick chat with Kate before I sleep. I still haven't heard from her. I'm trying not to worry. Instead I picture her fast asleep in our bed and then I imagine myself wrapping my arms and legs around her. Much nicer than thinking about what I will have to face in the morning.

JONESY

The day of the hijack

Jonesy throws himself out of bed as soon as the alarm goes off. He knows it's going to be a complicated set-up today. There's no time to waste.

He pops his head out of the window to see what the weather is like. It's cold but not wet. He can deal with that. Rain is a broadcasting team's worst nightmare. Even if the filming is inside, the truck needs to be on the outside to get the signal. Wind and rain can really bugger that up for the team. Doesn't look like they need to worry about that today, though.

Sandy is already loading the truck in the car park.

'Morning, gorgeous,' Jonesy bellows cheerfully out of the window.

'Shhhh, people will be sleeping, Jonesy. Anyway, get a move on, it's gonna be a total ball-ache today.'

Jonesy packs up and heads to his van. The broadcast location is a fifteen-minute drive away. And Sandy is right, this is not going to be straightforward.

The crew is used to jumping through lots of security hoops on their broadcasts involving high-profile people, but today's operation is next level. It's less about protecting the people in the building and much more about protecting what is made there.

When Jonesy searched for the location on Google Maps last night, the site looked huge, but today he is struggling to find it. He assumes it's not the type of place that has big signs announcing its location.

Before long he reaches the entrance to an industrial estate. Around him there are hundreds of tiny units, from a welding firm to a bespoke cake-maker, arranged in grid formation. It's not somewhere you would expect to find one of the world's most valuable businesses.

Jonesy is starting to worry that he is in the wrong place, but as he turns a corner he sees a small sign in front of him: *RAS*.

He laughs to himself. This is nothing like the fortress he was expecting. Jonesy pulls up at the security barriers just as Sandy turns in behind him. There is a small security hut.

'ID please,' comes a voice from the window of the hut.

Sandy jumps out of the truck first and hands over her press pass and passport. Seeing her maiden name, her real name, on her documents again makes her happy. Thank God she got rid of that dickhead Darren.

The security guard looks like he couldn't give two shits what the ID says, but that doesn't matter. She smiles anyway.

Meanwhile, Jonesy is frantically searching through every pocket in his trench coat and patting himself down as though it's a new type of dance craze.

They'd been told that they would need to provide several forms of ID, so it's no shock to be asked for it now. Given the hoops they have already been through before they had even arrived, this request should be one of the least stressful.

Jonesy thought he'd put his passport in his coat pocket when he left his house. Today it isn't there. He heads back to the van and opens his boot. He then gets out a screwdriver and proceeds to unscrew a panel in the floor of his van.

'What are you doing?' Sandy asks.

'I'm just getting my ID.'

'In a secret panel? What else do you keep in there? Dead bodies?'

'Yep, and Jaffa Cakes.'

They both laugh. Jonesy heads back to the window and hands over another passport that he keeps as a spare.

'You can't have had much sleep,' says the guard to Jonesy.

Jonesy knows he looks like shit today, but that was a bit below the belt, he thinks.

The security guard continues, barely looking up from the computer he is typing away at.

'Was a good result in the end, mind. Up the Boro.'

Jonesy is not into sport, but he looks like one of those blokes who is, so people always talk to him about the footie and the rugby.

Jonesy nods in agreement and a few moments later the security guard lifts the barrier and points them in the direction of another building about a hundred yards in front of them.

'Well, that was easy enough,' Sandy says as she walks back to the truck.

'I know, I thought it would be much more complicated than that.'

They drive through the barrier and see a man waving and pointing. Sandy parks the truck up next to him in one of the spaces he was gesturing to and Jonesy pulls in beside.

'Morning, I'm Russell, one of your chaperones today. Come on in and we'll start the security process.'

Jonesy and Sandy look at each other and roll their eyes. Of course there's more they need to go through.

'I need to scan you, search you, get your fingerprints and take your mobile phones,' Russell explains as he leads them into the building.

Jonesy is expecting it to look like some type of mission-control room inside, but there is nothing exceptional about it at all. It's an office. A very underwhelming one.

They head into a room that looks like a boardroom. Sitting at the table is Rose.

Sandy and Jonesy both look shocked to see her. The reporters never normally get there before the rest of the crew.

'Bloody hell. What's happened? Why are you here so early? Is everything all right?'

'Yeah, chill out. I just wanted to get cracking. We've got no producer – Zoya is ill – and, well, I just want to nail it today.'

Russell clears his throat.

'Each of you will have a chaperone who will be with you wherever you go – and I mean everywhere.'

Without a word said between them, Sandy and Jonesy stand back up. They have obviously decided it's probably best to go to the loo now and hopefully reduce the chance of needing to go again when Luke, Marcus or Russell, their newly assigned chaperones, will have to join them.

It's going to be an unusual morning for all of them.

ROSE

The day of the hijack

Two hours until I am live on air.

I'm in a local taxi on my way to today's broadcast location. The industrial estate we're driving through looks so familiar. I'm sure it's where my dad brought me when I was learning to drive. Oh, shit. I didn't tell my parents I would be doing a broadcast nearby today. They'll be annoyed, when they see me on the telly, that I didn't tell them I was in the area. Bugger. I'll have to call them later.

I ask the driver to turn up the volume on the radio just in time for the headlines.

It's 4 a.m. and you're listening to Live Time News. *A report into the deaths of more than a thousand babies at Liverpool Children's Hospital has found that there was poor care for over a decade, which led to unnecessary infant fatality.*

Bloody hell. This is sickening. I find it hard to listen to stories about kids now I've got one of my own.

The inquiry, led by Dame Liz Bourne, concluded that there were key failings in a number of areas. One father gave his reaction:

'We lost our beautiful son because of their incompetence. Then the government tried to cover it up. They have blood on their hands and this proves it. We won't let them forget it.'

The poor parents. I can't begin to imagine what hell they're going through. I wouldn't be able to cope if anything happened to my son.

The Department of Health welcomes the report and said it will implement the recommendations immediately. It denies there was a cover-up.

'What a load of shite. More bollocks from the government,' says the taxi driver, who is understandably outraged, like I am.

I don't reply. It's important I stay impartial in situations like this, even though I want to have a full-on rant. You never know who the driver might tell about what I've said in the car.

The newsreader starts the next story.

There have been outbreaks of violence around the country over-night, directed towards media outlets. Leeds Live was one of a number of TV stations to be vandalized. It comes following comments made by disgraced politician Janet Jacobs.

'Now I like her, mind, that Janet. Stands up for folk.'

I try not to react when the driver says this. I definitely don't want to get into that debate with him. Not about her.

Jacobs, who is currently on trial for money laundering, told fans outside the High Court that 'everyone has a right to be heard and they need to reclaim the media in whatever way they can'. Twenty-five people have been arrested.

'Aye, she's been stitched up there, like. Bet she's done nowt. That's the establishment wanting to stop her.'

I bite my tongue. I desperately want to get out of the taxi now before he finds out what my job is.

Health officials are warning that the service will collapse if the government continues with its plans to freeze the healthcare budget, announced by the chancellor yesterday. The Institute for Fiscal Studies said that government is trying to curb its excessive borrowing, but it could come at a huge cost to some of our most important services.

'A bunch of crooks, those politicians.'

He can't let any story go without giving an extreme opinion on it. I am now wishing I hadn't asked for the volume to be turned up.

Abdul Khalid, who was released from prison yesterday, has . . .

The driver doesn't even let the newsreader finish before he launches into another rant.

'See, they want to put Janet away, but they let out those—'

'Can we turn it off, please, I need to make a call.' I purpose-fully interrupt him before he says something racist. I've had enough of listening to his commentary now.

I call my programme team. The phone is ringing for ages before anyone answers. They're obviously busy.

'Hey, Rose, all OK? We're manic this morn.' The output producer, Danielle, is clearly quite stressed by all the breaking news coming in.

'Yeah, all is fine, just wanted to talk timings and—'

Before I can finish, Danielle stops listening and starts shouting across the newsroom to someone else.

'No, I've said fifteen times now, you need to blur the faces of the kids. Jesus Christ! And, Chris, can you check Becky has done her hostile environment training? It looks like this Janet Jacobs stuff outside the High Court will be nasty.'

She stops shouting.

'What were you saying, Rose?'

'I just want to make sure I'm getting enough time this morning. We have amazing access. And—'

I'm interrupted again.

'No, we don't need the pictures of the missing penguins – they found them, you imbecile. Don't you read the fucking news before you come in? . . . Yes, I know you were sleeping, but a quick fucking google won't kill you.'

'Sorry, Rose, Gen Z – so fucking work-shy, it's driving me bats. Anyway, headlines on the hour, then three mins at six-forty. Then I'm giving you eight at seven-ten.'

Oh, that's good news, my interview with the chancellor at ten past seven is now getting eight minutes instead of the original six minutes. More time to nail him.

Danielle is still in full flow.

'We need a news line, so go hard on healthcare, but also get a line on Khalid, and the Janet Jacobs case. After that, we'll play it by ear. Oh, actually, the chancellor is a bit of a thick twat, isn't he – it might be worth asking him the bread and milk price questions too, cos he'll probably fuck them up.'

'And the missing penguins?' I joke.

She laughs and then hangs up.

I hadn't realized that the taxi had stopped while I was on the phone. We're outside one of the units in the industrial estate with a sign saying *Plumpy's Palace* above it.

'Erm, sorry, but I don't think we're in the right place.'

'Really? This is where I drop off most of you lasses.'

Oh, bloody hell. The taxi driver thinks I'm a sex worker. Not again.

'No, no, it's not that kind of work. I do actually want to go to RAS, the address I gave you.'

'Oh, right, sorry, love, I just assumed, given the time and with you saying you were working. Well, I just thought . . .'

'Yeah, I know.'

An awkward silence follows.

As we drive away, another car pulls up at Plumpy's. I'm practically breaking my neck to see who is going to get out. I'm always fascinated by the types of people who go to these places. I don't know what I'm expecting to see, but I am desperate to have a look. I see the silhouette of a person, but no more. And, just as they are about to get out, we've turned a corner and are outside RAS.

After showing my ID at the security gate, I head through to a boardroom where I'm told to wait. I'm the first one there. I scroll through my phone until a grumpy bloke walks in.

'Right, I'm Luke. I'll be your chaperone today.'

'Oh, wonderful. Thank you so much, Luke. And cheers for letting us in to do the broadcast. It's amazing to get this access. And, well, we are all so grateful—'

He cuts me off as I'm midway through my charm offensive.

'If I had my way you wouldn't be here at all. But we've got a new boss who wants us to be more open with the media and, well, here we are. My job is damage limitation. Phone, please.'

'I have to hand it in now?'

Luke holds out a sandwich bag for me to put it in.

'Yep.'

'But I will need to talk to my team back at base.'

'There are landlines you can use.'

'Right, but I've signed all the security stuff, what's the harm?'

'Listen, this is one of the most secure places on the planet. We can't have you wandering around with a camera in your pocket and the ability to show the world what goes on in here.'

'Eh, it may have escaped your notice, but I'm taking a live TV camera in, so that rule makes no sense at all.'

'Yes, more's the pity, but I can control where you point that. You will have designated places where you can film and we will move staff so you won't see their faces.'

'What, even the staff have to be kept secret?'

'Of course they do. They could be taken hostage and forced into compromising security. Phone – now.'

People being taken hostage? It all sounds so far-fetched. This fella is definitely a jobsworth.

However, I don't need to be told again.

I send a quick text to Kate and pop the phone in the bag Luke is holding out. I still haven't heard from her.

She obviously went to bed early last night and isn't awake yet, so she won't have seen my messages.

It's as simple as that. It's got to be.

ARABELLA

4 a.m.

The day of the hijack

'Right, as discussed yesterday, you've got three broadcast and two newspaper interviews.'

Arabella has just arrived in the hotel room where the chancellor is having his breakfast.

Charles Barrow looks up from his newspaper and puts down the croissant he is eating. The plate is balancing on his belly, which in turn is being propped up by the table. Arabella can't help but notice that his shirt looks as if it has only been ironed at the front. The sleeves are still creased and no doubt the back of the shirt will be too. A visual reminder that this man only ever does the bare minimum to get by.

'You couldn't pop a bit more hot water in that tea, could you?'

Arabella ignores this request and continues with the briefing. As his special adviser – SPAD for short – she has to help him prepare for his media interviews. She hasn't got long. She cuts straight to the point.

'Your first one is our priority. The Rose Steedman interview.'

Arabella knows Rose well. Their paths have crossed at various points in their careers. When they were starting out, they worked in the same newsroom together as producers. Arabella focused on politics and Rose on business.

They didn't hate each other as such – despite their different backgrounds they were weirdly alike – but the newsroom bosses seemed to take great pleasure in pitting them against each other in that poor-versus-rich vibe. And Arabella played up to that.

By all accounts, Arabella was, and still is, a total bitch to Rose. It did not mean that she didn't think she was good at her job, though.

Arabella knows this is the interview that her boss will get caught out on.

The chancellor, who has barely moved since she walked in, looks at her blankly for a moment before his eyes start to dart around as if he is manually going through every filing cabinet in his brain to pull out information on Rose Steedman.

After a few seconds, he clearly finds what he is looking for.

'Ah, yes, that common woman. What is she? Northern?'

'She is northern, yes, and today you're being interviewed by her in her home territory, so you need to be super-positive about the North.'

'I always am.'

'You just called her common.'

'You know what I mean.'

Arabella is no stranger to men like the chancellor. After her stint in journalism, Arabella went to work for a hedge fund in Canary Wharf. It was full of powerful men whose stinking arrogance would smack you in the face as soon as you walked into a room they were in. Like the smell of a punchy cheese when you open the fridge door.

This man wasn't quite at Stinking Bishop level, but he wasn't far off. It didn't bother Arabella. Politics wasn't much different to finance in terms of its make-up. The 'earls and girls' recruitment was how one of her old bosses described it.

The chancellor was definitely self-entitled and occasionally patronizing, but the public loved him. He had a great way with people and always made them feel like they were important to him, even if he was a bit thick.

What she had struggled to work out, though, was whether he was one of the 'handsy ones'.

They were the men in the office who you had to avoid being alone with. The ones who thought nothing of casually groping you as they passed by. In her last job, any woman who spoke out would quickly disappear, probably with a nice pay-off, but with nothing ever done to stop the sexual assaults continuing for the next female recruits.

Arabella often joked with her group of girl mates in the City about why so many of the men looked like walruses. In fact that became the code name for the worst offenders. They had a WhatsApp group called 'Walrus Watchers', where they would share funny stories with each other about the stupid things the walruses did and said.

One of the men overheard them talking about it once. Arabella's quick-thinking friend Lucy pretended they were discussing a new shade of lipstick that MAC had brought out called Walrus Hue. This backfired when he then tried to buy the non-existent shade for his mistress. Still, he never worked out what they were really talking about.

Despite their ability to laugh at these awful men, the group messages also provided a safe space and an important support network.

So far the chancellor hadn't been worthy of a mention in the group chat. He hadn't even flirted with Arabella, which was unusual for her. Despite getting a first-class honours in Philosophy, Politics and Economics from Oxford, she knew it was her looks that disarmed men.

It was a poisoned chalice, being pretty, her mother had told her. You get everything you want apart from respect. Arabella's mother had been an air hostess and part-time model who met her banker father on a flight to New York. They were rich and, because of that, Arabella and her sister had a great life. They went to private school in term time, spent their summers in the south of France, their winters in the Caribbean and the ski season in Verbier. She was the 'ultimate posh lass', as one of her uni friends from Hull described her.

Her looks and privilege seemed to mean nothing to the chancellor, though. Which was a rarity.

And, despite all the bravado and self-entitlement, he did listen to her. She knew he needed her, and that would help Arabella get her job done today.

'Do you remember the last time Rose Steedman interviewed you?'

The chancellor whips down the newspaper, knocking off the croissant crumbs from his belly. They land on Arabella's open-toed shoes. She tries to hide her disgust at the debris now in her toe cleavage.

'Surely you don't expect me to remember every single interview I've ever done?'

'Perhaps not, Chancellor, but this one was particularly bad. Let me remind you. You were at the launch of a cultural event in Newcastle and you were on with a famous author. She asked you about funding for libraries.'

'Libraries? Who gives a shit about libraries?'

Arabella sighs; she knows he is joking.

'You suggested northerners didn't need libraries because they couldn't read. There was a huge backlash.'

The chancellor laughs and goes back to reading his paper.

'Right, don't mention libraries then,' he says from behind the paper, still laughing as he says it.

'No! Don't make any derogatory jokes about northerners – or anyone, for that matter. That would be my advice anyway.'

Arabella's done her bit now.

It's up to him to deal with what comes next.

JONESY

The day of the hijack

t's a foggy morning at the RAS site, which makes it impossible to get a sense of the scale of the place.

The route they're taking in the golf buggy suggests it's not a site you could easily walk around.

The journey gives Russell the chance to tell Jonesy all about the history of the place, which had originally been home to a munitions plant in the Second World War. Unsurprisingly, given Jonesy's background in the military, he is firing a million questions at his chaperone.

Jonesy's delighted to learn that it had been the famous Royal Ordnance Factory where thousands of people worked filling shells and bullets, as well as assembling detonators and fuses.

'It was even visited by Winston Churchill during the war,' Russell proudly explains as he continues with more tales from the past, as though they're on one of those Universal Studio tours.

'We're here,' Luke announces as he slams the brakes on the buggy, making everyone lurch forward.

Russell's tone changes from one of 'tour guide' to 'squadron leader'.

Before Rose and Jonesy have even stepped out of the buggy,

Luke and Russell have leapt out ahead of them and are aggressively pointing to the lines on the floor.

'See these lines. You have to stay in them.'

It's just the four of them now outside what looks like another office door.

The satellite truck, which had been following the buggy, is now heading around to a fire door at the back of the building. Sandy and her chaperone Marcus are aiming to get the truck into a decent broadcast position. They need to park it outside to get a signal, but still be close enough to where Rose and Jonesy will be filming inside, so wires can be put through to connect everything together and get them on air.

Jonesy grabs his camera, tripod and 'bag of bits', as he calls it, off the back of the golf buggy and heads to the door with Rose following behind. The darkness and fog mean they still haven't been able to judge the size of the building they are going into.

Luke, who is slightly ahead, gestures for them to go through into the lobby area, where they are scanned again.

It is eerily quiet and Jonesy is starting to question whether this is actually what they think it's going to be.

Luke uses his pass to open another door into a corridor that has security gates. They look a bit like the ones you get at the airport, which only let you go one way. This time they each take it in turns to have their face scanned, which then activates the gate to open into another long corridor.

At the end of that is a huge, vault-like door.

It opens slowly.

The atmosphere changes in an instant.

'Fuck me,' says Jonesy, his eyes lighting up like he's in a sex shop.

'It's unbelievable,' replies Rose, who, despite her many visits to businesses all over the world, has never seen anything like this.

They are gobsmacked by the scale of the operation in front of them. It is a different world. Like they've stepped through the wardrobe into Narnia.

This is the first time the public are going to see inside one of the most extraordinary factories in the world.

This is the place where money is printed.

Millions of pounds' worth of notes are rolling off the presses around them.

Rose and Jonesy stand open-mouthed.

There are only a handful of factories like this in the world and this is by far the biggest.

There are people everywhere, looking busy and important. And the sound is overwhelming. Huge machines working full pelt, which explains why the temperature has gone up a notch too.

Among the machines, an army of people are carefully scouring the sheets flying off the production lines.

Luke moves them on quickly.

'Right, no time for gawping, let's get to your broadcast point. Please stick to the lines on the ground and don't touch anything!'

By now, Jonesy has already wandered off and is chatting to one of the lads at a press that is pumping out Iranian rial.

His chaperone, Russell, is manhandling him back into line.

'Rose, guess how much one of those sheets is worth? Ten thousand pounds! That is fucking mental. That one sheet of paper could solve all my problems.'

'Now you know why they won't let us go to the loo on our own, Jonesy. You'd probably try to ram one of those sheets down your pants.'

'Nah, nah, I wouldn't, there's no room down there – know what I'm saying?'

Rose rolls her eyes. She hasn't got time for Jonesy's jokes, not when she's got the most important interview of her career coming up.

As fun as this tour is and as astonishing as the audience are going to find it, she needs to get in position and focus.

ROSE

Thirty minutes until I am live on air.

The camera is now set up and connected to the wires that Sandy has pulled through the fire door. I check the two microphones we have are working. They are. I put mine on. I loop it up through my jumper, out through the neck, clip the mic on the edge and then attach the pack to my trousers. Fortunately the high-vis jacket covers the box at the back.

We still only have one talkback unit, which Jonesy is currently frowning at.

'The talkback is playing silly buggers. It's only letting me go to one channel. It's like it's stuck. Should still work, though, just won't be the usual channel.'

'Maybe it got a bit damp in the van. Give it here.'

I connect my earpiece to the talkback unit and after fiddling with the volume I suddenly hear Sandy laughing in my ear.

'All OK out there, Sandy?' I ask.

'Yes, I'm just pissing myself at this sign I can see over the hedge.'

'Oh God, let me guess – is it Plumpy's Palace?'

'Yes, do you know it? Is it what I think it is?'

'A strip club, yes.'

Jonesy interrupts. He is only hearing my side of the conversation.

'Plumpy's Palace? That's where I met my ex-wife.'

'Ah, Jonesy, man, your gags are too predictable.'

It's a relief that the talkback is working. Now we're waiting for Sandy to get the signal she needs to connect us to the programme. She's not far off.

It's weird. We're much further on than we'd normally be at this time. I should take comfort in this, but actually it unnerves me. It's such a big day.

I keep reaching into my pocket to get my phone that isn't there. I'm desperate to find out if Kate has replied to my message yet. I also really need to talk to my team back at base. It feels too long to wait until Sandy gets the line connected, so I decide to find the landline.

'Luke, this phone you mentioned, where is it? I need to call my team.'

'Just over there,' he replies, gesturing towards a machine with a desk next to it.

'Ah, great. What's the number for getting through to it so I can let my team know?'

'No one can call in.'

'Eh?'

'It's a one-way phone. Dial 9 to get an external line. I'll have to stand next to you while you make the call, mind.'

Someone picks up the phone straight away. It's Sharif; he must be in charge of the outside broadcasts again today.

'Ah, Rose, the boss has been trying to get hold of you. You're not answering your phone.'

'No, we've had to hand them in. I'm on a landline. Is everything all right?'

'Yeah, fine, but have you seen the newswires?'

'No, like I said, I don't have a phone. What is it?'

'Janet Jacobs has been found dead.'

Dead. What?

My brain is struggling to process the information. I should be used to dramatic news in this job, but sometimes things still floor me, especially when the news is about people I know.

'Has she been murdered?'

I can't help but assume a woman who has driven such division and hatred between people must be on some type of hit list.

'No idea, we're just waiting on details. We've not been able to double-source it yet. It's just doing the rounds on Twitter. We're calling Jacobs' agent now. But, Rose, there's more I need to tell you.'

'I know, I know, you're cutting my time and bumping me down the running order. I get it, this is big news, blah blah blah. My stuff is boring. Yeah, I get it.'

'No, Rose, it's not about that. It's about you.'

'Eh, what do you mean, it's about me?'

I'm confused. How the hell am I connected to this?

'Rose . . .'

'Sharif, why do you keep saying my name like that?'

'Erm, people are saying on social media that she had a stalker and it might be something to do with him.'

'I suspect she had a lot of stalkers. She's got a whole load of weirdos who follow her around, but why does that matter to me?'

'His name is Big B . . . Billy Rubin.'

JONESY

5.35 a.m.

The day of the hijack

'You can't go outside,' says Russell, who is following Jonesy to the fire exit.

'But I need to check we've got the signal sorted.'

'If you go outside then you'll have to go through the whole security process again. Only your engineer is allowed in and out, because she's got the authority for that.'

Jonesy is getting stressed.

'You're making my job very hard, you know, mate. I'm not trying to nick owt, I'm just trying to make sure we get on air.'

Russell crosses his arms and steps in front of the door.

'Yeah, and you're making my job hard by trying to breach our strict security procedures.'

Jonesy gives up and walks away from the door. He is not happy.

'I'm going to fart in about ten minutes too – I suppose you'll need to be there for that as well.'

At that point Rose reappears next to them with her chaperone, Luke.

Jonesy takes it as another chance to moan about the strict security.

'I'm just telling one of the Chuckle Brothers here that we're not going to be able to do our job properly unless they chill out a bit.'

'Listen, we knew it was going to be hard so we just need to do what we can.'

Rose's response is a bit more abrupt than Jonesy is expecting.

'Are you all right?'

'Yeah, yeah. Just some weird news, that's all. That loon Janet Jacobs is dead.'

Russell and Luke both drop the teacher act momentarily and stare at Rose in shock.

Unsurprisingly, Jonesy is the first to speak.

'Wow, well, I suppose she was bound to get bumped off eventually. Miserable old bitch.'

Before anyone else can say anything, a loud crackle comes out of the talkback box that Rose is holding. This is followed by voices chatting away to themselves, as if they're suddenly eavesdropping on someone else's conversation.

'Ah, brilliant, we have a signal,' says Jonesy, who is now picking up the camera ready for action. 'Come on, love, let's get ourselves into position.'

As if at the flick of a switch, Jonesy watches Rose go into reporter mode, clearly turning off the bit of her brain that is worrying about something. He's known her long enough to see her do this on a number of occasions.

It's fifteen minutes until they are live on national television from a location that's never been seen before on screen. This is going to blow the audience's mind.

ROSE

'CUE ROSE,' I hear in my ear.

'Good morning from the world's biggest money-printing factory. Seventy different currencies are made here, from dollars to pounds to yen. Today I'll be talking to the man in charge of the country's money . . .'

Before I can finish I hear a crackle and then a voice saying 'testing, testing' in my ear, then another crackle. It throws me off for a moment, so I slightly stumble over the last few words of my sentence.

'. . . the chancellor, to find out more about his plans for our economy.'

I carry on staring into the camera with a fixed smile until someone tells me I'm not on air any more.

'And we're off you. Thanks, Rose. Back with you at six forty,' says Sharif in my ear.

I'm glad that first headline is out of the way, but I'm annoyed that I slightly stumbled.

Who was that? Someone must have accidentally come through to my earpiece. It happened to me a couple of weeks ago too, when one of the people in the gallery thought they were talking to our weather presenter. They had pressed the wrong talkback button so they came through to me when I was live on air. Trying to talk about liability-driven investments while being given a rundown on squally clouds was tricky, to say the least.

I need to get through this morning without any hitches.

That also means not worrying about all the other stuff in my head, including Kate and Rory. Or Billy.

It's surprising how often I have to do that. I always need to look bright and cheerful on the telly. I can't ever let the world see what might really be going on in my life. Nope, the nation expects and pays for Rose the wonder woman, who isn't stressed about a man stalking her, or her family going AWOL. I'm being dramatic, but the point stands. No matter what is going on, or how stressed or worried I am, I can never let the nation see it. On telly, I always have to be cool, calm and collected.

Luke, who agreed to stand out of vision during that headline, is now back next to me.

'Charlotte said they're happy with that first bit and she'll be down shortly once the chancellor arrives.'

'Right you are. If Charlotte is happy then that's great news. Remind me, who is Charlotte again?'

Luke looks at me like I'm an idiot.

'She's from the PR team.'

I'm already picturing some young posh lass who has come up from London and will probably do our heads in.

We've got about thirty-five minutes until I'm next on. I should probably check in with the team back at base. We've had to power down the kit to conserve battery, so I'm going to have to call from the landline again.

I get through to Jake, who is one of the producers on the team. He sounds harassed.

'It's not ideal not being able to contact you, Rose. Anyway,

Danielle is wanting you to talk to some of the staff there in your next hit.'

'We're not allowed to show the faces of any of the staff, Jake. It's part of the security, just like the no phone rule.'

'Surely there must be a way around it? Use your imagination, Rose.'

What a cheeky little shit. Use my imagination. Producers who never leave the office drive me bats. They have no concept of what it's like on the ground.

'You know what, Jake, I probably shouldn't even be using this landline and you sound busy anyway, so I'll just stick with my plans unless someone says something different in my ear.'

And I hang up.

Jonesy and I plan the next hit. We're battling with the noise a bit, so we wander around to find the best spot. Luke and Russell are still monitoring our every move. Apart from that, though, everything feels very straightforward. It's weird, but despite all the drama happening outside this building, it feels strangely calm inside. The sound of the machines whirring away is actually quite therapeutic. Jonesy and I are doing what we're best at. Sandy keeps us in the loop of what's happening from her position in the truck.

Between the three of us, we have everything under control. And I am enjoying it.

Before we know it, we're back on air. I'm doing a show-and-tell, picking up sheets of notes and explaining how the machines run 24/7 to make them. As I walk from one machine to the next, I talk about the extraordinary layers of security they have here. Even the notes themselves have twenty-five different security features on them. The presenters in the studio are clearly engaged with this story because they start firing questions at me about what happens if there are misprints. I explain how, instead of just throwing them away, they have to shred them in front of a representative from the country the currency is from.

I end the three minutes I've had on air by telling everyone that in thirty minutes' time I'll be interviewing the chancellor live on the show.

I'm ready.

ROSE

Seconds after finishing my seven o'clock headline I see the chancellor and his entourage walking through the factory towards me.

There are four of them in total. One is obviously their chaperone, given the lanyard he is wearing, and the other three are straight from Westminster central casting.

At the front is Charles Barrow. In one respect he looks like your typical male, pale, stale politician, but in another he is someone who commands your attention.

In my many years as a journalist, interviewing lots of leaders from the world of business and politics, I have observed a commonality. When they walk into a room, they have gravitas, irrespective of whether they are good at their job. People stop what they're doing and look at them. Not necessarily because they have any extraordinary physical attributes; it's something less tangible – they just somehow seem to own the space.

Charles Barrow has that. Although in this moment he is giving me Village People vibes, thanks to his pink neon high-vis jacket sitting clumsily over his suit, which seems on the tight side. Also I am pretty sure there are crumbs on his tie, which is resting awkwardly on his rotund belly. As my mates at home would say, 'He looks a right clip.'

What Charles also has to his advantage is wealth. He is posh. And with that comes connections. I am sure I read somewhere that he is a distant relation of the king, but then aren't they all, these posh folk?

Talking of posh, so are the people he has hired to advise him. I can spot them a mile off. The SPADs. First up is a young lad in a tailored suit with matching waistcoat and pocket watch, who couldn't look more out of place if he tried. His face tells me he is about twenty, but his clothes date him to the early twentieth century. He's a good-looking lad with that classic solid and defined jaw, angular nose and deep-set eyes. On top of which sits a mop of beautifully quaffed auburn hair. No doubt he washes it in unicorn tears to get that shine. I definitely would have remembered him if I'd seen him before, so he must be new. He actually looks like he could be on work experience, but I think that's more about me feeling old than him being young.

With him, surveying the scene like a stunning jaguar about to hunt down its prey, is the tall, svelte and immaculately put-together Arabella Pinchinthorpe – or Lady Macbeth, as we call her in the newsroom.

We go way back. Behind our fake smiles is a fierce rivalry. You could say we were made to dislike each other in order to survive and get on in our careers. But we just can't seem to drop it.

For a while, we worked together as producers and then, one day, she suddenly left journalism for a job in the City. There were rumours that she'd had an affair with one of our news editors and it had all gone a bit sour, but who knows? There wasn't a straight man in the newsroom who didn't fancy Arabella, and I wouldn't be surprised if she had slept her way to the top.

I wouldn't blame her either; she had the looks and the brains to make most men succumb. I, on the other hand, think I got on because the blokes saw me as their bit of rough. I was nowhere near as good-looking as Arabella, but I was decent at my make-up and could hold my own when we were out drinking. This led to me being on the receiving end of a few inappropriate comments at staff parties. Nothing I couldn't handle, though.

Looking back, we should have bonded over the way we were seen by the men in the office, but we never did and we never will.

A lot has changed since our early twenties. Just look at her now – not just a SPAD, but the Chancellor of the Exchequer's chief of staff. An incredible rise to power and a reminder, given it's my job to hold the government to account, that the rivalry definitely hasn't gone.

As soon as the chancellor and the entourage approach me, the atmosphere changes in an instant.

I go to greet Charles with my hand extended to shake it. He ignores this and instead gives me a wry smile as Arabella steps forward instead.

'Arrogant twat' is what I want to say, but I hold back. Instead, it's time to start the game of cat and mouse with Lady Macbeth.

'Good morning, Rose. So, to confirm, you will have exactly eight minutes with the chancellor. Can you tell me your line of questioning?'

'Arabella, so lovely to see you. You know we don't tell you what we're going to ask. I'm sure a man of Mr Barrow's experience will be more than prepared for whatever may come up.'

'As you and I both know, Rose, it makes for a much better interview if the minister is fully briefed on what you are going to ask.'

The men around us watch the conversation unfold like they're following a rally at Wimbledon. I actually don't know why I am being so polite to her. I'm not taking this shit from her. Especially not today.

'As you and I both know, Arabella, that's bullshit.'

Arabella gives me one of her classic fake smiles I've seen a hundred times before, then turns on her heel towards the chancellor, who is looking very smug.

I bet they're shagging. It wouldn't be the first time a politician was having an affair with an aide.

Anyway, round one is complete. I think I might have just won that one. As if I was going to give her the questions I'll be asking. What planet is she on?

Jonesy appears next to me with a huge grin on his face. He's clearly observed the whole thing.

'I love seeing you two together.'

I roll my eyes. Jonesy worked with Arabella in the newsroom too and knows all about our rivalry.

'Listen, I know she's a bit fierce and all that, but I like that in a woman. It's why I love you so much. Plus the sexual chemistry between you – you've got to feel it.'

'Fuck off, Jonesy, you're doing my head in.'

Jonesy goes from laughing to instantly looking pissed off.

'I'll tell you what's doing my head in. That corrupt bastard on the phone.'

Jonesy is gesturing to the chancellor, who is a few metres away, deep in conversation on his mobile. Fortunately, no one hears Jonesy calling the minister corrupt, which is just as well because I really don't want another debate with the government about whether our news organization is biased.

Jonesy turns to his chaperone.

'Why the frig is *he* allowed his phone, eh?'

Russell is clearly not in the mood for any more of Jonesy's moaning and snaps back at him.

'Because he's the chancellor, duh. He's hardly gonna nick money from here, is he?'

'Are you kidding? He's a politician, they're more dodgy than the rest of us put together. Bloody double standards.'

'Mate, I don't make the big decisions. To be honest, if I had my way he wouldn't have a phone either, but you know, the bosses told me he doesn't have to follow the same rules.'

'"He doesn't have to follow the same rules" – that fucking sums it up, doesn't it.'

I hear a crackle in my ear. Sandy's voice booms through.

'Rose, it sounds like it's not long until you're on. I'm going to connect you.'

I take a deep breath.

Time to nail him.

ROSE

'm ready.

Through my earpiece I can hear the presenters in the studio introducing me. I don't want to waste a single second of my time with the minister. So as soon as they throw to me I start the interview.

'Good morning, everyone. I'm here in Teesside at the world's biggest money-printing factory along with the Chancellor of the Exchequer, Charles Barrow. Good morning, Chancellor, thanks for joining us. I'll get straight to it. You announced a freeze on healthcare spending. The IFS says this is a 10 per cent cut in real terms. Why are you cutting healthcare spending?'

'Good morning, Rose, thanks for having me on the show. Let me start by saying what a great honour it is to be here at RAS, a great British engineering success story, bringing in millions to our economy every year, as well as providing jobs in the North East. In fact, this very site has a wonderful manufacturing legacy, having been home to some seventeen thousand workers, mainly women, who helped to make munitions for the Second World War.'

Typical delay tactic. He knows this will eat into some of the time I have with him.

Time to jump in.

'Yes, Chancellor, British manufacturing at its best. So let's talk healthcare cuts.'

The chancellor gives a smug nod and continues.

'Yesterday I announced a raft of ways we will be boosting the economy, which will bring in more money for the long term . . .'

It's obvious that he is going to continue to ignore what I ask and just bang on with his own agenda. I am not having it.

'With respect' – I have no idea why I am saying this but I continue anyway – 'what about the cuts, in real terms?'

I hear 'six minutes' in my ear. He's already waffled through two minutes of our time. I need to start punching through.

'Chancellor, why have you cut healthcare spending?'

The chancellor carries on talking about the importance of construction. I see in the corner of my eye that Arabella is nodding at him, which suggests she's pleased with how it's going. That's annoying. I need to land something here. I will. I know what I'm doing.

I interrupt again.

'Chancellor, answer the question—'

'Well, Rose, I think what matters now is not . . .'

There's a crackle in my ear and I hear another voice, but I can't think who it is.

'Rose, you need to ask my questions now.'

That's weird, who the fuck is saying that? Anyway, it doesn't matter, I need to concentrate on what the chancellor is saying. I ignore the voice and push further. I've moved on to ask about Abdul Khalid.

'Listen to me, I'm in control now,' says the voice in my earpiece.

What the fuck is going on? I ignore the voice once more. I mustn't lose my concentration on what is being said by Charles Barrow. But I hear them in my earpiece again.

'Rose, I have your wife and son.'

Eh? Is this a pisstake? I can't believe what I'm hearing. This must be some daft prank. Or am I having some type of stroke live on telly? I've heard about that happening. Still, I continue to ignore whoever is in my ear. This is the biggest interview of my career. I cannot let it be derailed by some prankster who keeps talking to me in my earpiece.

'You need to carry on as normal, but I am in control now.'

The chancellor is waffling on about launching an inquiry.

I need to get this back under control.

The voice speaks again.

'Rose, listen to me. I have Kate and Rory, I took them from your house in Didsbury. Your son did not go to Busy Bees Nursery this morning because I have him.'

I feel a pain inside like I have been hit by a double-decker bus.

Rory. Kate. Didsbury. Busy Bees. What the fuck?

This is real.

'I have him.' The words are ringing in my ears.

'You must not react,' says the voice.

I am frozen with fear.

Whoever this is, they know too much for this to be fake. Very few people know what my son is called, never mind where I live and what nursery he goes to.

'Rose, do exactly as I say and no one will get hurt.'

I am live on telly. I cannot react. I must not react.

PART TWO

Five years before the hijack

OLLIE

Ollie Croft was fifteen when his school was put into special measures.

A new headteacher had been appointed, who was desperate to turn things around and make a name for herself. Harriet Waters knew that if she could get Newton Banks Academy back on track, like she had done with all her other schools, she would be a shoo-in for an OBE. She'd been told as much by the chair of the academy trust, who had a say in the local honours nominations. He had convinced her to take on this one last job before she retired. Harriet wasn't arsed about getting an OBE, but she knew her dad would be made up if she got one, so she said yes. Plus she was a sucker for trying to help kids that others had given up on.

Like most schools in deprived areas, it wasn't that the kids or the teachers were bad, it was that lots of the pupils didn't have the structure in their lives to allow them to be good at the academic assessments they were constantly put through.

Harriet hated that the British education system measured everyone purely by academic achievements and not by the practical stuff that the kids she worked with needed and were good at.

More often than not the young people in schools like hers were clever – they had to be in order to survive – but because they weren't necessarily the bookish 'clever' that everyone banged on about all the time, they were written off.

Two thirds of the kids who went to Newton Banks Academy were on free school meals, nearly triple the national average. And about a third were 'looked-after children', meaning they were in the care system in some form or another.

The teachers at this school spent more time dealing with child protection issues than they did giving curriculum-driven lessons. But it didn't seem to matter to the inspectors when they visited. There was a bit of lip service paid to the school for the work they did in what they called the 'softer' areas of teaching, but all that mattered was whether the pupils were getting the grades. They weren't, so the school was deemed as failing.

Harriet was determined to change that.

She was a firm believer in the 'fake it till you make it' mantra. If she could get the kids and the teachers to pretend that they were just as good as the students and staff in the other local schools, then eventually they would be.

Ollie Croft was one of those students. He'd been told by his form tutor that he was lucky because he came from what his teacher said was a 'good home'; in other words, his parents were still together and they both had jobs. He didn't feel lucky, though. His mam had cancer and his dad worked away all the time.

Ollie was, more often than not, the person in charge at home, looking after his younger brothers and his poorly mam.

The responsibility was both suffocating and isolating.

Ollie was desperate to escape. Not in the middle of the night as a runaway kid; that was definitely not an option. His family would be heartbroken, plus where would he go and how would he survive? Apart from the money he'd been given by various neighbours from the odd jobs he'd done, like sorting out their phone and laptop problems, he was skint.

He had £50 to his name. Not enough to escape.

Plus he had no idea what he wanted to do with his life even if he could get away.

Loads of his mates wanted to be footballers or reality stars or, in his best mate CJ's case, an influencer. None of that interested him. Also, he was rubbish at sport and was embarrassingly shy, not least because he seemed to be miles behind his classmates when it came to his physical development. He hated looking younger than everyone else. His mam kept telling him he'd catch up and, given she was a nurse, he could only hope she was right.

No, he needed to find something else. His dad reckoned he could sort him out with a job at the company he worked for. He quite liked that idea, but he knew that would mean he'd still be stuck at home.

It wasn't that Ollie hated his family or the place he lived, even though everyone referred to it as Newton Bronx. He just hated that his life was so constrained.

When his dad was away, which was at least three days a week, it was Ollie's job to get his brothers fed and organized for school. He also had to make sure that they got there and back safely, had clean clothes to wear and went to bed at a reasonable hour. His mam tried to take some of the burden when she could, but between her nursing shifts and the cancer treatment she was either not there or too weak.

It was too much, but he knew everyone was trying their best and he didn't want to add to his parents' worries.

He felt guilty for even thinking about wanting to leave.

It wasn't that long ago Ollie had heard his dad crying in the bathroom after a visit to the local foodbank. He'd always told them that only lazy people had to rely on handouts. And now he was having to use one. He knew his dad was crying with shame.

Ollie tried to offer him the £50 he'd been saving, but he refused to accept it.

'No, son, this is not your problem, and you've grafted for that,' his dad had said as he stuffed the dog-eared ten-pound notes back in Ollie's school shirt pocket.

Ollie didn't know what to say. He could see his dad's eyes fill with tears again.

He gave Ollie a quick ruffle of his hair before leaving the room. Ollie wondered if he had done the wrong thing by offering the money; maybe he'd just made his dad's shame worse.

This whole situation was a mess.

And Ollie wanted a way out for them all.

Harriet had a plan for the school and it started with a visit from a politician.

The MP coming to Newton Banks Academy was a local man named Steve Evans. Like the kids he was seeing today, he knew what it was like to come from a place that is constantly being slated. Steve had started his career in engineering as an apprentice welder and over the course of two decades had climbed the ranks to become the managing director of a global fabrication firm. From there he'd set up his own business, which he then ended up selling for a tidy sum to the company he'd started out at. Steve had defied the odds and, as a result, he was now a wealthy man.

'He coulda straight-up retired with his dough,' Ollie said to his mate CJ, who was one of several pupils who had been told to go to the school library and google 'Steve Evans MP'.

'What does MP mean – massive penis?' laughed CJ, who had interpreted the request by his teacher to go to the library as free rein for him to muck about for a couple of hours.

'It's Member of Parliament, bellend.'

'Same thing.'

Ollie laughed as he continued to scroll through all the articles that had come up about Steve Evans. He'd never had the want, or need, to research a politician before, but he was actually enjoying it.

'Y'know what, he seems sound,' Ollie said to CJ, having just read an article about Steve selling his business and giving a load of money to a local foodbank.

'Why'd he go into politics then? I'd be freestylin' a Ferrari round Newton Bronx, pickin' up the laaaadies,' CJ said, putting on a stupid voice as though he was an American gangster.

Ollie nudged CJ.

'Hold up, Waters the Plants is coming.'

The lads tried to stifle their laughs. They had been quick to agree on their headteacher's nickname when she started at the school three weeks ago. Every time one of them said it out loud they were hit with a fit of giggles. Harriet Waters had heard it all before; in fact, it was what her friends called her too. Every year on her birthday she'd receive a parcel addressed to 'Lady Waters the Plants'. Her mates refused to let her live down the comedy value of her name.

'Are you ready to give Mr Evans a tour?' Harriet said to Ollie.

'Yeah, s'ppose so,' Ollie replied, having reverted back to teenage lad stereotype now he was in the presence of a teacher.

The students who had gathered in the library had been chosen for a reason. In a move that had surprised the school department heads, Harriet hadn't asked for a list of the most well-behaved pupils. Quite the opposite. She'd asked for two distinct sets of students. First up, the gobby kids who fell into the class-clown and/or school-bully category. In addition, she wanted the names of the students who weren't necessarily good or bad, but who often got lost in the shadows of the school.

The teachers who had compiled the lists assumed that their new headteacher was crackers. One of them said as much in the staffroom over lunch: 'It's like she wants to make this place look even more of a shitshow than it already is.'

Harriet knew it was a risky plan, but that's what she did: she took risks. There was a strategy behind every decision she made. Even when it made her look like she had lost her mind, she didn't explain her rationale.

She wanted them to see it all play out.

Harriet cleared her throat and delivered what she hoped would be an empowering statement to rally the students assembled in the library.

'Right, I've been told that you lot are the ones who everyone should meet when they visit this school because you know everything that's going on here and you're not afraid to ask the difficult questions.'

The students, of whom only half were listening, looked confused, clearly unsure as to why they were even there.

'What's the mad cow on about?' said one girl under her breath. Her mate was too busy trying to scratch her name into the library table with a compass she'd nicked from her maths class to take any notice.

Harriet continued: 'Today I want you to be you. Not the version the teachers expect of you. The real you. That means telling the MP everything about yourselves and this school, in your own way.'

'What, y'mean tell him we're all scruffy cunts and this is a shithole?' laughed Dean, who as far as Ollie and CJ were concerned was one of the scariest people on the planet.

'Yes, if that's what you think – as long as you explain why you think it's a shithole too.'

The room gasped and the girls at the back giggled.

'Yer jokin', arn' ya?' Dean said in the broadest possible accent. Even Harriet, who was from the North East, had to give herself a moment to play back in her head what he'd just said.

'No, I'm not joking,' she eventually replied.

She could see that Dean was not only shocked that a teacher had sworn, but that they had also agreed with him. That was no doubt a first for Dean.

Dean was sixteen, with a full-grown beard and half his ear missing, rumoured to have been bitten off in a fight. Everyone in the school, kids and staff alike, was scared of Dean, apart from Harriet. Before teaching she'd been a probation officer. She'd met plenty of impulsive and in-your-face teenagers who constantly tested the boundaries. From what Harriet had heard, Dean was another young lad let down by the system.

Harriet moved on to ask the rest of the group to offer their input.

This time CJ piped up with a cheeky smile on his face.

'Yep – I wanna know what car he drives.'

'Great, anything else?'

CJ was left speechless that his suggestion hadn't been shot down as being stupid.

'Erm, I wanna know if he's got pets,' said Courtney, another kid on the gobby list.

'Oh, and what phone he has. Oh, and whether he vapes,' she was quick to add.

'I wanna know what he's done with all his money,' said Courtney's mate Ellie, who had suddenly become more interested in the chat after hearing a teacher swear.

With the headteacher not discounting any of the questions they were suggesting, the gobby students were throwing out all kinds of ideas for things they could ask. This was exactly what Harriet wanted. They were enthusiastic and, more importantly, focused.

They chatted more about the questions they wanted to ask and then agreed on a route they would take the MP on to give him a proper school tour, with Courtney insisting that he'd definitely want to see the locker area where all the best fights happened. Not an ideal suggestion, Harriet thought, but what the hell, it was their reality and the headteacher knew at this point it was important not to dampen their confidence.

Harriet could see out of the library window that the MP was arriving with an entourage.

'Right, you lot, time to get answers to all those burning questions you came up with. Also, grab some name badges to wear. Oh, and I don't know if I mentioned, but this is going to be filmed for TV.'

'WHAT THE ACTUAL—'

The door to the library flew open just in time to stop Dean and several other kids dropping an almighty chorus of F-bombs.

'Your visitors are here, Miss Waters,' said the stressed receptionist, who was trying to get into the library while a load of kids piled past her, desperate to go to the loos to check their hair and put on more make-up.

'We're gonna be famous!' screamed Ellie, who was now climbing over her mate Courtney in an attempt to be first out of the door. Meanwhile Courtney was on her hands and knees looking for her e-cigarette, which had dropped out of her pocket in all the commotion.

The 'gobby kids' were all wired up and ready to go. Now Harriet needed to do the same with the 'forgotten kids'.

As they walked towards the reception, Harriet whispered to a handful of the particularly shy kids who were at the back of the pack.

'Do me a favour and work out whether this guy is a typical wanker politician or one of the good guys? I know you'll be able to suss him out – you're the clever lot.'

Ollie was stunned. Did she just say 'wanker'? This woman was unlike any other teacher he had ever met. Also, she was asking them to suss the guy out.

What a surreal morning he was having.

One that was about to get even stranger.

Harriet introduced herself to the MP and TV crew, then made her excuses and left the students to it.

She was met by open mouths when she walked into the staffroom a few minutes later.

'Have you really just left our pupils on their own with a politician and a camera crew?' exclaimed Mrs Inchley, who was stirring her coffee rigorously.

'Jesus Christ! It sounds like the start of a very bad joke. A politician, a TV crew and a load on unruly kids walk into a—'

'A fucking nightmare, that's what we're all walking into here,' interrupted Mr Stanton, who had just thrown his cup into the sink and was now making his way to the door.

Harriet tried to reassure them. She knew it was a gamble, but she didn't want them knowing that.

'Yes, I have left them to it. And do you know what? I think they're going to be brilliant at this – just watch them.'

ZOYA

Zoya couldn't believe what she was reading.

Never did she think that one day the retelling of her life story would land her an apprenticeship with a major TV news network and prestigious college.

Today she had the email proving it:

Dear Ms Aflani, we would like to offer you the position of trainee journalist on our Diversity in Media Scheme.

Zoya read the line over and over again.

A journalist. A job she thought was out of reach for someone like her.

She'd heard about the scheme on the radio. The aim was to try to get more people from different backgrounds into mainstream media. They said that you didn't need to have any qualifications or experience, you just needed to be a great storyteller with a passion for original journalism.

She didn't know if she was a good storyteller or not, but she knew she had an original tale to tell.

Her own story about escaping the war.

Zoya had started a diary on her tenth birthday, the week after her family fled a chemical attack near her hometown in Syria. Her account of her family's resettlement in Manchester via a refugee camp in Lebanon was a powerful story. The email confirming the job said as much.

This was the new start Zoya needed after a tough few years. Her father, despite all his success as a scientist in Syria, ended up working all hours as an HGV driver in the UK. This meant she was left in charge at home.

Zoya didn't mind. For the first time in a long time, she had her own bedroom, was able to hang her clothes up in a wardrobe and take warm showers. That felt like heaven to her.

School was tricky, though. Not just the obvious language and cultural barriers, but the time and structure that was needed to do well was hard for Zoya.

In the end, it was the TV news shows she watched late at night that would be her teacher. Zoya couldn't get enough of them. She loved nothing more than getting her little brother and elderly nana off to bed early so she could park herself in front of the telly and binge on the endless news channels. Hearing journalists slagging off the people in power – and not getting in trouble for it, like they would in Syria – took a little bit of getting used to. So did all the colourful accents. Her favourite was a reporter called Rose. She had no idea where she was from, but she loved how she said the word 'poor'.

So, when Zoya heard about the journalism trainee scheme that was being offered at the news organization where Rose Steedman worked, she saw it as her best chance to be part of a world she loved.

Zoya's retelling of her life story based on the journal she had kept in the refugee camp got her an interview.

She knew it was a risky tactic, telling one of the world's biggest news networks that she didn't rate some of their coverage. But that's how she felt. Very rarely did she see a story about the Muslim community that didn't focus on some type of extremist element. And she was sick of constantly hearing about the oppression of women like her.

Zoya blamed the media for the toxic division she saw and the racial profiling her family was put through on a daily basis.

This was a chance to be part of changing that. Be a force for good. And today's email was giving her an opportunity.

Zoya went straight to tell her father. He cried. He had been racked with guilt and worry about his daughter. She had missed so much of her education; he'd been afraid that would prevent her from reaching a decent profession.

Now she had got onto the first rung of the ladder at a well-respected global news organization.

This was going to be life-changing.

OLLIE

The tour with the politician and the TV crew was nothing like what Ollie was expecting.

For a start, the TV people who'd turned up seemed normal. They looked and sounded like they could have been students in the school. Obviously they weren't teenagers, but they weren't old-old, like in their thirties and forties. And they weren't dead posh either.

What he also found weird was everyone's reaction to them being there. Ollie thought his classmates would all be going wild, shouting and launching themselves in front of the camera.

The opposite was happening.

Despite all the bravado shown in the library and all their proclamations about it being their chance to be famous, their gobbiness just seemed to evaporate.

Everyone was being respectful. Nothing like when the police raided the school last year after Dean's mate Gamo brought a gun in. Before anyone realized it was a replica, a major incident was declared. Even with armed police pointing guns at the gates, the likes of Courtney and her mates were still dicking about, shouting at the police officers to 'show us yer weapons'.

Today felt very different.

Ollie watched as Dean went from being angry and feared to someone who was being warm and gracious. The presence of a TV crew had obviously sparked something in him.

Dean was asking them all about the kit they had and was then explaining how he made music videos at home, which included creating his own sound equipment to give him 'incredible reverb', as he described it. Ollie had no idea that Dean did anything other than scare the shit out of people. This was a mind-blowing change of character.

The girls were much calmer than normal too. Granted, they weren't really listening to what anyone was saying and were constantly touching their hair and looking at anything that would provide them with a reflection of themselves, whether that be a passing window or their mobile phones. But they weren't playing up.

Similarly, Ollie had never known a situation where his daft mate CJ hadn't made his presence known, whether by saying something stupid or doing something silly.

It was like a spell had been put over the school.

He was sure it wouldn't last.

STEVE

Steve was nervous around TV cameras; it was a new thing for him, all this press interest. For years, as a local businessman, he had slipped under the radar. But now he was a politician, people wanted to know more about him and what he was doing.

He was accountable.

Plus the seat he'd won was a controversial one. It had been held for many years by Janet Jacobs, a local woman who had become a divisive figure in politics. She'd stirred up a lot of hate with her extreme views on immigration. And, even though she'd been voted out, she had a scary following of loyal fans.

All of this put him, and the area he represented, under a lot of scrutiny.

Despite this, Steve had decided that it was a good thing that there would be cameras there today. He felt comfortable in a school like this, plus he could see the kids were enjoying the fuss that was being made.

The students didn't say much to him to start with, seemingly more interested in how they looked on camera than anything else, so he had taken the lead. He chatted away as they wandered around the school, stopping every so often for the crew to get extra shots from different angles.

Then, about fifteen minutes in, a young lad, who looked like a typical spotty teenager, piped up with a question – one he asked directly to the camera rather than to Steve.

'Isn't it boring, yer job?' said the lad wearing a badge with the name *Christoper-James* crossed out and the letters *CJ* scrawled next to it.

Steve smiled as he answered.

'It can be sometimes, yes, CJ, but all jobs have boring bits. I do loads of exciting stuff too and get to vote on big decisions that impact everyone's lives.'

CJ continued to stare down the lens of the camera, even though the TV crew had gestured for him to look at Steve when he was talking to him.

'We watched ya earlier, proppa going for that fella with the beard.'

Steve had no idea where this was going or where to look, given that CJ still wasn't looking at him.

'In that room with the massive green benches.'

'Oh, the House of Commons,' Steve said now, laughing. 'I was in a debate.'

'Looked like the start of a punch-up to me, mate. Also, why is it called the House of Commons? Is it actually a house? Where people live? And they all look proppa posh to me, like, not common.' CJ wasn't holding back as he delivered his lines to the camera.

It prompted the others to start joining in. Soon they were bombarding him, asking the stuff that everyone wants to know but is too afraid to ask, like how much was he paid, what perks came with the job and who was the most famous person he had met. It was all very different to the private school he'd been made to speak at last month because one of the parents was a party donor. There, a kid had asked whether he thought the Bank of England should keep its independence given the current problems with inflation and monetary policy. Steve was pretty sure the student hadn't thought of the question himself. If he had, then that was even weirder.

Today, talking to the kids at Newton Banks Academy was a breath of fresh air. The school was rough, there was no doubt about that, and he was sure some of them would be mixed up in some shady stuff, but this wasn't too dissimilar to where he grew up. So the kids actually made him feel at home, much more so than the political cesspit he now inhabited.

'Are yer gnashers real?' asked Courtney, who had finally stopped checking herself in her mobile phone screen.

Steve laughed. His teeth weren't real, they were veneers. He'd had terrible teeth his whole life so one of the first things he did when he sold his business was get a dental overhaul. No one had ever asked him about his teeth before, and yet, in this moment, he suddenly thought that loads of people had probably been wondering the same thing when they'd seen his new pearly whites.

He answered honestly, which led to a chorus of kids announcing that they'd known it all along.

'What phone ya got?' was another pertinent question from a girl who he'd overheard arguing with her mates about which make and model was best. Steve was sure that the answer would determine whether he was cool or not, though even using the word 'cool' was no doubt uncool these days. It was a language minefield.

'Why'd you become a politician?' This time the question came from a lad at the rear of the group.

'Because I wanted to make a difference,' Steve replied, turning to face the direction the voice had come from. Most of the kids at the back avoided eye contact, so it was hard for Steve to work out who had actually said it.

'A difference to what?' the lad said, now choosing to look at Steve as he spoke.

'Erm, well, a difference to the people in this area, so that, you know, it's a great place to live and there are better services for everyone, no matter what their background.' Steve slightly stumbled.

A big lad with half his ear missing piped up next: 'Sounds like bollocks to me. Yous 'ave been around ages and this place is still a shithole.'

Steve knew the lad had a point.

'Well, yeah, politicians have been around a long time, but I've only been in this job a year. I am trying. Plus I don't think this place is . . . erm, how you described.'

Steve wanted to say 'shithole', but couldn't bring himself to swear at the kids on camera.

He felt a bit pathetic.

'So have *you* made a difference yet?' It was the quiet lad at the back who was asking questions now.

Steve managed to get a glimpse of his name badge.

'Are you in interested in politics, Oliver?'

'It's Ollie, and no. Yer the first politician I've met and I don't get what yous lot actually do.'

Steve thought this was quite the outburst from a lad who'd been all but mute for most of the tour. He'd lulled Steve into a false sense of security and then skewered him.

These kids would give any good journalist a run for their money.

Steve went on to explain to them how he wasn't happy with the way the country was being run, so he'd decided to have a go at it himself.

It was half true. The other side of the story, which he wasn't going to tell them, was that he'd needed an escape from his troubles at home. Five bouts of IVF had taken their toll on him and his wife. They had all the money they were ever going to need, but not the family they so desperately wanted. They were at breaking point with it all. Politics, he thought, was something that could give meaning to his life, or at the very least, distraction. And it seemed to be working.

Chatting to the kids showed him once again just how little access young people had to politics, especially those in deprived areas. He wanted to change that and try to open some doors for them.

'Listen, would you lot like to come to London to see where I work and what I do?' He made this suggestion not knowing if that was going to be possible.

'Trip to London? Get in!' said one of the students whose eyes had widened. 'We can go to the Ministry of Sound. Our Grace said it's sick in there.'

'I'm not sure about the Ministry of Sound, given your age, but I could definitely sort out another ministry visit. Ministry of Defence, maybe?' Steve was well aware of how naff he sounded, trying to link a nightclub to a government department, but he was at that age where dad jokes were not something he could hold in any more.

'How?' said the big lad, looking suspiciously at Steve. 'How we gonna get there? How much is it gonna set us back? We're skint, bro.'

All good questions, Steve thought, half regretting having suggested it without talking to someone official about it first. That didn't stop him committing further.

'I'll sort your travel,' he announced, knowing he could afford to pay for it, but not knowing whether he'd be allowed to. There were so many rules in politics, especially when it came to money.

Still, he'd said it now. He was determined to make this trip happen.

At that point he didn't realize what a mistake it would turn out to be.

HARRIET

Harriet knew that a local MP visiting the school on his own would do nothing for the kids. No offence to Steve Evans, he seemed like a decent fella and she knew he had an interesting background, but now he was a wealthy white man of a certain age. The majority of the kids would take one look at him and discount anything he had to say.

The visit needed more layers to create a meaningful experience around it, something that would impress the kids. Harriet thought a TV crew would do just the job.

Given the press interest in the school, Harriet had contemplated the idea of getting a local TV news crew in. However, it was an option that came with problems. The students at Newton Banks had complicated family lives, which meant that quite a large proportion of them were not allowed to feature in any publicity material. No pictures on the website, no photos in the papers and definitely no appearing on telly. It wasn't relevant to all of the students, but there were enough pupils with child protection issues for it to be a problem. If a real TV crew came in, Harriet would have to keep all those kids out of the way of the cameras, which would be near impossible. It was definitely more trouble than it was worth. Plus the kids who would benefit the most from this were unsurprisingly the ones with the safeguarding needs.

Harriet had another plan.

Her partner, who was a sports reporter, did some part-time lecturing at a college with a well-respected film and TV production department. Harriet convinced them to let her borrow four of the trainees.

Not only were they CRB checked, which meant they could work with kids, but their course was part of a prestigious national news network apprenticeship. So to all intents and purposes they were a proper TV crew.

Her idea was to get them to come with all the usual TV kit and pretend they were filming for the local news. It would look and feel like real telly, and in a way it was, but the apprentices would use the experience as a practice run for their coursework, rather than broadcasting anything publicly. After it had been graded, all the footage would go back to Harriet. It was a win-win for all involved.

No one needed to know that it wasn't being broadcast. Not even the MP. She wanted the whole thing to be as authentic as possible.

It was working.

The TV crew had generated a real buzz about the place. And not a buzz that leads to the police turning up in riot gear. For a change, it was a positive one.

Plus Harriet was delighted to see that the crew were what she would call 'normal'. It turned out they were part of some Diversity in Media initiative, which meant they came from backgrounds like the kids in her school. This was a massive bonus. They were relatable.

Despite reservations from the staff and even her own worries about this backfiring, Harriet had pretty much predicted what would happen. Her carefully put-together plan was all about giving the students responsibility they weren't used to, but in a controlled setting.

It started with the types of students she had chosen.

In Harriet's experience, gobby kids, despite appearances, did actually care about how they looked to their peers. They wanted to make people laugh, but they didn't want to look stupid. So she hoped the TV element would stop them playing up in the moment. And by encouraging them to ask whatever they wanted, they would have confidence in their own ability to think of interesting stuff.

The 'forgotten kids' were the absolute opposite. They were subservient in many ways, but harder to control psychologically. They needed a confidence boost and Harriet thought that would come from giving them responsibility. The kids were asked for their opinions all the time in a traditional academic sense, but not about a person they were meeting. And definitely not about someone in authority. It was a simple flip in their mindset so that, for a change, they were doing the judging rather than being judged. Along with critical thinking, they'd also have to verbally communicate it all back to her, flexing another muscle these particular kids avoided using at school.

There was a further important component to this live experiment Harriet had undertaken in the school.

The teachers could not be involved. Taking them out of the equation would give the students more confidence to speak freely and put them on a level playing field with the adults. It would take away the hierarchy of the school system and hopefully mean that they would show each other mutual respect. Most of them had to function as adults outside of the school in order to survive, so this was an acknowledgment of that.

That was her theory, anyway.

Harriet knew her plan wouldn't work with all the kids. It was only the first step in changing mindsets. Even if it only triggered a handful of them to think a little bit differently about themselves and the role they had in life, then it would be worth it.

It was too difficult to explain all this to the teachers, and she was aware it sounded like cod psychology, but she'd seen this work in the probation service with some of the most fucked-up teenagers in the country.

If handled well, it could be life-changing.

For Ollie, it was.

ZOYA

Zoya could barely sleep the night she got the email confirming her new job as a broadcast journalist. Her mind was alive, thinking about all the things her future now might hold.

She'd double-checked this wasn't a scam or a prank or anything like that. It was real.

Despite her excitement, she had decided not to tell the rest of the family straight away, not least because she didn't want to overshadow her cousin Adeel's wedding, which was happening that weekend.

Unlike Zoya and her younger brother Bilal, her two cousins had been born and bred near Manchester. Her dad's brother and his two sons had a very different experience of life. Yeah, they went to the same mosque and would see each other occasionally, but they were worlds apart.

Truth be told, it was only their nana keeping the wider family together.

Zoya adored her grandmother.

So, when the wedding weekend came, Zoya made sure she played the role of dutiful granddaughter. She rallied around her nana, making her cups of tea and helping her up the stairs to the toilet when needed. This also meant spending a lot of time at her uncle Majid's house where the main wedding prep was happening.

And it was there where it all kicked off.

Zoya had noticed that morning the groom's younger brother was behaving quite erratically. He kept leaving the room to use his phone and was dead jumpy every time someone spoke to him. She wondered if he'd got an inappropriate girlfriend he didn't want the family to know about. Maybe, but it didn't quite explain all of the weird behaviour.

It was while she was filling up the kettle at the kitchen sink that she discovered the truth.

Her cousin was in the garden on the phone, pacing up and down. The window was partially open and she could hear a little of what he was saying. Her nosiness got the better of her so she opened the back door a smidge and held her ear towards the gap.

What she was hearing didn't make sense.

This was a coded conversation. And not a good one.

Her mind was racing, trying to work out all the rational explanations for why he might be saying what he was saying.

But the more she heard, the more convinced she became that her cousin was up to his neck in it.

Then, when he finished the call, he took the SIM card out of the phone and destroyed it.

This was bad. Really bad.

OLLIE

The MP visit to Newton Banks Academy had left an unusual atmosphere in the school. Ollie couldn't quite put his finger on it, but there was a new vibe about the place. A nice one.

Dean's change in behaviour was the most telling. Instead of spending his break times fighting with people, he was getting them to help him film spin-off music videos to put on TikTok. Apparently, one of the TV crew had explained how he'd got into the industry by making stuff at school and putting it out online. His work got spotted by an events company who helped get him on a TV production scheme, as well as giving him a part-time job.

It was as though Dean had been given a treasure map to follow.

Similarly Courtney and Ellie, who had never talked about careers before – unless having a baby and getting a council house counted as a profession – had started looking into what they might be able to do behind the scenes in telly. They'd bonded with one of the TV crew who they'd spotted having a sneaky cigarette after filming, even though she was clearly Muslim. She'd told them the explosive news that there are people paid to help stars get ready for TV shows by picking their clothes and doing their hair and make-up. It was like an epiphany for Ellie, who suddenly realized she might be able to get a job shopping. Courtney was also buzzing about the make-up side of things, so they decided to get involved in Dean's music videos too.

Peppered among the chaos of the school were now pockets of productivity. Young people who were not moaning or kicking off because they were bored. They were actually doing stuff they were enjoying and being recognized for it too. Their social media accounts were getting more followers and even the teachers were offering to help.

Tempers were still occasionally lost and the students weren't necessarily doing any better in their exams, but they were behaving – and that was definitely a shift in what everyone was used to.

Ollie couldn't deny that he had changed too. He still couldn't believe that he'd challenged an MP in front of the TV cameras. And, what's more, he'd enjoyed it. Not the TV side, but the political debate they'd had. Finding out what Steve got paid was also a massive eye-opener for him. Three times what his mam got as a nurse, plus he got to live in two homes, one of them in London. Ollie thought that sounded brilliant. He'd have enough money to help his family out so his dad wouldn't have to work away, and by having two places to live he'd be able to escape without completely abandoning his family.

CJ laughed out loud when Ollie told him he wanted to be a politician.

'Mate, ya can't even talk to a teacher without pissing yer pants, how ya gonna do speeches and all that mad shit in the common house?'

'House of Commons, ya twat.'

'Yeah, whatever. Yer my mate, right, I rate ya, but yer gonna need to work on yer banter to crack it.'

Ollie knew CJ was right.

His lack of confidence was always what held him back.

He needed to change, and the upcoming trip to London would be his first step in doing that.

STEVE

Fifteen teenagers from Newton Banks Academy were now wandering around the House of Commons. They were asking questions and taking pictures. Steve felt like they were genuinely getting something out of this trip he had organized for them.

About two hours in, the group were stopped by a SPAD who Steve recognized from the cabinet office.

'Are they yours?' asked the SPAD.

'The kids? Yes, they're mine.'

'You have been a busy boy.'

'Ah, no, they're not my actual children, they're part of a school group. I'm trying to organize trips for those from' – Steve whispered the last bit so as not to offend the children – 'tough backgrounds.'

'Oh, wow, this is brilliant.'

Steve was surprised to hear genuine praise from the SPAD, who had a bit of a reputation for being a bitch, which was why she'd been given the moniker 'the Killer Quill'.

'And they're northern, right?'

'Erm, yeah, from my constituency.'

Steve had no idea where this was going.

'And you got all the clearance needed to bring them into Parliament?' The SPAD was getting more and more excited.

'Well, yes, obviously, because they're here.'

'Oh, this is just great! Do you think I might be able to borrow them later?'

'What do you mean?'

The SPAD raised her voice and this time directed her words to everyone in the group.

'I'm organizing an event at Number 10 this afternoon and an opportunity has come up to invite some extra students. I know the prime minister would love to have as many children there as possible to enjoy the free food and drinks. Might you wonderful youngsters be able to help?'

It was the school headteacher, Harriet Waters, who jumped in to answer.

'We would be absolutely delighted to stay on for the event. Of course, in order to do this, you'll need to change our trains and organize taxis for all the students to get home from the station.'

The SPAD was taken aback by the requests, but agreed to them.

Steve couldn't believe his luck. This was a chance for him to shine in front of the prime minister and take these kids into a world that people like them never got to see.

Three hours later, inside Number 10, all hell broke loose.

OLLIE

Ollie could not believe he was finally getting out of Newton Banks, even if it was just for the day. His parents had pulled out all the stops to make it happen. His dad even took time off work, which was unheard of.

Ollie felt free. Standing on the railway platform that morning was like an out-of-body experience. And not just for Ollie.

None of the students had been on a train before, apart from Ellie, who travelled once a month to see her dad in prison. In fact most of them hadn't ever left their home town.

The travel alone was a mind-blowing experience for them.

Especially for Courtney, who had nicked a couple of cans of her dad's extra-strong lager to drink on the way. She'd necked one in the train toilet just before they arrived. That, coupled with the heat and speed of the London Underground, meant that when the doors opened at Westminster she chucked up on some fella's shoes. Weirdly, he didn't seem bothered. Just tutted and then pushed his way past.

Their headteacher, however, was not impressed. As well as emptying out the other cans Courtney had stashed in her bag, she made her drink a full bottle of water with something she'd put in it called milk thistle. Apparently that would help sober her up. And, to be fair, it looked like it had. Although it didn't hide the shame Courtney was feeling. Pulling a booze-fuelled whitey in front of her mates was something she'd never live down.

Westminster was like nothing Ollie had ever seen before. The hustle and bustle. The size and grandeur of the buildings. It was both exciting and intimidating.

Then walking through the 'corridors of power', as the MP Steve had called them, was like being in a movie.

Ollie tried to picture himself there in ten years' time, thinking about what he would be wearing and who he might be talking to. It was mad to let his mind wander into a new life. He had never dared do that before.

And now they were walking into Downing Street. This day was just getting more and more surreal.

For the second time today they had managed to pass the armed guards without any drama. Ollie was sure that Dean or one of the lasses might try to crack a gag that would land them in the shit. But they didn't; they just took it in their stride and went through all the security procedures with ease.

Then they were standing on one of the most famous streets in the world.

'This is just like our nanna's gaff,' said CJ, who didn't seem impressed at all. It was all a bit 'old world' to him. He'd much rather be at the headquarters of TikTok. He'd heard they had a slide in the office and free food.

'Sh'up, it's a terraced street. Apart from that, it's nowt like yer nanna's.'

'I just don't get what the fuss is. I thought the boss would be loaded, livin' in some kinda mansion.'

The headteacher laughed.

'If it's so unimpressive, Christopher-James, you won't want to be in the photo. Everyone else, gather around.'

The other students reluctantly lined up in front of the door of Number 10. They hated having their picture taken when it wasn't on their terms.

'What filter yer putting on it, miss?' asked Courtney as the headteacher pointed her camera phone at them.

'No filters, Courtney.'

'What, not even the Paris filter?' Courtney replied with a note of alarm in her voice.

'No. I just want a normal, natural photo of everyone.'

'Miss, nooo, ya can't do that, I'm gonna look shocking,' moaned Ellie, who had already taken about twenty selfies with various filters giving her a mix of dog ears, wings and some type of freckled face.

Ollie didn't get the whole filter thing and hated having his photo taken, so this carry-on outside the door of Number 10 was doing his head in. Still, he assumed the photo wasn't allowed to be posted anywhere, so hopefully no one would see it.

Just as the photo was about to be taken, the door behind them opened and a cat ran between their feet. Several of them jumped, causing Ollie to drop his phone out of his hand. A tall man with a massive belly who had appeared in front of them picked it up.

'I think this belongs to you, sir?' he said as he handed Ollie the phone and walked through the door into Number 10.

'Did you recognize that man, Ollie?' asked Harriet. 'He's quite a famous politician.'

'Ah, right, yeah,' Ollie lied. He had no idea who the man was. He made a mental note to google him later. He wanted to learn as much as he could about this world and all the people in it.

'He called ya sir. Deffo a loon!' CJ said, laughing.

At that moment the door to Number 10 swung open again and out came the woman they'd seen earlier. She was now holding a clipboard.

'Hello, Newton Banks Academy, my name is Penelope Pencil.'

There was an uncontrollable roar of laughter from the students, which Penelope ignored.

'I'll be looking after you this afternoon. So let's start by getting you all inside.'

Ollie stepped through the door, which was being held open by a policeman.

He was expecting to be wowed. He wasn't. To him it looked like a museum, and not even an interesting one.

'See, it's a proppa old fogey's gaff, this,' CJ announced before the door had even closed behind them.

And to be fair, Ollie couldn't disagree.

He didn't know why, but he'd assumed it would be much more modern and hi-tech. There was a small room off to the right with a load of security cameras in it, but other than that it looked old-fashioned.

Still, it was fascinating to Ollie.

The bright yellow walls leading up the grand staircase were covered in pictures of people, nearly all men, from hundreds of years ago. Ollie recognized some of them from the googling he'd been obsessively doing since deciding he wanted to become a politician. He wanted to learn about them all.

'They're the stairs Hugh Grant dances down in *Love Actually*,' explained their headteacher. 'You know, the film where he plays the prime minister,' she continued.

'Oh, he is well fit for an old bloke,' Courtney said as she positioned herself in front of the staircase, ready to take a selfie.

The police officer put his hand across the phone lens Courtney was pointing at her face.

'No phones inside. Pack them in your bags and then pop them over there, please,' the officer said, gesturing to a wall with wooden cubbyholes.

The students did as he said, apart from CJ, who Ollie noticed had just shoved his phone down the front of his pants.

'Right, let's get you into the Pillared Room,' said the posh pencil woman who was now guiding them along a corridor into a huge room full of old paintings, uncomfortable-looking furniture and a massive chandelier hanging down from the ceiling.

Despite it looking old, Ollie knew everything in this building was probably worth a small fortune.

It was intimidating, and not just because of how posh it was.

The room was also packed with people, mainly men in suits. And scattered among them was a handful of school kids of varying ages, all in very smart uniforms.

The Newton Banks kids stood out for all the wrong reasons. Not only were they not wearing uniforms, which they barely had at their school anyway, but they also looked shabbier than everyone else. A lot shabbier.

Until this moment Ollie had never considered himself to be scruffy. He always tried to make an effort with how he looked, mainly to make up for feeling so puny in stature compared to his classmates. In this setting his trainers looked battered and his clothes looked faded. His navy hoodie looked more of a dishwater colour against the vibrant blazers the posh kids were wearing. And their shoes were so clean he wondered if they were box fresh.

Ollie looked down at his feet. He'd opted for his white Adidas shell tops for the trip. The only other shoes he owned were school ones and he'd have been tortured by his mates if he'd turned up in them.

Ollie loved his shell tops. They'd been a Christmas present off his parents – or Santa, as his brothers had been told. Ollie looked after them, but there was only so much he could do to rescue them as the months passed.

For the first time in his life, Ollie desperately wanted to be in a uniform so he could blend into the background. His jeans, hoodie and trainers looked so out of place in this grand room full of rich people.

The Newton Banks students could see the posh kids sniggering at them as they walked among them. Even the adults paused their conversations to look them up and down.

CJ didn't look remotely bothered. He was much more interested in following the woman who was carrying a tray of free food.

'Have ya seen this, Ol? It's proppa titchy food.' CJ was staring at the puff pastry snack he'd lifted off the tray in total wonder.

'It looks like Minion food,' said Courtney, which prompted CJ to go into full Minion character mode.

Normally CJ's impressions would make Ollie laugh out loud, but his display had prompted lots of people to turn and look at them. All Ollie felt was another pang of embarrassment.

It got worse.

'Ah, man, that's proppa mingin', that. Bbbbork!' said Courtney, who was now spitting the food out into her hand and over-exaggerating her retching.

Ollie was desperate to get away from the crowd.

At the back of the room there was a table of drinks. He could see that Dean had already made his way there.

Ollie beckoned CJ to go over to the drinks table too and get away from the main crowd of people.

The lad behind the table was explaining the drink options to Dean.

'We've got wine, beer and elderflower spritz.'

Ollie had no idea what the last one was.

'A beer, please,' said Dean confidently.

Ollie and CJ could not believe he had the balls to do that.

The lad handed him a beer.

Open-mouthed at what they had just witnessed, CJ and Ollie looked around to see whether there were any teachers watching.

Dean had got away with it.

CJ then piped up and tried to ask for the same. The waiter looked him up and down. CJ looked a lot younger than Dean, but hopefully because he wasn't in a school uniform he would get away with it too.

They heard a laugh behind them.

'I think you might be pushing your luck there, gentlemen,' said the voice, which they turned around to see belonged to the man who had picked up Ollie's phone.

'You're probably better asking your friend to get them for you,' he said, laughing as he reached between them to take a glass of wine for himself. 'That's what I'd do, if I were you,' he added with a wink, before walking off.

Ollie's eyes followed him out of the door. It wasn't the way they had come in, so he wanted to know where it led. Another corridor to another room that no doubt had great stories to tell. This place was a maze and much bigger than it looked from the outside. He wanted to explore all of it.

'I can't believe he didn't grass us up there,' said CJ.

'I know, weird. He seems all right, doesn't he?' Ollie replied.

'I dunno like, he's still a posh old twat. But I reckon he's spot on about asking Deano. Worth a shot.'

They were still scared of Dean, but he'd been a lot kinder to them since they'd been brought together by recent events.

Five minutes later, Dean came back with a beer for them to share.

Ollie was reluctant to drink any at first, but once he'd seen CJ take a swig without any issue, he took the risk and did the same. He could not believe that they were standing in the prime minister's house drinking beer. And no one was stopping them.

Ollie started to wonder if he was even there at all. His day-dreaming was interrupted by Penelope Pencil, who was now back standing next to them alongside their headteacher, who was grinning inanely.

Ollie managed to put the bottle behind his back before anyone noticed. And, in a sleight-of-hand movement that any magician would be proud of, CJ discreetly slipped the bottle out of Ollie's grasp and put it on the table near them. All without turning away from the adults now in front of them. First the disappearing phone and now the vanishing drink. Ollie admired CJ's carefully honed skills and his defiance of the rules. He could never be that brave.

'I am just gathering everyone together for a photograph with the prime minister,' Penelope said, ushering them towards the door.

Ollie realized he hadn't actually seen the prime minister yet. Now, all of a sudden, one of the most powerful men in the world was walking towards them. He wasn't what Ollie was expecting and didn't really look like he did on the telly. He was smaller for a start, and somehow less powerful-looking. Ollie's conclusion was that the prime minister just looked really normal, albeit posh-normal, not normal-normal.

This did nothing to calm Ollie's nerves, though. The magnitude of the moment hit him. And then the worst thing happened. The prime minister directed his first question to Ollie.

'So how are you finding Downing Street?'

'Me?! Erm, it's, I dunno, well, dunno, erm . . .' Ollie blustered his way through a terrible answer and unintentionally let his sentence drift off.

What did he think of Downing Street? He was so out of his comfort zone he hadn't even formed an opinion, not one he'd tell the prime minister anyway. All the thoughts going through his head made him sound daft.

He slowly tried to edge himself back into the crowd that had gathered in the hope that the other students, who were clearly desperate to speak to the prime minister, would push themselves forward and hide him.

'Mate, ya look like Homer when he's backing into the bush,' CJ tried to whisper while holding in a giggle.

'Homer? Who mentioned Homer?' the prime minister asked, directing the question at Ollie and CJ.

CJ was totally unfazed by this whole scenario, whereas Ollie, who felt like he was having a panic attack, was desperate for the prime minister to stop talking to them.

'Me. Why, like?' said CJ.

'Are you studying Homer? My favourite is the *Odyssey*.'

'Studying? Eee, yous have a mad way of talking. I've not seen *Odyssey*, like. My favourite episode is "Who Shot Mr Burns?".'

There was a burst of laughter from the students in uniforms. CJ assumed the people around him agreed about the best episode of *The Simpsons*. Their laughter was obviously testament to that.

'I'm studying Homer, Prime Minister,' piped up one of the posh kids. 'Wouldn't you say, Prime Minister, that Odysseus's ten-year struggle to return home after the Trojan War is not too dissimilar to the geopolitical situation we find ourselves in now?'

CJ started to laugh. Fortunately, the prime minister's attention was now solely on the posh kid. Ollie's heart was still racing.

They didn't belong here and he needed to get out.

He looked around the room for an exit or a least a sign for the loo.

Penelope Pencil could see him looking uneasy and pulled him to one side.

'What on earth is the matter?' she said angrily.

'Do you know where the toilet is, please?' Ollie said, burying his head into his chest. He felt stupid.

She gestured to a door as she replied, 'Just through there on the left, but hurry up, I need a photo of you all when you get back.'

Ollie moved quickly towards the door. He felt like he was

going to pass out. Maybe it was the drink, although he was used to drinking more than this with his mates.

He headed out of the room and into the corridor. He propped himself against the wall and closed his eyes for a second.

'Are you OK, young chap?' said a voice that made him jump and open his eyes. It was the man who had given Ollie his phone back earlier and also encouraged their underage drinking. He was standing just outside the door Ollie had come out of and was smiling at him, which Ollie found weird.

'Er, yeah, just looking for the toilet?' Ollie replied.

'It's through that door.'

Ollie went to walk off and then Phone Man spoke again.

'Listen, this place can be quite daunting.'

Ollie turned around and half smiled as Phone Man continued: 'It's full of posh old wankers like me.'

Ollie let out an involuntary splutter, which he managed to turn into a fake cough. Did he really just say wanker? He wondered if this was some kind of joke. He looked around him to see if the man was actually speaking to someone else, but apart from a couple of security guards further down the corridor, there was no one near them. Nor were there any cameras, so it definitely wasn't one of Ant and Dec's 'gotcha' moments.

He must have misheard him. There is no way this famous politician had just called himself a wanker. And then it came again.

'We're all wankers really.'

Ollie stood there motionless with his eyes as wide as saucers. It was as if he had been turned to stone by the word 'wanker'. A word he had heard countless times, but one that sounded so weird in a posh voice and in this setting.

He had no idea how to react, so said nothing.

'My point is we're all the same, despite appearances. I get the squits when I eat a dodgy curry, I sweat when I'm nervous and I make a terrible fool of myself when I drink too much.'

As the monologue continued, Ollie went from being paralysed by fear to reaching a point where he could no longer control his laughter at the mad things this man was saying to him. Especially the next bit.

'I want you to remember something. Whenever you feel intimidated by someone because they're rich, or scary or whatever else, just think of the three 's'es. Everyone shits, shags and shaves.'

'Ya what?' Ollie erupted with laughter.

'You weren't expecting me to say that, were you? But it's true. We're all the same, us supposed grown-ups. We all shit, shag and shave.'

This man was nuts; he'd never met anyone like him.

'Yer not normal,' Ollie said while laughing.

'Well, yes, there is lots about my life that isn't normal, but also an enormous amount that is.'

'Like what?'

'Well, for example, I worry about things, and sometimes wonder what I am doing with my life.'

'No way, yer dead posh 'n' clever, what've *you* gotta worry about?' Ollie had shocked himself with his punchy reply. Without his realizing it, Phone Man had disarmed him.

'Listen, everyone worries about things, no matter how rich they are. And how do you know I'm clever? I bet you're cleverer. I'm also sure you could do a better job than me.'

'Nah, I wouldn't have a clue.'

'Do you think I do?'

'But I'm nowt like you.'

'And that's a good thing. I bet your life is more interesting than mine.'

'Nah, my life is dull.'

'I bet it isn't. Tell me about it.'

'I just look after my family.'

'So tell me about them.'

Before Ollie knew it, he was telling the man about his family life. About his mam being ill and the pressures on him to look after his brothers. He talked about wanting to get away but not knowing what he was good at or where to even start.

It was as if this man had unlocked something in Ollie.

The boy who never opened up was spilling his guts to a man he'd never met before. A man who was so different to him, and yet seemed to understand him in a way no one else had.

Phone Man listened intently, nodding and occasionally asking questions, while also telling him about his own family pressures.

The panic Ollie felt earlier had gone; in fact, he felt completely at ease talking to Phone Man in this moment, despite how strange it was.

It all came to an abrupt end when the door next to them was flung open and Ollie's headteacher came marching out with Penelope Pencil shouting behind her.

HARRIET

'I need to get this photo of the prime minister with the children. I'm not asking you, I am telling you,' shouted Penelope as she tried to catch up with Harriet, who had walked out of the room when the conversation had started to get heated.

'And I am telling you that taking the photo is fine, but you cannot publish it,' Harriet said sternly, but without raising her voice.

'It's being sent to the press this evening and it's been agreed it will run in *The Times* tomorrow morning.'

'That's fine, then do a separate photo without my lot in the picture.'

'No, I need those kids in it. They make it look . . .' Penelope paused.

Harriet knew she was trying to find the right words to say what was now obvious to her: they needed the 'diversity' that the kids from her school brought.

Harriet interrupted her before she could insult them.

'Miss Pencil, do you not understand some of my students are vulnerable kids whose lives I would be putting at risk if I allowed their faces to be plastered all over *The Times*? It could be read by any number of people we are trying to keep them away from.'

'Reading – ha! I doubt they do much of that,' Penelope laughed.

It took all of Harriet's might not to punch Penelope in the face.

'So explain to me exactly what you mean by that?'

Harriet knew what Penelope meant. The snobbery enraged her, but she was determined not to let it show and lose the moral high ground she was currently standing on.

'Listen, let's leave out the vulnerable kids and do a photo with the rest?' Penelope coaxed, not deigning to acknowledge the fact that she had insulted Harriet and her students.

'I will not segregate my students like that.'

At this point Ollie, who Harriet hadn't noticed was also standing in the corridor, piped up.

'Miss, I don't mind not being in the photo, if that helps.'

'Thank you, Ollie, but it's not just you that can't be in the pictures. Also, you deserve better. Listen, get yourself back in the main room and I'll be along in a minute. They're serving puddings now.'

'Oh, the puddings in here are marvellous. Come on, Ollie, let's leave these two ladies to it,' said Phone Man.

Harriet looked at Ollie, marvelling how great it was that one of her students was on first-name terms with a famous politician. She smiled to herself for a moment as she watched them walk back into the room. Then she turned her attention back to Penelope Pencil.

'These kids deserve better. We came here to learn more about the people who run our country and hopefully help to inspire the next generation of politicians. They could be our future ministers.'

Penelope laughed again. 'Future ministers? More like future inmates.'

That was the final straw for Harriet.

'Wow, so that's what you think of us. You really did only want us here as a box-ticking exercise for your press campaign. Well, I cannot wait to tell the press all about this visit.'

'As if they're going to believe you,' Penelope said under her breath as she turned on her heel and walked back into the room.

Harriet was ready to bring this pointy pencil bitch down.

ZOYA

Zoya was in no doubt she was doing the right thing by contacting the police.

She'd read enough news stories to know that what she'd overheard her cousin talking about on the phone was terrorism.

She had to stop him.

After making her excuses to get out of her uncle's house, Zoya looked up the hotline number she'd seen on buses for reporting suspicious behaviour. She told them enough to be taken seriously and within thirty minutes a detective in the regional counterterrorism team was calling her from a withheld number.

The officer wanted to meet, but there was no way she was going to take that risk. He asked her lots of questions about her cousin, who his friends were, which mosque he went to and, of course, what exactly she had heard.

She answered them all as best as she could.

Then there was nothing for two days. The family wedding came and went. Zoya had avoided her cousin for most of it and, as far as she could see, nothing seemed out of the ordinary. That freaked her out.

Had the police spoken to him or not? She had no idea. Maybe this was just a big misunderstanding.

Zoya was really hoping she'd got this all wrong. Then, a week later, her uncle's house was raided. It was all over the news.

It turned out the information Zoya had given the police was the missing link they said they needed on a cell they had been trying to infiltrate.

Abdul Khalid, her cousin, was a terrorist.

It tore their family apart.

Zoya's father couldn't understand how a boy who'd grown up in a safe country, having never seen the true terrors of war like they had, could have ended up wanting to kill innocent people.

It didn't make sense to any of them.

No one wanted to accept it.

Some of them, including her nana and brother, refused to.

'It's a stitch-up,' said Bilal.

'It's not, Bee.'

'Happens all the time to people like us.'

'Bilal, it was a unanimous verdict. Not a single person on the jury was in any doubt that Abdul was planning to blow up Wembley.'

'I know, but they could have been tricked by the police.'

'Oh, man. You're not falling for all this shit from Uncle Majid about the police being racist, are you?'

'They are, though.'

Zoya so desperately wanted to explain to her brother why it was true, but she couldn't.

The police had agreed, based on the intelligence Zoya had given them, that she would have to be protected. Her name was redacted in all the evidence shown to the court.

No one could ever know that she had been part of this. Especially her family. That meant letting them all carry on believing that the police had got it wrong.

It was hard, though.

Zoya felt like she was living a double life. At home, she would listen to her family's endless conversations about Abdul's innocence; then, at work, she pretended not to know him. Not that anyone asked if she did.

Zoya was flying high in her job. Not only had she passed her traineeship with a special award from the head of news, but she now had a full-time position in Rose Steedman's team too. Her role was office-based for now, but Zoya knew that if she worked hard enough it wouldn't be long before she'd be sent out on the road as one of Rose's producers. It was a position she was determined to secure.

However, keeping the family secret was tough.

And eventually she caved.

The day of Abdul's sentencing was unbearable. Her nana was distraught and the men in her family were angry. Zoya didn't want to be at home. So she left.

She drove and drove until she arrived at Rose and Kate's house. She wasn't planning on going there, but it's where she ended up. Kate was the only person in the world she could trust. She also knew that Rose was away filming.

Zoya had never expected to get so close to Kate. A chance meeting at Rose's house led to a discovery of shared interests and, from that, a friendship Zoya hadn't realized she needed. Kate listened to her in a way that no one else did. And, in return, Zoya tried to be there for her as much as possible, especially when Rose was away and Kate was trying to juggle childcare alongside her own demanding job. Zoya enjoyed helping; whether it was taking Rory to the park or dropping around a plate of her nana's food. She wanted to lighten the load for Kate, in the way that Kate did for her emotionally.

Zoya looked up to Kate as a kind of big-sister figure, although she sometimes wondered if she wanted more than that from Kate. Not that she'd ever go there.

It was this bond that took Zoya to Kate that night. Telling her what had happened with her cousin instantly lifted the weight of the secret from her shoulders.

Kate promised never to tell a soul. Not even Rose.

But the next day Zoya regretted it.

Her selfishness could have put a target on Kate's back.

OLLIE

t had been four days since the London trip. Four uneventful days.

Ollie didn't know exactly what he was expecting to happen when he got home, but he didn't think things would just go back to normal.

They did, though. His dad was working away and he'd gone straight into carer mode.

He didn't even get the chance to tell his parents about the trip so he could enjoy reliving it all. His dad had left before he got home and his mam was bedbound again with another infection. He'd fallen into his usual routine. He was sure his mam would rally again soon, like she always did, but in the meantime it was up to him to hold things together at home.

Even school was dull now. There was nothing to look forward to. No meetings about trips they were yet to go on or discussions between the students about how they were going to sneak alcohol in their bags. It was just the same old, same old. Even CJ wasn't around as much to annoy him. He'd clearly taken inspiration from Dean and was now spending all his free time making stupid TikToks.

Ollie was fed up.

The chat with Phone Man was rattling around his head. He wished he could talk to him and find out what he should do next. Then Ollie felt silly for even thinking that someone like him would be able to contact a famous politician.

But maybe there was a chance with social media. Cristiano Ronaldo once 'liked' a comment that Roman in Year 9 had left on one of his posts. No one could believe it, but it was definitely real, so there was a chance Phone Man might read his message if he sent one.

Ollie had nothing to lose. So that night he looked him up on social media, found his account and set about writing a direct message to him.

He googled *how you should start a message to an MP.*

Dear Right Honourable

He deleted it and sat and thought about it again, then had another go.

Hello, I met you at Downing Street on Monday.

He paused. What did he actually want to say? He thought about it for another few minutes and then continued.

I just wanted to say thanks for talking to me. It was really helpful. Bye then. Ollie (who you talked to in the corridor)

It had taken him nearly twenty minutes to write a couple of lines and he still wasn't sure whether it was the right thing to say or not. He pressed send anyway and then waited. He instantly regretted ending it with 'bye then', but it was too late.

Then, to his shock, within moments of sending his message, a reply appeared. His stomach did a flip.

Thank you for your message. We'll respond to your enquiry in due course.

It was an automated reply. Ollie felt daft. Of course someone like Phone Man wouldn't respond to these messages personally. What an idiot he had been, getting his hopes up like that. He was annoyed at himself for letting that happen.

Ollie was back at square one.

He went into school the next day angry. And for the first time ever, he let his emotions show.

'Now then, here comes the next prime minister,' CJ had joked as Ollie walked through the school gates.

'Shut up, prick,' Ollie had barked back.

'What the fuck is wrong with you?' CJ said, confused at why his mate was being so defensive.

'You, being a dick,' Ollie replied.

'Whoa, mate, why ya fucking calling me a dick?'

'Because you are one,' Ollie shouted back at him.

'Er, you're the dick who is doing fuck all with yer life, apart from pretending yer gonna be summat yer not.'

And it was at that point that Ollie punched CJ in the face, which in turn led to a full-on wrestling match between them.

Within seconds a crowd had gathered and the words 'fight, fight, fight' were being chanted from all directions.

'Lads, what the hell is going on here?' said their PE teacher as he tried to pull them apart. 'I thought you two were mates?'

Both lads stood up and dusted themselves down. CJ's nose was bleeding and Ollie had a rip in his shirt.

Ollie was desperate to cry. But he couldn't. Not now.

Instead he ran off. Ran as fast and as far as he could until he reached the outer perimeter of the school.

His life was a mess.

Three days after the fight with his best friend, Ollie's mam died.

It was all quite sudden in the end. She'd had cancer since he was ten, on and off. Every time he was told to expect the worst, she rallied. He just assumed the same would happen this time. She always bounced back when she went into hospital. There was nothing to suggest to Ollie that she wouldn't this time too.

And now she was dead.

No one explained the exact cause of death to him, though he'd overheard someone talking about sepsis. He wanted to know the truth, but was just given some shit analogy about his mam being a butterfly who had spread her wings so she could fly to a better place.

It was all bollocks, but he had to keep up the pretence for the sake of his younger brothers.

And yet, while he was trying to keep things together, his dad was falling apart.

Ollie didn't even cry at the funeral. He couldn't. His dad was a mess again. He'd got so drunk he was no use to any of them.

That meant Ollie was the one who had to comfort his brothers as their mother's coffin disappeared behind the crematorium curtain. Although that actual moment had made Ollie want to laugh, not cry. The person in control of the conveyor belt must have pressed the wrong button because at first the coffin started moving towards them and looked like it was going to tip off the front. There were various gasps and wails from the small gathering of family and friends as the coffin jerked over the edge and then went back the other way. His mam would have laughed her head off at that. She loved a good giggle, although she hadn't done much laughing in the last year of her life.

His dad, however, had slept through the whole thing. Slumped in a chair at the back like a corpse who hadn't been allocated a coffin yet.

Things were spiralling out of control. His school had tried to help him, but he didn't want them interfering, so he lied about how bad things were.

He could handle this on his own. And right now, he had to.

Ollie's dad was rarely at home and when he was there it was the same pattern of chaos over and over again. First the beers, then the whisky, then the tears. Each time ending with him falling asleep on the sofa completely wasted and covered in his own snot and slobber.

Ollie barely slept, constantly worried that his dad would choke and end up dying too. And when he did sleep, he had regular nightmares about crazy things, like his brothers getting run over as he walked them home from school. His mind was all over the shop and yet he knew that he had to stay in control.

Ollie always made sure he was up early enough to get his dad off the sofa before his brothers saw him. But it was exhausting, and any sympathy he had for his dad disappeared the day he came downstairs and found him asleep covered in his own piss.

He left for school that day vowing never to go home again. But as soon as the last bell of the day went, he felt guilty, knowing if he didn't go and collect his brothers, no one would, and he couldn't go on the run with them. So he went home.

Ollie reckoned his dad must have felt guilty too, because when they arrived home that afternoon there was a puppy waiting for them in the kitchen. Ollie's brothers were over the moon, but he knew it would be another thing for him to look after.

That night in bed, he was staring at the ceiling, listening to his dad clattering about downstairs and hoping that he might have learned his lesson and not be pissed. Unlikely.

Then his phone pinged.

It was an Instagram notification telling him he had a direct message. He didn't recognize the name @magnuscanis or the profile picture, which was a photo of a big dog.

He opened the message.

Hey Ollie, sorry for the slow reply, it's been rather frantic at work. Thank you so much for your message. I thoroughly enjoyed our chat a few weeks ago.

There was no name and nothing on the profile page to identify them – no followers, no posts, nothing.

Then another message popped up underneath.

Alas, I should have said, this is my personal account.

There was only one person he knew who would use words like 'alas' or 'frantic'. It had to be Phone Man.

Ollie stared at the screen. Of course someone like him would have two social media accounts. One official and one personal.

It had to be him.

Phone Man did remember him.

He started to type out a reply, careful to use proper words and sentences rather than his usual text speak.

Hello, I'm OK. What have you been doing at work?

Ollie could see the dots underneath the message as soon as he had sent it, which proved he was online right now, replying to him. Ollie's stomach flipped.

He couldn't believe he was sitting in his bedroom talking to a famous politician.

Another reply popped up.

Just the usual. I hope your mum is in good health and your brothers are behaving. Have you conquered the world yet?

As if.
Ollie started to reply.

No, my mam died.

As soon as he wrote it, he deleted the last three words. He didn't want pity. He left it at a single word and pressed send.
The dots appeared again.

Well, it won't be long before you do, I'm sure. You've got this!

He wanted to tell him everything that had happened since they had met, but he didn't know where to start.

Thanks

He was going to stop there, but his fingers just carried on typing.

My mam died and my dad is a twat.

He stared at his phone.
The dots came, then went again. Ollie panicked that he'd said too much. He shouldn't have told him about his mam and he definitely shouldn't have called his dad a twat.
Then the dots came back and a reply popped up.

My goodness. This is terrible.

Ollie was so relieved to see the reply. Then the floodgates opened. The messages between them continued for another ten minutes with Ollie detailing all that had happened.

And then the replies stopped. Ollie sent a couple more messages, but nothing came back. He stared at his phone for another ten minutes, thinking about how brilliant it was to have someone to talk to. He felt a calmness he hadn't felt for a long, long time.

His eyes started to get heavy until eventually they closed and his phone dropped out of his hand on to the floor.

Nearly nine hours later he woke with a jolt. He picked up his phone to check the time, but the battery had died. He'd forgotten to put it on charge. He plugged it in and then ran downstairs to make sure his dad was off the sofa.

To his surprise, there was no one downstairs. He shouted for his dad and brothers, but there was no response. Where was everyone?

Then he looked at the clock on the oven. It was 8.45 a.m.

'Shit!' he shouted.

He was going to be late for school and his brothers were too.

He started to run upstairs when the front door opened and his dad walked through with the puppy in his arms.

'Where've ya been?' Ollie shouted, completely bemused by the whole situation.

'To drop the boys off at school and give the dog some fresh air.'

'Eh?' None of this made sense to Ollie. It was like he'd woken up in a different house. A normal one.

'Why didn't ya wake us?'

'Sorry, mate, ya looked like ya needed the extra kip. Don't stress. Yer smart, you'll catch up.'

His dad didn't get it. Ollie didn't want to get behind at school, not now he wanted to be a politician.

He legged it back up the stairs and threw on his clothes, grabbing his phone and bag and running out of the door.

He ran past the front of his house and could see his dad through the window, playing with the dog. This sudden change in his behaviour was welcome, but it made no sense to Ollie.

His phone hadn't had long to charge, but it was enough for him to turn it on and see that there was another notification about a message from @magnuscanis:

Sorry, was at an event so had to dash off. You've been through a rough time. But, as I said, you've got this. Let's message later. I'd like to help.

Ollie's stomach did another somersault. Could this really be happening? Ollie no longer cared that he was late for school. All he was bothered about was getting home to carry on talking to Phone Man.

And, sure enough, that night Ollie chatted to him again online through a series of social media messages. The conversation started as a simple exchange of questions about their day. Ollie loved it. He knew his mates would probably find it boring, and a bit weird, but Ollie found it thrilling. In these moments with Phone Man he could forget all about his responsibilities. He felt like he could be a normal person, an adult even. Although he was very aware there was nothing normal about talking to a famous politician.

Because of that, Ollie made sure he'd watched the news that evening so he could ask political questions, look informed. Phone Man didn't actually answer them, though. He seemed to be much more interested in asking about Ollie's life, which was a new experience for Ollie. No one ever asked him stuff about himself.

Like the night before, the conversation lasted for about ten minutes and then the messages abruptly stopped. And just like the previous morning, he woke the next day to another message telling him that he'd had to go and he'd be in touch again soon.

Ollie had to wait a few days before the next message exchange. He didn't mind, though; he could see from the news that Phone Man was busy.

Ollie had put a news alert on his phone so that every time the famous politician's name was mentioned in any stories he would get a notification. He couldn't believe how many videos and articles kept popping up about him.

For a laugh, he'd also put an alert on his name and CJ's. Unsurprisingly, nothing had come up.

Ollie wondered though if one day people would write about him. As much as he was shy and hated public speaking or anything like that, he hoped he would eventually get to a point where he'd be good at it. He wasn't sure he was ever going to enjoy it, and he still didn't think he wanted to be famous, but he would like to be doing important stuff that people would want to talk about. He hoped his new friendship – if that's what you'd call it – would help him to achieve that.

His conversations with Phone Man, which were now happening a couple of times a week, became a regular part of Ollie's life.

For the first time ever, Ollie felt confident and even excited about his future.

HARRIET

Harriet had stayed true to her word. As soon as she got back from the trip she called the newspapers to tell them how Newton Banks students had been treated by the prime minister's office.

The journalists were initially interested in the story, but it was dropped like a stone when Downing Street officials denied that it had happened and instead accused her of hijacking the event in protest at the school being put in special measures.

Penelope Pencil had been right. No one believed her. And worse still, the whole thing was putting her reputation in danger. A reputation she had built for over thirty years in education.

Harriet was furious at the injustice of it all. She was struggling to sleep, kept awake every night wondering how she could get the truth out there. But it was only her word against Penelope's.

As the days and weeks passed, Harriet felt more and more powerless.

Her friends and family had all told her to stop wasting her time and energy on the story and instead focus on what she was brilliant at: improving the school that desperately needed her help. That was the way to bring about change, they said.

And it turned out, they were right. Harriet didn't actually need to do anything to get revenge.

It was the kids everyone else had underestimated who were about to blow this whole thing open.

OLLIE

Phone Man next messaged Ollie on a Saturday night.

His dad had taken his brothers to visit their gran, but Ollie didn't want to go. Instead he spent the weekend with CJ. Their scrap at school was long forgotten. In fact, neither of them had even mentioned it since. They just fell straight back into their usual routine together, hanging out at CJ's house.

CJ had become obsessed with making TikTok videos. He'd started with about ten followers in his early days posting videos, but since the London trip his short films were getting more and more attention. Especially the one of Courtney throwing up on the tube. He'd managed to capture the exact moment it happened, which he then edited to make it look like Courtney was an alien on the tube who communicated with people by throwing up on them. It was funny, and a thousand people seemed to agree, judging by the number of likes he'd had.

Courtney was raging, though, not just because he'd filmed her throwing up, but because he'd given her googly eyes. Still, CJ didn't care. Quite the opposite, in fact; he saw this as his chance to become a professional TikToker.

That afternoon CJ was working on another London-inspired video. Ollie hadn't taken much notice of it; he was more interested in reading news stories about the latest developments in Westminster.

It was funny to think how much their lives had changed because of that visit by the MP and their trip to London.

At 10.12 p.m., Ollie's phone buzzed with a notification.

Well, tell me, how has your week been? Surely you're closer to world domination now?

Ollie laughed as he read the message. CJ had his headphones on so didn't notice. He knew Phone Man was half joking about the world domination thing, but it did always give Ollie a little confidence boost.

Another message popped up before he could reply.

Listen, I am going to be in your area the week after next for an event. Would you like to come along?

'Fucking hell!' Ollie shouted in total disbelief at what he was reading. It was loud enough for CJ to take off his headphones and ask what was going on.

Ollie had never told anyone about the messages between him and Phone Man. He was pretty sure no one would believe him and, even if they did, they would probably take the piss. But now that there was a meeting on the cards, he was desperate to tell someone. And it had to be his best mate.

As soon as Ollie told CJ, he regretted it.

'So what yer sayin' is some old posh bloke slid into yer DMs and now wants to meet up. That's a bit fucked up, mate. He sounds like a perv to me. One of those groomers.'

'No, it's not like that. And anyway, I messaged him first.'

'So you're the one creeping? Y'know, if lads are yer bag – and I don't give a shit if they are – ya can do betta than 'im.'

Ollie was mortified by CJ's reaction.

'Eugh, it's not like that.'

'How d'ya know it's even him messaging?'

'Of course it is – who else would it be?'

'I dunno, some other dirty perv who wants yer arse?'

'I keep tellin' ya, the messages are nowt like that. He's helping me with my career.'

'As what tho? A posh bloke's bitch?'

'Oh, fuck off, CJ. Just fuck off.'

Ollie walked out of CJ's bedroom and headed into the bathroom with his phone.

'Don't be sendin any dick pics from my bathroom,' CJ shouted behind him.

Ollie ignored him. He locked the door, put the toilet lid down and sat on it. He re-read the chats he'd been having with Phone Man. It had to be him; there was no other explanation. And, as for the messages being dodgy, there wasn't anything sexual in their conversations; not a single message had implied anything like that. Plus the guy was married with kids. He'd seen pictures of them all together online.

Still, the row with CJ had planted a tiny seed of doubt in Ollie's head and now he didn't know what to reply. He wondered if he should play it a bit cooler and suss out if there was something more sinister going on. He didn't want to believe it, but thought he should probably test CJ's theory.

Ollie typed out his reply.

Hi, yeah this event, I'll obviously need to get permission from my dad and headteacher.

The reply bubbles appeared straight away:

Oh gosh, I didn't think a public event after school would require such formalities. It sounds like this could lead to an awful lot of bureaucratic hassle for my team.

Ollie wasn't sure how to take this reaction, plus as usual he needed to google a couple of the words in the message before he could fully understand it. If nothing else his vocabulary and overall writing had improved remarkably since he'd started messaging Phone Man.

Another message appeared before he had written a reply.

On reflection, perhaps we should just leave it. I was only trying to help, but if you are uncomfortable meeting me and my colleagues at a public event without having to seek permission then best to forget it.

Shit! Ollie had called this wrong. He felt like a fool. Why had he listened to CJ and his stupid theory? If he was a dodgy perv, Phone Man wouldn't be inviting him to an event with other people. Now Ollie looked like a stupid kid.

Ollie let out a slow sigh, wondering what the hell to do next. He tried to rectify the situation as best he could:

Ah sorry, of course I don't need permission.

Ollie considered writing more, but he didn't know what to say. He pressed send before he could overthink this. Then watched the bubbles. He felt nervous, afraid of what Phone Man was going to say next.

Marvellous, I will be in touch in due course with more details.

Ollie jumped up from the toilet seat and punched the air. This was so exciting. He was halfway through writing a reply to thank Phone Man when suddenly someone started braying at the door.

'Ollie, Ollie, quick, get out. My phone is going mental.'

'Shit, what? It's not my dad, is it? Is he OK?'

Ever since Ollie lost his mam he was in constant fear that someone else he loved would die suddenly and every time a phone rang he always had a momentary panic that it was a call to tell him someone was dead.

'Eh? It's nowt to do with yer dad. It's the video I posted – it's had ten thousand likes!'

'What? The alien one?'

'No, the new one I put up this afternoon.'

'Jesus Christ, let me see.'

It was a twenty-four-second video that was about to put the school on the front pages of all the newspapers and throw a grenade right into the heart of government.

HARRIET

Harriet knew nothing about the video when it was first posted. It was only when more than 3 million people had seen it that it came to her attention.

She was in the kitchen cooking a Sunday roast for her family. It was rare to get them together so Harriet wanted to make the most of it. She could overhear her partner and brother-in-law in the living room, arguing about whether the football financial fair play rules were indeed fair. Eventually her sister Claire got so bored of it all that she came into the kitchen for a chat.

'So, sis, still not going to retire any time soon?'

'That's a punchy opening question, even for you, Claire.'

'Well, you did say at the last school you were going to give it up.'

'I know, but I'm obviously not ready to yet.'

'Let's not forget what happened to Mum . . .'

'Yeah, she retired at sixty, died at sixty-one. That's exactly why I don't want to stop, thank you very much,' Harriet snapped back.

'OK, fair point. I do think you need to slow down a bit,

though. Geoff was telling me you're still doing quite a bit of work with that missing person charity too.'

'Who the hell is Geoff?' Harriet hated people talking about her private life and the frustration was clear in her voice.

'Geoff from the rambling club. Anyway, my point is you're doing too much.'

'Listen, you know exactly why that charity work is important to me. And, quite frankly, Geoff from the rambling club needs to keep his neb out of my business.'

'I know, I know, it's just all that emotional pressure at the charity and then running a tough school on top. Haz, it's a lot.'

'OK, OK, you've made your point. Let's just enjoy the afternoon, shall we, and—'

Before Harriet could finish her sentence, her niece, who had been sitting in the corner of the room on her phone in complete silence, let out a gasp and then screamed as if Harry Styles had just walked into the room.

'What the hell is it, Liv?' asked Claire.

Olivia ignored her mam, jumped up from her chair and ran over to Harriet.

'Auntie Haz, I think this is you!' she screamed in a high-pitched and slightly overbearing tone.

'What you talking about?' Harriet took off her oven gloves and picked up her reading glasses.

'Look, look . . . that's you . . . on this TikTok,' Olivia said, pointing at the screen on her phone.

Harriet was staring at the phone but couldn't make out what was happening. It looked like a graphic of a pencil being drowned in water.

'Oh my God, look at how many views you've had! Over three million.'

'Is there any volume?' asked Claire, who was struggling to see the screen despite squeezing herself in between her sister and daughter.

Olivia turned up the volume and started the video again.

Miss Pencil, do you not understand . . .

As soon as Harriet heard the first few words, she dropped the phone to the floor. The video was still playing.

. . . some of my students are vulnerable kids whose lives I would be putting at risk if I allowed their faces to be plastered all over The Times? It could be read by any number of people we are trying to keep them away from.'

There was no doubting that was Harriet's voice. Claire picked up the phone to carry on watching. Harriet stood in shock with her hands clasped to her face.

Reading – ha! I doubt they do much of that.

Claire then gasped at hearing these words from the second voice on the video.

'Jesus Christ, Haz, is this a video of what happened in Downing Street?' Claire asked.

Harriet couldn't believe what she was seeing.

All the commotion had now caught the attention of Harriet's partner and brother-in-law, who had come in from the living room.

'What the hell is going on?' screamed Scott, Claire's husband, who was well-meaning but always reacted so dramatically even to the most minor things.

'I have proof. I have undeniable fucking proof to shove right up the government's big fat hairy arse!' said Harriet, who was now doing what she would call ugly crying.

Olivia burst out laughing at all the swear words coming out of her headteacher auntie's mouth.

Harriet's partner took the phone off Claire and watched the video from the start. It was near enough the whole conversation that Harriet had had with Penelope Pencil about not doing the photos with her pupils. The audio was there in full, but their images had been edited to make Penelope look like a giant pencil and Harriet a hosepipe.

'This is dynamite!' shouted Harriet.

'A big massive huge fuck-off stick of it!'

OLLIE

Unbeknown to Ollie, or anyone for that matter, CJ had started filming when he saw the headteacher arguing with the lady from the government. He then managed to open the door to the corridor just enough to squeeze his phone through and capture the whole row without being seen.

CJ edited it, added music and put graphics on. He'd had 100,000 views within three hours of posting it. By the time they woke up on Sunday morning, it was at 1.2 million.

'Mate, this is off the scale,' said Ollie, watching the number go up in real time.

CJ, who was in the bunk bed above him, leaned over the side to reply.

'I know, right, I'm gonna be a TikTok millionaire.'

'No one knows it's you, though, do they?'

'Nah, I didn't wanna run-in with the feds.'

'The feds? You talk some shite! I think ya need to take credit for the video, y'know, otherwise some other fucker will.'

'Shit, ya right, I'd not thought of that. The lasses are never gonna believe it's me with no profile pic.'

CJ spent the next five minutes looking for a decent photo of himself, which they both knew didn't exist. Eventually he gave up looking and took one of him doing the peace sign with his tongue out. He uploaded it and added his surname to his profile too.

'Done. Let's go down the shops and get some Monsters? We're gonna fucking need it today!' The excitement in CJ's voice was through the roof.

Ollie threw on his clothes and put his phone on charge. He felt a pang of sadness. His mam had always told him he drank too many energy drinks. As much as he hated hearing her say it, knowing she never would again really hurt.

On the whole, he thought he was coping quite well with his mam not being there any more. But it was the little things, like the Monster drink reference, that were a gut-punch of a reminder.

Fortunately their trip to the shops soon distracted him.

'Whoa, hotties straight ahead,' CJ said, referencing the girls from the year below who were gathered outside the shops looking at their phones.

One of them looked up and spotted CJ.

'OMG, there he is – CJ!' shouted the girl. This was then followed by high-pitched squeals from the others who had all looked up to see him.

En masse, the whole gang ran at CJ while simultaneously screaming questions at him.

'Ladies, ladies, yous don't need to throw yerselves at us, I've got time for y'all. Now, what d'ya wanna know?' CJ said, lifting his arms up as if he was delivering a sermon to a crowd of disciples.

'Is it really you who did the TikTok?' asked one of the girls who had edged herself to the front of the pack.

'Yes, I filmed it all myself and then used my editing suite at home to produce the final piece for your enjoyment. I was flying under the radar online, y'know, to keep the feds off my back. But fuck them. They're more scared of me than I am of them.'

'It's had millions of views. Yer famous,' she said, this time slightly leaning on CJ's arm as she talked and took a selfie.

'Yeah, I know, it was only a matter of time. I've been asked loads of times to make films for people and, well, Hollywood have been in touch again about doing stuff with them. Y'know, ladies, you get used to all the attention when you're in my business.'

'Oh my God, you're going to Hollywood! Can I come?' said another girl, who had just walked out of the shop and overheard CJ's speech.

'Of course, of course. You can all come.'

The screams started up again.

Like a great orator of his generation, CJ had his audience eating out of the palm of his hand. All desperate for more. And yet not one of them questioned the bullshit and exaggeration CJ was feeding them or the weird posh voice he'd put on. Ollie couldn't help but admire him for that. He felt like he was watching a masterclass in how a teenage boy can do well with the girls.

'Listen, ladies, I'd love to stay and chat, but Spielberg is calling me soon so I'm just gonna get my Monster and do one. You understand?' CJ said as he headed into the shop and gestured for Ollie to follow him.

Fortunately for Ollie there was a limit on how many teenagers were allowed in the shop at the same time, so the girls had to wait outside. As much as Ollie was pleased for CJ, he was grateful for the respite from the chaos.

'Well, that name-change did the trick. The lasses were absolutely gagging for me, bro.'

Ollie laughed. How funny their lives were now, he thought to himself.

By the time they got back it was gone 2 p.m.

'Where have you been? Your headteacher has been on the

phone about some bloody video,' said CJ's dad, who was not happy.

'Shit, I'm fucked,' CJ said under his breath.

His dad handed him his phone.

'You need to ring her back now.'

Ollie went upstairs to get his own phone off charge and saw that he had a dozen or so news alerts. Phone Man must have said or done something, he thought as he unlocked it and clicked on the alerts.

Ollie stood opened-mouthed as he stared at his phone.

He could not believe what he was reading.

It wasn't Phone Man who the stories were about. It was CJ.

'CJ man, yer in the news!' Ollie shouted down the stairs, but CJ couldn't hear him. He was still on the phone to their head-teacher.

Ollie was speed-reading the stories. They were all about their school and CJ's video.

He could feel himself starting to get anxious the more he read.

Loads of people were raging about how the kids from his school had been treated in Downing Street. Some were even saying the prime minister should quit.

What had they done?

Ollie was in full panic mode. His mind automatically went to worst-case scenario; if all hell had broken loose in government because of CJ's video, then Phone Man would be furious with him. In fact, he might as well kiss goodbye to ever hearing from him again.

Ollie was regretting having suggested that CJ update his profile with his real name and picture. Phone Man knew CJ was his best mate, they'd talked about it in messages before. This was a total disaster as far as Ollie was concerned.

CJ came running up the stairs to find Ollie on the landing.

'Well, yer never gonna fucking believe this: Waters the Plants thinks my video is the best thing she's ever seen. She reckons I've saved the school and wants me to send the unedited film so she can use it as evidence.'

'What the actual fuck?! Evidence for what?'

'I dunno, proving the prime minister's a cunt?'

'Shit, ya can't send it.'

'Eh, why?'

'Cos I'm in it, talking to—'

'Oh, yeah, yer boyfriend. Guessin' yer don't want people knowing yer dirty secret?' CJ laughed, not realizing how stressed Ollie was by all this.

'No, oh fuck off, I just don't wanna get him in trouble. And stop sayin' he's my boyfriend – there's nowt going on. He's married with kids, for fuck's sake.'

'Well, I've said I'll send it, but I'll look after ya, bro, and cut that bit out.'

'Will ya? Cheers, mate.' Ollie breathed out a sigh of relief. He knew Phone Man would still be pissed off, but at least now it wouldn't implicate him as being right in the middle of the row.

Ollie didn't know whether to message him or not. In the end he thought it best to leave it for now. He didn't want to make things worse.

That night neither of them slept. CJ was constantly refreshing his phone screen to see how many likes his video was getting and Ollie was going over and over what he might say to Phone Man to repair the friendship he was pretty sure he'd ruined.

By the time they set off for school on Monday, it was at 4.3 million views and growing, which CJ proudly announced as he was locking the door of his house.

'Not only am I gonna be rich, I'm gonna be a fucking super-hero.'

'Waters the Plants called you a people's hero, not a superhero.'

'Same thing. I've never been so buzzing to go into school in all my life. I'm a walking thirst trap. This is gonna be epic.'

Ollie was trying to look like he was enjoying it all too, but he wasn't. He could not shake off the thought that he had pissed off Phone Man and ruined his chances of getting the help he needed to get out of here.

HARRIET

Harriet woke on Monday morning the happiest she had been for a long time. She got up early so she could be at the shops as soon as they opened. She normally read the newspapers online, but today she wanted the physical copies to savour and possibly frame. It's not every day you end up on the front page.

The headlines had her howling with laughter. The journalists must have loved the fact they both had such silly names.

Not the sharpest Pencil in PM's pot

PM's Pencil in poverty porn row

Waters going on here? PM's Pencil erased by
maverick headteacher

Given all the stress and endless calls Harriet had gone through trying to get the papers to publish the story initially, she was shocked by how quickly things had blown up in the past twenty-four hours.

After finding out the video had been made and put online by

Christopher-James Garrens, one of her Year 11 pupils, she was able to get the unedited version to pass on to the press and government. He'd sent it to her in two parts. She didn't care why. All that mattered now was that she had proof.

The government had unsurprisingly dismissed it as a deepfake, but the same journalists she had spoken to originally could see she had been telling the truth. Plus the video had already gone viral, so this had become a massive story even without their input.

The press stories, although very much on her side, were still annoying her. There was a lot of focus on the negative things, like the fact the school was in special measures and the area had high crime rates and drug use. None of this was relevant to the story, but the journalists loved littering their pieces with it anyway.

Overall, she was happy that the truth was now out there. The next big thing was going to be dealing with the broadcast interviews she had coming up that morning.

She had been heavily briefed by her partner about all the dos and don'ts of live interviews. Harriet had seen Nic do countless interviews on the telly. Admittedly about sport, but still the basics were the same for any kind of TV interview.

The school trust's governing body had tried to stop Harriet saying anything else publicly, but she was adamant that she should be allowed to give her unedited side of the story. As a compromise, Harriet agreed to them sending a PR person. They tried to dress it up as someone who would be able to help with all the interviews, but Harriet knew that they would probably try to control her.

Harriet had five back-to-back broadcast interviews and then a sit-down profile piece with *The Times*.

She could see out of her office window that the TV crews had already started gathering.

'Some of them have been here since last night,' said Kevin, the school caretaker, who lived in the estate opposite. He had followed Harriet into her office as soon as he saw her arrive, desperate to tell her what had been going on.

'I was making a cuppa for Maureen, then all of a sudden she started shouting about the school being on the news. I said, "Yer jokin', arn' ya," and she said, "No, Kev, I'm not, come and have a look." I honestly thought she'd lost her marbles, but, bugger me, I looked out of the window and there they were. All these people with cameras and lights and all sorts. And these big vans with big dishes on the top. Eee, well, I couldn't believe it.'

Harriet smiled at Kevin. It was funny how this whole thing impacted them all in so many different ways. He was clearly loving it, although she could do with him toning down the excitement a bit so he could focus on his job.

'I need you to keep an eye on the TV crews today, Kevin, and stop them filming any of our kids' faces. Don't let them talk to them either. They can be sneaky buggers, these journalists.'

Kevin nodded in agreement as Harriet carried on speaking:

'I really don't want to have to go through the whole safe-guarding thing again. Much easier if they don't film the kids at all. They'll inevitably want to get the backs of their heads at least. I'll send a couple of teachers out with you.'

'Yeah, no problem, Miss Waters. I will be on it like a bonnet.'

'Right, great. OK, team, time to face the nation!' Harriet straightened her suit jacket and headed to the door of her office.

'We need to talk through your strategy, Miss Waters,' said a voice from the corner of the room. Harriet had completely forgotten about the PR person with them.

'The strategy is simple, Vivek: I tell them the truth about what happened.'

Harriet was still pissed off that the trust had sent someone to babysit her and so she was now being needlessly passive-aggressive.

Vivek, who looked about twenty-one but was probably about

forty, was not afraid to stand up to Harriet and so continued to talk at her.

'From my research I have concluded that you are highly likely to get some tough questions about events on the London trip other than the Downing Street row. For example, there is a video online of a Newton Banks Academy pupil vomiting on the tube. This is believed to have happened after she had consumed lager in the toilet of the train, which is illegal.'

'Yes, I know that, Vivek.' Harriet was beginning to get annoyed.

'Then there is the fact that the students were kept later than they should have been and the parents were not given enough notice of changes.'

His formal delivery was making Harriet feel like she was in a police interrogation.

'All right, all right, enough with the cop routine.'

Harriet sat back down at her desk and reluctantly asked him to run through his thoughts on it all.

As much as she hated to admit it, Vivek did have a point. Of course she was going to get grilled on other stuff. She'd been so wrapped up in her one-woman crusade proving the government's discrimination against her students, she hadn't thought about all the other elements the press might be interested in.

After listening to fifteen minutes of Vivek forensically dissecting every line of questioning and delivering full briefings on each interviewer, Harriet felt more prepared than she had done for anything in her life.

Outside, crowds had gathered behind the cameras. Locals from the estate were watching it all unfold. Harriet felt a pang of nerves as she stepped out of the school entrance.

Cameras started to flash.

'This is what it must feel like to be Madonna,' Harriet joked.

'I wouldn't know,' replied Vivek, deadpan.

They walked over to the first TV crew. The camerawoman

explained that Harriet would need to wear an earpiece in order to be able to hear the questions the presenters in the studio were going to ask her.

The earpiece was a weird-looking rubber thing that was meant to fit around your ear and then sit comfortably inside it. It didn't feel comfortable at all and kept popping out. When it was finally in place, Harriet heard a crackle and then a man's voice speaking to her.

'Hi, Harriet, it's Lewis here, directing. The presenters will be coming to you shortly.'

The camerawoman prompted her to look down the camera lens. It felt weird, but Harriet tried to relax and pretend the camera was a person's face, which is what her partner had told her to do.

Now, in her ear, she could hear the presenters talking. They weren't talking to her, it was a bit like hearing a TV on in another room. She assumed she must be hearing the programme going out. Then another voice started speaking.

'Coming to you now, Harriet.'

She nodded at the camera and could hear the presenters giving a summary of what had happened before they came to her with the first question.

Four minutes later and it was all done. Harriet hadn't said all the things she had wanted to, but there were no tricky questions, so she was grateful for that.

Vivek gave her a reassuring nod, then she handed the earpiece back and went straight to the next TV crew. It was only a metre on from where she'd just done the last one. For this interview, there was a reporter standing by to ask the questions. That was much easier. No earpiece to worry about, or weird thing about where to look. That interview went much better, she thought.

Within thirty-five minutes Harriet had done all the interviews and was heading back to her office.

'That was an exemplary performance,' declared Vivek.

'Thanks, it made a big difference having you helping – I appreciate it. I feel like I could sit a GCSE on it now.'

'Erm, I don't think so. I don't believe there is a GCSE on this topic.'

'Never mind, it was a joke.'

'Ah, right, I'm not great at understanding jokes,' Vivek replied sheepishly.

Harriet looked at Vivek with a smile. For the first time, she understood. She kicked herself for not spotting it earlier. She'd worked with loads of neurodiverse kids over the years, so she should have seen the signs.

Her phone buzzed again, as it had been doing relentlessly since they had got back to the office. She picked it up to see endless message notifications from family and friends saying what a great job she had done.

Harriet was over the moon.

She should have stopped there.

OLLIE

Ollie and CJ arrived at school to what could best be described as a media circus.

'Fuck me, this is insane!' said CJ, who was standing with Ollie on the opposite side of the road, taking it all in.

In front of them were a dozen or so TV camera crews huddled around the school sign and the school gate. Each camera had a person behind operating it and a smartly dressed person in front speaking into it. There were also a load of harassed-looking people wandering around with their phones clasped to their ears.

And then there were about twenty people, most still in their pyjamas, who had gathered behind the cameras to gawp.

'Half the estate's out,' Ollie exclaimed.

'Eee, look at Courtney's mam in her nightie – I can see her nips!'

'Oh, man, that's minging.'

'So you are gay?'

'No, I'm fucking not, I just don't like old women's tits.'

'Just old men ya like, is it?'

'Oh, shut up. Shouldn't you be getting ready to be interviewed?'

'Nah, Waters the Plants said no kids or parents – summat to do with child protection. Wants all the glory, I reckon.'

The school caretaker, who they had nicknamed Rambo, was now running up and down trying to stop the camera teams from blocking the road into the school. Their PE teacher, Mr Stanton, was rugby-tackling students who were trying to get themselves in front of the cameras.

It was chaos.

Mesmerized by the scene in front of them, the two lads continued to stand and stare until Dean appeared next to them. They both involuntarily jumped and took a sharp intake of breath. Despite being on good terms with Dean now, he still scared the shit out of them.

'CJ, this shit is unreal, mate.'

'Thanks,' said CJ, who took this as a compliment.

'My TikTok has blown up too. Loadsa people wanna know more about the Newton Banks bitches, thanks to yer dumbass post.'

Again, despite the insults and slight aggression in Dean's tone, CJ took this as a positive reaction.

Ollie could see how much everyone was benefitting from CJ's video, but the whole business was making him feel sick. He still hadn't heard from Phone Man. He wondered whether he was annoyed with him. Would he still want Ollie to go along to the event this week? Or had he blown it? He had no idea. The not knowing was what was freaking him out.

He questioned again whether he should message him, but he thought it might be too soon.

He tried to tell himself that he needed to be patient, not least because lots of the news stories were about the government being in chaos, so Phone Man was obviously going to be busy dealing with that.

The last message he'd had from him had implied that he'd be

in touch soon, and that was only forty hours ago. Although obviously a lot had happened in those forty hours.

He just couldn't help feeling stressed by it all.

The only thing that was keeping him from having a total meltdown about it was the fact that CJ had chopped out the middle bit of the video. The bit that featured them both in the corridor. As far as Ollie could see, the press hadn't mentioned Phone Man in any of the stories about what had happened on that fateful trip to London. And he was confident that he would know if they had because he would have had an alert on his phone.

He needed to calm down, he kept telling himself.

After a hectic morning, the media storm died down. The people from the estate had quickly got bored and gone back indoors. And quite a few of the cameras and trucks outside had gone too.

When Ollie got home, his dad was in a bit of a state. The weekend at his gran's had meant facing the reality of his mam's death all over again. His dad was already on his second beer when Ollie walked through the door with his brothers, just after 4 p.m.

All the optimism Ollie had felt about his life had pretty much disappeared in the past twenty-four hours. Seeing his dad drinking again only compounded that. He wasn't drunk yet, but Ollie knew it was only a matter of time before he'd have to carry him to bed.

He made tea for his brothers and went back to searching online to see if he could find any details about the event Phone Man was supposed to be attending. There was nothing at all.

'Yer obsessed with that bloody phone! Get yerself out with the dog, get some fresh air.'

'I'm all right here. Anyway, he can't go on walks yet. He hasn't had his jabs, has he?'

'Oh, he'll be all right for a quick run. Just keep him away from other dogs and don't let him stand in anything.'

'Dad, I don't wanna.'

'Tough. Go. Get yerself out. It'll do y'good, son. And leave y'phone.'

Reluctantly, Ollie pulled on his coat and picked up the dog. It was too small to put on a lead so he just carried him around the park instead. Despite his initial reservations about his dad bringing home a puppy, he was enjoying his company. The puppy was the only one in their family who was always pleased to see him.

It was quiet in the park, aside from a couple of local drunks who were passing around a bottle of cheap cider. He worried his dad was going to end up like them. Although, looking at them now, laughing, they seemed a lot happier than his dad did.

Maybe he should get his dad some help. Get him to one of those groups. After all, he wasn't really an alcoholic, just a man who was gutted he'd lost his wife.

When Ollie walked back in the house, his dad was shouting out what he believed to be the answer to a question that had just been asked on the TV quiz show *Pointless*.

'Tuvalu, it's Tuvalu! I'm tellin' y'now, it's Tuvalu.'

Ollie had no idea what the question was or whether his dad was right or not. He hadn't even heard the word Tuvalu before.

Just at the moment the answer was due to be revealed, the programme cut from the *Pointless* studio to a woman in another studio sitting at a desk.

'Oi, what the fuck's happening?' Ollie's dad shouted, throwing the cushion he'd been holding at the screen.

'Shhhhh,' Ollie said. 'I wanna hear her.'

We interrupt this programme to bring you some breaking news. In the past few minutes Downing Street has released a statement to say that the prime minister will be standing down with immediate effect . . .

'What?' Ollie said with a gasp. Surely CJ's video hadn't caused this? There had to be some other explanation.

'Who cares!' Ollie's dad said with a groan. 'I wanna know if Tuvalu is a pointless answer!'

'Dad, I wanna listen, shut up.' Ollie had missed the last bit of what the newsreader was saying and only caught the tail end of the goodbye.

We'll have all the latest at six o'clock.

Then it cut straight back to the TV show, where the host explained that the best answer for a country beginning TU was Tuvalu.

'YES! I told ya!' shouted Ollie's dad, punching the air in victory.

Ollie's dad was a mystery to him. So clever, yet not remotely interested in current affairs or politics. He didn't think his dad had even registered what had been going on since the school trip to London. In a way, though, Ollie was glad, because it meant he wasn't being questioned by him.

'I'm gonna go up to my room, Dad. Please don't drink too much.'

'Course not, son. Just one more can, I promise.'

Ollie knew that was a promise he was unlikely to keep.

'I've been thinking, you could get some . . .'

Ollie let his sentence trail off. His dad wasn't listening, too engrossed in guessing the next answer on the TV quiz.

He headed up the stairs. His phone was pinging in his pocket. He couldn't wait to catch up on everything that had been happening.

He clicked on the first headline in the long list that was now showing on his phone home screen.

PM QUITS OVER SCHOOL TRIP DEBACLE

He waited for the story to load, which was taking ages. The Wi-Fi in their house was shit at the best of times, but today it was excruciatingly slow.

If the prime minister quitting hadn't shocked Ollie enough, the next part of the story nearly made him fall out of bed with laughter.

Phone Man was being named as the front-runner to take over.

The man he had become friends with online was potentially going to be the next prime minister, one of the most powerful people in the world! Ollie's mind was blown.

It was totally incomprehensible to him, and he started to wonder whether the last few weeks had even been real. Had he really been messaging the next prime minister? Or had someone been playing a cruel joke on him? But who would do that, and why?

He opened his social media page and went straight to the direct messages. He clicked on his chat with @magnuscanis and re-read the whole exchange right from the very beginning. It had to be him. There were things he'd said in the messages that only Phone Man would have known from their chat in the corridor of Number 10.

This latest development also suggested to Ollie that, if Phone Man had been angry with him, he probably wouldn't be any more.

He felt it was the right time to send a message. He started to type.

I've just seen the news. That's amazing. I hope you win.

He kept it short and simple then waited to see if any bubbles appeared, but there was nothing.

It was about the time of day they'd normally message each other, but he guessed it would be a long shot to expect him to be free to reply straight away.

He waited a few more minutes and then debated whether to send another message about the event.

He started to type again.

Are you still coming to Newton Banks next week?

He pressed send and went back to reading as many news stories as he could about what was going to happen next. But no amount of reading could ever prepare him for what was to come.

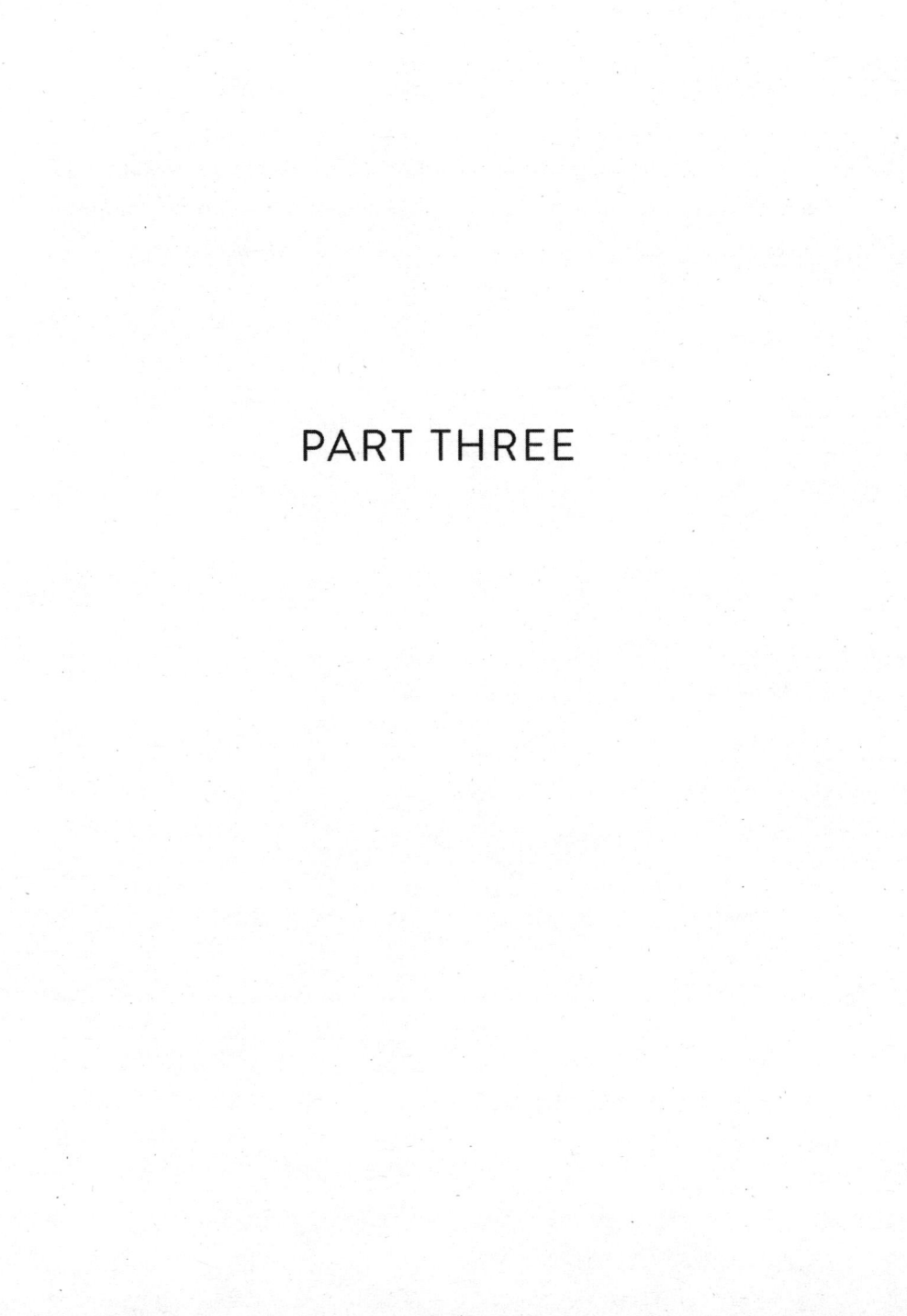

PART THREE

ZOYA

3 p.m.

The day before the hijack

Zoya left the hotel the crew were in. There was no way she could stay. Not after the family drama that had erupted.

She knew leaving could cost her her job and she was dropping Rose in it, but she had to sort this out.

She had a three-hour drive home to work out what to do. Her battered Peugeot was the perfect place to do that. Although you wouldn't think it to look at it, awash with empty cigarette packets, apple cores, muddy boots and general 'life on the road' debris. She'd felt a tinge of embarrassment that morning when the security lad from the site had got in to help her sort out the car battery. But not enough to do anything about it.

Weirdly she found comfort in the chaos of her car. It was her space away from the rest of the world. However, she needed to talk to her boss before she could escape into her thoughts.

She didn't want to lie to her boss, but she had to. If what her brother had told her was right, and her cousin knew, then she was in great danger, but she couldn't tell her boss that without unravelling a massive shitshow of a situation.

'Hi, Gary, it's Zoya, I'm' — she paused to cough — 'not feeling great.' She coughed again.

'Right,' was his response.

Zoya wasn't sure she was going to get away with it, but she was committed now. She continued in the pathetic croaky voice she'd put on for the call.

'I think I've come down with something.'

Silence. Zoya could feel her heart racing. Then her boss spoke.

'Where are you?'

'Erm, I'm in my car,' she said sheepishly, realizing now she should have called from her hotel room if she wanted this to sound more convincing.

'I'm, er, looking for a pharmacy,' she lied as she took the slip road for the motorway.

'Are you sure you're OK to drive?' Gary asked in a voice that made it clear he'd detected her bullshit.

'Er yeah, I'll be fine once I get some drugs in me. I think I should probably head home, though, boss. I don't want to pass it on.'

'Well, it sounds like you're already on your way home, Zoya. But listen, whatever it is, look after yourself. I'll call you tomorrow.'

And he hung up.

Zoya knew she'd been busted, but if she didn't sort out this mess with her cousin, her job would be the least of her worries.

She longed to ring Kate, but daren't. She couldn't risk involving her any more than she already had.

She put her foot down and let out a long sigh.

She was driving into a nightmare.

OLLIE

Four and a half years before the hijack

I t had been over a week since CJ first posted the video, setting the ball rolling for one of the most dramatic weeks, not just for their school, but for the whole nation. At least in a political sense.

Although the TV cameras had gone, there was still a lot of activity in the aftermath of their press exposure. For a start, there were lots of visitors coming and going. All very smartly dressed and all being shown around the school by students. No one knew who they were, but Ollie had overheard one of their PE teachers talking about the chance to get some decent kit.

Dean and CJ were still riding high on their newfound TikTok fame. There was even talk of them getting agents. They'd been told that the school had been inundated with brands wanting to work with them. They'd also been sent a load of free stuff, which CJ was selling off on the sly. And, for the first time in CJ's life, he now had a girlfriend.

For Ollie, though, life had pretty much gone back to normal. He still hadn't heard from Phone Man and was now convinced that the event he was meant to be going to in Newton Banks had been cancelled. Even if it was happening, which Ollie could find no evidence of, he certainly didn't expect to get an invite now. To say he was gutted was an understatement. It was like their friendship had never happened. If he didn't have the messages to prove it, he wouldn't have believed it himself.

It didn't stop Ollie's obsession with him, though. He busied himself with learning everything he could about the leadership contest. He read countless articles on all the potential candidates. He wanted to understand more about how everyone had got to where they were in their careers. Depressingly, all their backgrounds were very similar. There was no one like him, he thought, which is what Phone Man had said to him in the corridor that time.

All but one of them had gone to a private school and three out of five of them had studied the same thing at university; Politics, Philosophy and Economics. Ollie looked up the places where you could study it and what grades you'd need to get in. He would have to up his game at school if he was ever going to be in with a chance of being able to apply. Also, he'd probably need to sell a kidney to be able to afford it.

There were other similarities in the candidates' careers too. Two of them, including Phone Man, had been in politics their whole lives, one of them had set up and sold various businesses and the other had been the boss of a trade union. Ollie read that it was very unusual for someone in that particular party to have had that background. He didn't really know what that meant, but he remembered he'd once heard his dad trying to convince his mam to join the nursing union, so he asked him about it. It was probably the first time in ages he'd had a normal chat with his dad. Admittedly, it was just before he was about to set off for work, so he was sober, which was good, but it was all a bit rushed.

Ollie could see from the news that Phone Man was doing a lot of travelling. He often imagined what his life was like when the cameras weren't rolling. It must be exciting, he thought, sleeping in different hotels every night. Ollie hadn't been on holiday for years, not since before his mam got sick, and he was so young then he couldn't remember ever staying in a hotel.

He tried to search for information on Phone Man's family again, but there wasn't much. There were only a handful of pictures and they looked like they were from a long time ago. He wondered what the kids looked and sounded like now. Obviously posh, but were they nice? And did they miss their dad when he was away? He assumed they wouldn't go with him because they'd have school. But then he thought that maybe rich families take teachers with them. He let his imagination run wild with all the iterations of Phone Man's family dynamic. He couldn't imagine their life would be anything like his when his dad was away.

Ollie's dad had left that morning; he would be away again until Friday. The responsibility of looking after his brothers and the dog had fallen to him. No change there.

He'd put his brothers to bed and nipped out with the dog. He tried to leave his phone at home when he went out to the park; weirdly, his dad had been right about it making him feel better. This time, however, he couldn't resist taking it with him. There was too much going on and he didn't want to miss anything.

While he was sat on the bench scrolling through his phone, he saw a story he hadn't noticed before. There were now so many stories about Phone Man, the alert he'd had on his name had become a bit pointless. The notifications were never-ending and it was killing his battery, so he'd taken the decision to turn it off and instead just google him whenever he wanted to know what was going on.

The story was an old one from two days ago. He had no idea how he had missed it. It said that Phone Man was going to be in Newton Banks on Tuesday for the opening of a new arts and theatre centre. That was tomorrow.

The event was happening. The event he was meant to be at. Ollie stared at his phone in disbelief.

He weighed up his options. He could just stay at home and do nothing, he could message Phone Man to see if he could get him in, or he could just turn up and see what happened.

He quickly ruled out option one; there was no way he was missing out on this.

So should he message him or not? That was the question he was struggling to make a decision on.

Ollie looked back at their conversation. The last message he'd had from Phone Man was on the Saturday night just after CJ had published the video, but before it had gone viral. He re-read it:

Marvellous, I will be in touch in due course with more details.

Despite messaging him twice since then, once about the news of him being the front-runner for prime minister and the second with a direct question about the event, he hadn't heard from him.

There was a chance, given the chaos, he had just forgotten to reply, so if Ollie messaged it might remind him and then he'd sort out him getting into the event. However, it might also prompt him to tell Ollie he couldn't come, and then where would that leave him? He didn't want to risk being told not to go.

It was getting late. He needed to get back home.

He looked at their conversation for a final time. He wasn't going to message. He was just going to turn up. *What's the worst that can happen?* he asked himself.

As he headed back, he messaged CJ to see if he was up for coming too. He knew he'd take the piss out of him, but it was worth it if it meant he would go with him. He would feel too shy going on his own.

Moments after sending the message, just as he was putting

his phone in his pocket, he saw that CJ was FaceTiming him, which was unusual for either of them to do with each other.

'Shit, I forgot to tell ya,' CJ said.

'Tell me what?' Ollie sounded confused.

'We're already going.'

'What d'ya mean?'

'Waters the Plants gave us some tickets at the end of geography. You'd gone for yer brothers, so she gave 'em to me.'

'Tickets? What d'ya mean? Tickets for what?'

'Tickets for the BRITs, obviously,' CJ said sarcastically.

'I don't get it.'

'Keep up, dipshit! Tickets for that poncey theatre thing tomorrow night. The one yer boyfriend is gonna be at.'

Ollie was struggling to process what CJ had said.

'Where did Waters get 'em from?'

'I don't fucking know. We've got the tickets, bro, that's all that matters.'

CJ was right, but Ollie couldn't hide his annoyance that Phone Man hadn't messaged him to tell him any of this himself.

'I thought you'd be buzzing, mate,' said CJ, surprised by Ollie's reaction.

'I am, I am.'

'Well, tell yer fucking face that.'

CJ hung up.

HARRIET

Four and a half years before the hijack

Harriet had spent nearly two weeks fielding calls from every Tom, Dick and Harry wanting to visit Newton Banks Academy. Big brands sent free school equipment, local businesses offered to sponsor the sports teams, and politicians, of all flavours, wanted to be there to show that they were focused on meeting the needs of the students. Or, as one of them put it, 'they wanted to show their unwavering support for the beating heart of the local community'.

What a load of tosh, Harriet thought. She knew what they wanted and it was nothing to do with helping the school. It was political point scoring. As for the businesses, it was purely a marketing tool.

'Send money and free stuff to the poor kids and then everyone will think your brand is lovely,' Harriet had said in her office that afternoon.

'I'm detecting some cynicism, Miss Waters,' said Vivek, her newly appointed communications manager.

'I'm not, I'm just a lot older than you. And can you please stop calling me "miss"? You're making me feel even older than I am,' Harriet replied.

'I'm being professional,' Vivek said in a tone that suggested he really didn't see what the problem was.

'Grown-ups call me Harriet and my friends call me Haz. I think you fall into at least one of those categories now, Vivek. Maybe I should start calling you Viv now to make it easier?

'No. Vivek, please.'

Harriet laughed. She'd grown to love Vivek's no-nonsense straight-talking. Apart from the occasional misunderstanding, normally caused by Harriet's sarcasm, they had formed a strong bond.

The media frenzy Harriet was living through would have been impossible on her own. She hated to admit it, but she did need the hand-holding that Vivek provided. The radio and TV studios were much more intimidating than she'd anticipated. And Vivek's attention to detail meant that she went into every interview prepared for whatever was thrown at her.

Harriet was acutely aware that the media interest and the freebies from businesses wouldn't last long, so she had to make the most out of it now. She said yes to pretty much everything, apart from the chance to go on a reality show – that was a step too far. Also her partner Nic didn't look too impressed when she floated the idea at dinner the night before.

The past couple of weeks had been exhausting, but she could see that the whole thing had genuinely lifted the atmosphere in the school. Obviously it hadn't solved all their problems, but it had certainly helped some students start realizing their own self-worth. Plus the increase in resources meant that the staff were a bit happier too, for now at least.

'So this theatre trip tonight,' Vivek piped up.

Harriet could feel one of his explainers coming on.

'We are taking twenty students and five adults including myself and you.'

'Correct.'

'So I foresee a couple of problems.'

'Go on.'

'The culture minister is going and he is one of the candidates running for leader.'

'Yes, I believe the invite came from his office.'

'There is a lot of press interest in him at the moment so we can assume that there will be a lot of cameras. I also think it is likely that you will be doorstepped on the way in.'

'Doorstopped?'

'Doorstepped – it means approached by journalists either outside or inside the venue, to be asked your opinion on things.'

'Oh, right.'

'There is also a chance that the students will be photographed and filmed.'

'I've already said to the relevant government department that they can't do that.'

'Yes, and their camera team won't. But there will be other camera crews there who they will have no control over. Also, some of the students here are known for disobeying rules so are unlikely to follow any guidance we give them about dealing with the cameras.'

'Right.'

'Plus this theatre was local MP Janet Jacobs' idea.'

'Oh God, of course. That evil old witch.'

'She's the same age as you and she's not a witch. She is, however, someone who attracts a lot of unwanted attention. There is a high likelihood of her being there, and this means there will be protestors outside the theatre too.'

'So what are you saying? We don't go?'

'No. I'm saying we don't go in through the main door. We go around the back, circumventing any camera crews or protestors. I've confirmed that there is a fire exit and I've arranged for them to let us in through there before the event starts.'

'Vivek, you are a genius.'

'I'm not. I don't fall within the ninety-eighth percentile on an IQ or standardized intelligence test.'

Harriet laughed.

This trip was just what the school needed.

OLLIE

School had been a blur. Ollie's sole focus was on the theatre trip.

'You told yer boyfriend we're coming tonight?'

'Nah, I've not heard owt from him.'

'Ah, lover's tiff?'

'For fuck's sake, CJ, can you just drop the whole fucking boyfriend thing. He's older than my dad.'

'Relax, I won't say owt in front of him.'

CJ saying the words 'in front of him' sent a shiver through Ollie's body. He was going to see Phone Man today, actually be *in front of him*. He'd be able to tell him all about the research he'd done on becoming a politician and how he'd been looking into studying PPE.

He felt a buzz of excitement, one he hadn't felt in the few weeks since the video went out.

And now their coach was pulling up at the rear of the theatre. Ollie had read that the event started at 5 p.m., but it was only 4.30 p.m. and they were already there. He didn't mind, though, he wanted to see all the comings and goings.

They were hurried through a door at the back of the venue.

There were loads of people inside. A bit like Downing Street, there seemed to be quite a few posh people with clipboards milling about. Various cameras had been set up at the front of the stage with people going on and off to test microphones.

Within thirty minutes the theatre was full. Someone came on stage to tell them what they needed to do if there was a fire and also to remind them not to use their phones.

'Fuck that,' CJ said under his breath.

All of a sudden a load of photographers ran from the back of the theatre to the front of the stage where they crouched down on the floor. Moments later, Phone Man walked on to the stage. The cameras all started flashing.

'Welcome, everyone, to the grand opening of the Banks Theatre. Isn't it wonderful?'

There was a cheer from the audience.

Then Phone Man looked directly at where they were sitting.

'I'm also delighted to welcome here the marvellous students from Newton Banks Academy.'

Ollie's headteacher turned to smile at them all. She was obviously over the moon at his mention of the school.

Phone Man continued, 'And let me tell you, there were no arguments about getting them along for this event! But don't worry, guys – no pressure to be in any photos.'

The audience laughed.

'He deffo looked at ya then,' CJ said, jabbing Ollie in the side with his elbow.

Ollie stayed silent and carried on listening to the speech.

He had never seen anything like it. The way Phone Man could stand on a stage and talk so effortlessly to a huge room full of people and not be nervous was incredible to watch. Yes, Ollie had seen teachers do it countless times in school assemblies, but this was totally different. Everyone was listening to him, and on top of that they were laughing and smiling too. He had the audience eating out of the palm of his hand. Ollie could never imagine himself doing that.

Ollie was in total awe, mesmerized by everything he did and said.

And what he was saying resonated with Ollie. This man was clearly passionate about bringing real change to stop the inequality that families like Ollie's were being held back by. He talked about all young people being given the opportunity to shine, no matter what their background. And he finished with the phrase he'd said to Ollie countless times in his messages, a phrase that always made him feel empowered:

'You've got this.'

They were Phone Man's final words after fifteen minutes of talking. He was applauded off the stage and was ushered to a seat a few rows in front of where Ollie was sitting.

Even CJ looked impressed by Phone Man's performance. To be able to make a roomful of people laugh like he just had was something CJ craved.

The performance began. Their ticket had said that it was a variety show with special guests, but he had no idea what that meant.

'I wonder who the special guests are gonna be,' CJ mused. 'I hope it's a hottie off the telly, like that lass who does *Love Island*.'

Ollie ignored CJ and instead stared at the back of Phone Man's head. He wanted to climb inside it and find out exactly what was going on in there. What was he thinking in this moment? And more importantly, had he seen Ollie? And if he had, how did he feel about seeing him? Was he glad he was there or was he still annoyed at him – assuming he ever was? Ollie hoped that he'd find all of this out at the end of the event.

He was desperate to talk to him and wasn't even bothered about watching the high-energy show that was now being performed on the stage in front of him. While the audience whooped and cheered and sang along to all the familiar songs, Ollie just carried on staring at Phone Man.

After the show finished the students were ushered to the front of the stage. They hadn't been told why, but Ollie assumed and hoped it must be to talk to Phone Man.

The rest of the audience were leaving and there was a team now sweeping up the glitter that had been shot out of a cannon in the final moments of the performance.

'Ah, Newton Banks Academy, I have heard so much about you. I trust one of you will be filming this,' Phone Man said as he stood up from his scat.

CJ stuck his phone in the air.

'Sure am. Carry on.'

Phone Man laughed.

'Well, it's lovely to meet you all. I've heard so much about your brilliant school and of course your marvellous teacher.'

Their headteacher stepped forward at this point and shook Phone Man's hand. Ollie could see that she was impressed by him.

Then, within seconds, another woman with a folder in her arms stepped forward to speak.

'We need to go, Minister.'

'Alas, work calls. Keep up the good work. You've got this.'

And he was gone.

Ollie was devastated.

HARRIET

Four and a half years before the hijack

'Well, that was weird,' Harriet said to Vivek as they took their seats next to each other on the coach.

'What do you mean? Why was it weird? It all went exactly as we had planned.'

'Yes, I know. I meant the minister was weird.'

'Weird in what way? He behaved exactly like all the ministers I have ever met.'

Harriet realized this was going to be a tricky one to explain. Something didn't sit right with Harriet about the meeting with the minister.

'I just found it odd that he introduced himself to us as if he had never met us before, when he had. He was there that day in Downing Street.'

'Maybe he had just forgotten. He must meet hundreds of people every week.'

'I know that, but he was actually there when the row happened. He was in the corridor talking to Ollie. In fact, now I remember: he said Ollie's name.'

Harriet turned around at this point to see if she could catch Ollie's eye. He was staring down at his phone.

'Ollie,' Harriet shouted.

'Yes, miss?' Ollie looked alarmed at being called.

'The minister today — you've met him before, haven't you? That time at Number 10?'

'Erm, dunno, miss, maybe,' Ollie replied.

'OK, right, I thought you were chatting to him in the corridor when the row kicked off?'

Ollie shrugged his shoulders and went back to looking at his phone. Harriet gave up on the chat and turned to face the front again.

'Well, if the student doesn't remember the encounter, chances are the minister won't either,' Vivek said, assuming this would now be the end of the matter.

Harriet understood what Vivek was saying, but there was something bothering her about it.

She made a mental note to talk to Ollie and make sure there wasn't more to this.

OLLIE

Four and a half years before the hijack

'Why'd ya not tell Waters the Plants the truth?' CJ asked when they got off the coach and were walking home.

'Dunno. Just don't want her poking round my business.' Ollie said this trying to hide how bothered he was by the whole thing. He had barely been able to control his emotions when Phone Man ignored him. Then to have his headteacher asking awkward questions about it as well . . . It was all too much.

He knew he couldn't avoid CJ's questions, though.

'Sounds dodge, mate. I know I take the piss, but he's not doing owt to ya, is he? Like summat he's told ya to keep tight about?'

'Oh, fuck, no. Nothing. We don't even message any more.'

'Ah, right. But ya sound, aren't ya? Cos he was deffo weird today, the way he looked at ya, like, when he was talking.'

'D'ya think?'

'Yes, mate. He 100 per cent looked at ya creepy, then fucking ignored ya. I wanted to knock him out.'

Ollie was pleased to hear that CJ had seen what he saw. Still, he was desperate to stop talking about it. That was just prolonging the pain.

'I don't think he even remembers me,' Ollie said, trying to close the conversation down.

'Of course he does. No one's gonna forget a legend like you.'

Ollie smiled. Despite all his gags and bravado, CJ actually cared – although this was as close as he was ever going to get to showing it.

'Listen, ya don't need him, the fat old twat. We're going places, y'know. Fuck this shithole and its bitches.'

Ollie laughed. Typical CJ: no sooner had he revealed his sensitive side than he went back to full daft-bugger mode.

When he got home, the house was empty. Ollie had arranged for his brothers to go for a sleepover at a friend's house after school. It was the first time he'd ever done that, but it was his only choice if he was going to be able to go to the event.

He wished he'd never gone.

He slumped down onto the sofa. Above the telly he could see his favourite picture of his mam. Taken before she got ill.

A wave of grief hit him.

He didn't stop crying until he went to bed.

Everything that had happened, everything he was feeling, had overwhelmed him.

And after crying for what felt like forever, he slipped into a state of emotional paralysis.

In the weeks that followed Ollie reverted back to how he was before the MP had ever visited his school. He'd still hang out with CJ during the day, but as soon as his lessons had finished he'd make his excuses and go home.

He stopped bothering to look at what was happening on the news and avoided anything to do with Phone Man. He'd lost all interest in politics too. He didn't see the point; he was never going to be part of that world.

His headteacher tried to intervene. She called him into her office a few days after the theatre trip for what she described as a 'chat'. A word that instantly made him feel uncomfortable.

After a few cursory questions about his studies, she brought up Phone Man. She mentioned seeing them talking in the corridor in Downing Street and how strange it had been at the theatre. She asked him whether he thought it was weird that he had not remembered meeting him.

Ollie gave nothing away. Partly because he didn't feel anything any more. Ollie was numb to life. He didn't even react when she told him Phone Man hadn't won the leadership contest. He didn't care.

After their chat she arranged to speak to his dad. Not that much came of it. There was talk of a grief counsellor, but Ollie kept finding ways to get out of it. His headteacher kept on at them, but Ollie's dad was very good at convincing people he was handling things better than he was.

It was weeks later, as he was sat on the park bench one evening, waiting for the dog to have a wee, that he heard a notification on his phone. He didn't get many of them these days.

He pulled his phone from his pocket and what he saw on the screen stopped him in his tracks.

It was a notification of a direct message from @magnuscanis. Phone Man.

Ollie clicked on the notification. It took him straight back to their chat. The one that had ended abruptly several weeks ago.

Hello stranger, how are you?

Without hesitation Ollie wrote a reply as if it was the most normal thing in the world for a fifteen-year-old to be talking to a senior politician.

Fine. How are you?

Bubbles appeared underneath.

Jolly good. Now, tell me, where are we at with your rise to stardom?

It was then that it hit him. He was back talking to Phone Man like nothing had ever happened. But loads had happened. He wanted to ask him why he hadn't messaged him before now and why he'd ignored him at the theatre, but he didn't have the courage.

Phone Man didn't owe him anything, but Ollie was still hurt at being ignored.

Before he could reply, another message appeared.

It was as if Phone Man had read his mind.

Are you annoyed with me, dear boy?

That's all it took to disarm Ollie and soften his annoyance. 'Dear boy' was such a funny thing to say. He smiled to himself as he typed out his reply.

No I'm not.

And to be fair, he wasn't annoyed any more. Excitement had taken over.

Ollie was so pleased to be talking to him again.

Their conversation continued all the way home from the park. Ollie told him about what had been happening at school.

The numbness had instantly evaporated.

Ollie felt on top of the world.

For now, at least.

ZOYA

The day before the hijack

Zoya had no idea what to expect when she walked into the house she shared with her father, brother and nana.

She could hear the TV, but apart from that it was quiet. The evening news was on.

Shit. Zoya suddenly realized she hadn't told Rose she was heading home. In all the drama of the day, she forgot. It was bad enough to be leaving her in the lurch like that on a huge broadcast, but to not even tell her she was going . . . That was bad form.

She'd be fine, though; Rose was a pro. Zoya would apologize once everything was sorted. She thought about Kate again, how she longed to talk to her. She'd know what to do. But she had to sort this out herself. It was a mess of her own making.

Zoya heard her nana's voice coming from the living room.

'Why is Abdul on the telly?'

Zoya assumed she must be talking to her dad. She couldn't hear a response.

Her nana's voice grew louder.

'Abdul is a good boy.'

Zoya realized as she walked into the room that her nana was talking to herself. Her confusion had only got worse since Abdul's arrest five years ago.

'Hello, Nana,' Zoya said, sitting down next to her.

She responded with a wave of her hand as if to dismiss her.

'You smell of smoke,' she said, without looking at Zoya.

'Ah, I've just walked past some lads smoking outside.'

'I will not be disrespected in my own home.'

Zoya rolled her eyes.

'Nana, it's just a bit of smoke.'

'You have disrespected my family.'

'Nana, I am your family.'

'Well, start behaving like it.'

The conversation wasn't making any sense. But Zoya was used to that. And her nana's dementia was the least of her worries right now. Her priority was finding Abdul.

'Nana, has he been here?'

'Who?'

'Abdul.'

Her nana turned to look at her now. She was angry.

'Your cousin, you mean?'

'Yes, Nana, my cousin. Has he been here?'

'Are you going to apologize to him?'

A wave of panic hit Zoya. What did she mean, apologize to him? What did she know? Did her nana also now know that she had been involved in Abdul's arrest? Surely not. She barely knew what day of the week it was.

'What do you mean?' Zoya asked, her heart racing.

'You lied to the police.'

'What?'

'He told me.'

'Nana, when did he tell you this?'

'Does it matter? You lied, Zoya.'

'Nana, did you see him?'

'Yes. He told me.'

'Where is he now?'

'Probably looking for you. I told him where you were.'

OLLIE

Four years before the hijack

O llie's sixteenth birthday was his best yet. He still didn't look his age, annoyingly, but nevertheless he was grateful to finally reach that important milestone.

He'd been enjoying school lately. Now he was back messaging with Phone Man, he'd got into current affairs again. Their conversations were sporadic, but Ollie didn't mind. His grades were good and his English teacher was blown away by how much his writing had improved. He still didn't know whether he'd get what he needed to do the A levels required to study PPE, but he was giving it his best shot.

His dad had made him a birthday breakfast and given him some money to get a McDonald's for his lunch. Ollie felt great.

He was less impressed by what CJ had done to his locker, though. To mark his birthday, he had covered the front in a load of obscene pictures, including a big-boobed woman holding a cake. Ollie nervously laughed as he quickly ripped them off before any of the teachers saw.

Inside his locker he found a parcel.

'Did you put this in here?' Ollie asked CJ.

'Nah, but look, someone's opened it,' CJ replied, pulling at the side of the envelope, which had been ripped. He continued talking as he carried on inspecting it. 'Must've been sent to the school – they check 'em for owt dodgy nowadays.'

'Do they?' Ollie asked.

'Yeah, after Ellie's dad sent her a bag of coke.'

'What the fuck? To the school! That's mental.'

'It burst open when Rambo shoved it in her locker. Gotta be the best day of his life that day. What a high.'

'How did I miss this?'

'You were in yer weird phase.'

'Ah, right, yeah.' Even though it had never been discussed, Ollie knew exactly what CJ meant. His lengthy disappearing act was something that happened but neither of them ever talked about.

'Anyway, since then, they've been opening any post we get.'

Ollie opened the parcel and inside was a green leather notebook with the words House of Commons written in gold lettering and with the logo underneath. It was the poshest notebook he had ever seen.

'A fucking book – what a shit present!' CJ exclaimed. 'Who's it from anyway?'

Ollie opened it and on the inside cover was a handwritten note:

You've got this!

Ollie's heart sped up. He knew exactly who it was from. They'd been talking about his birthday the week before.

'I dunno,' Ollie lied.

'Right, I'm going for a slash. See ya in maths.'

'Yeah,' Ollie said without looking up. He was slowly stroking his finger over the words inked onto the cream page and smiling.

That night, Ollie messaged Phone Man to thank him for the gift. He replied straight away.

Oh, I'm pleased you got it. How is your birthday? Are you drunk yet?

Ollie wasn't sure what to reply. His dad's drinking was enough to put him off for life. He didn't want to say he'd celebrated by having a burger and chips at lunch. But that was the truth.

I'm celebrating at the weekend

Oh, how nice. Listen, I was wondering if you would like to come to a little soirée I'm having with some of my political pals.

Ollie googled the word 'soirée' before he replied. His eyes lit up when he realized what it meant.

Yes I would like to, thank you.

Great. It will be a chance to meet up with some like-minded individuals, young and old, to discuss the great events of our time. If that doesn't sound too boring?

That sounds brilliant. When is it?

This Saturday, at my club.

You own a nightclub?

Ha! No, it's a private members' club in London. You do make me laugh.

Ollie felt a bit daft. He had so much to learn.

I have exclusive use of it that evening so there will be a free room for you to stay in, should you so wish. Perhaps you would like to bring along one of your chums.

The only time Ollie had heard the word 'chum' being used was when he was sent to get food for the dog. He realized that in this context Phone Man meant friend.

Ollie wondered whether CJ would go with him. He had a look to see if he was online so he could ask him before replying to Phone Man, but it was late and he wasn't. He'd have to wait until morning.

He made the assumption that CJ would say yes, but probably only if Ollie paid, because despite making a load of money from the videos, he was tight.

Ollie couldn't bring himself to use the word chum in his reply.

Thank you. I would love to bring someone.

The reply came back straight away and then the conversation ended.

Great. I'll message you the address and timings.

Ollie couldn't sleep that night. Excitement and trepidation flooded his brain. Could this really be happening? He was afraid to feel too much excitement because of what had gone on the last time they had arranged to meet.

This time felt different, though.

Despite saying yes straight away, he actually had no idea if he had the means to get there and back. There was a folder of money stashed at the back of his wardrobe. In it was the £50 he'd offered his dad all those months ago, plus a bit of birthday money he'd been given and then a few odds and sods he'd found when he was out and about. He counted it out. In total it came to £78.23.

He had no idea whether that would get him and CJ to London and back, so he spent the next hour planning out the route and costing all the travel options.

The train was out of the question. To travel anytime in the next couple of days was going to cost over £200 return for the two of them. Ollie had no idea trains were so expensive. It made him appreciate once again the MP who had paid for their London trip in the first place. He also made a mental note to make travel cheaper for people if he ever did become a politician.

He worked out the cheapest option was the bus, which he reckoned he could get for £15 return, but that was only if they got the bus back at a ridiculous time in the morning. Still, he had enough money and it would get them there on time.

His plan was to go to the bus station the next day to buy the tickets. He was frustrated that he couldn't just buy them online there and then. He realized he also needed to sort out a bank account if he was ever going to have the independence he desperately craved.

With the travel plans sorted, he let his mind drift to thoughts about who he might meet and what they might talk about. As Phone Man had pointed out, this was his chance to make some new 'like-minded' friends.

He had already been looking at the political youth groups near where he lived, but they weren't that close, plus he knew that his nerves would probably get the better of him and he'd never actually go through with meeting up with them when the time came. He hadn't even been able to bring himself to join their online forum. Instead he just looked at the things they posted on their social media pages, but at a distance. He never 'liked' or commented on them, for fear of exposing himself and bringing unwanted attention.

It was while he was looking at their pictures again that it suddenly dawned on him that he didn't have any suitable clothes to wear. He looked nothing like the people in the photos. He counted out his money again. After the bus fares, he would have £48.23; he needed some of that for food, but he reckoned he could easily use £40 of it to buy some decent clothes. Something else to add to his 'to do' list for the following day.

First on the list was 'Talk to CJ'.

CJ said yes before Ollie could even finish explaining.

'Get in! London, again, and yer paying. Mint. I don't even care how fucked up this is.'

'It's not fucked up.'

'It fucking is – that dirty old perv is inviting ya to a party in London after dicking ya about. I tell ya what, if he does owt dodgy I will have to deck him, like.'

'Oh, sh'up. I keep telling ya, he's not dodgy, he just likes helping people – that's what politicians do.'

'Aye, keep telling yerself that. Either way, it gives us a chance to do a load more TikToks.'

'I dunno if you'll be allowed to film the party, like.'

'I'll just do it on the sly, man, don't worry.'

'What d'ya reckon we say to our dads?'

'Fuck all. We're sixteen, we can do what the fuck we like,' CJ said defiantly.

'S'ppose, but I'm gonna have to say something – my dad'll be back.'

'Aw, man, just say yer at mine.'

'Yeah, good idea. I'm gonna go into town later to get bus tickets and some new gear. Wanna come?'

'Are ya buying?'

'If I can afford it, yeah.'

'Get in, I've had my eye on a Boss T-shirt.'

'I was thinking Primark, like.'

'Not real Boss. Keith down the Crown is selling knock-off ones for a fiver. Want me to get ya one too?'

'Nah, I'm gonna wear a black blazer.'

'It's a party not a fucking funeral.'

'I know, it's just my mam . . .' Ollie unexpectedly coughed, caught out by his emotion. He took a deep breath and continued: 'She always said I looked good in black.'

'Right, yeah, but a blazer? That's a bit weird.'

He didn't want to tell CJ that he'd been looking at what young politicians wear to help him decide on an outfit. It wasn't worth the piss-taking. Plus CJ wouldn't understand.

Ollie's sole focus now was impressing the people he knew could help change his life.

PART FOUR

The day of the hijack

ROSE

7.12 a.m.

'Rose, I have your wife and son.'

The words keep playing through my head while the chancellor continues to talk at me.

I'm not even listening to him now. My heart feels like it's going to explode. Who is this person speaking to me in my earpiece? And what do they want?

I have so many questions and no answers.

Do I know this person? I can't quite work it out. It doesn't sound like one of the usual people from the TV gallery back at base. Or does it? I have no idea.

Think.

Is it Billy? It's got to be. There is no other explanation.

He must have been watching my family to know where to find them.

Oh my God, Billy has got my family.

But what does he want? Why has he hijacked my broadcast?

And where have all the other noises gone that I normally hear in my earpiece? Aside from his voice, there is silence, not the usual hubbub of activity I'd expect.

Am I even on air any more?

I feel like my mind is playing tricks on me.

The voice speaks calmly and slowly again.

'Rose, if you want Rory and Kate to come home, you are going to have to do as I say. Nod if you understand.'

Rory and Kate. He has Rory and Kate. I cannot bear this.

That's why Kate didn't reply to me last night. She'd been kidnapped.

Oh my God. What if he hurts them? What if he has already done something to my son? Oh God, Rory, he must be so scared right now. I need to leave. I need to get to him right now.

But I can't do that, can I? The voice said to do as he says.

I feel a scream build inside of me. I can't let it out.

I need to stay calm. I can't stay calm.

He has my son. I am going to have to do whatever the fuck he wants.

I have no choice.

I slowly nod my head.

The chancellor stops speaking and looks at me. He's waiting for my next question. He has no idea that someone, a stranger, is trying to control this interview now.

Maybe nobody else knows. There's a chance it might only be me hearing this.

I can't speak. I feel like the whole world is looking at me. Actually, millions of people are. But none of that means anything in this moment. All that matters is that Rory and Kate are OK. And they're not going to be unless I do what this man is saying.

The chancellor takes my silence as a prompt to carry on talking.

I stare at him blankly. I have no idea what is going to happen next.

And then the voice speaks again.

'Rose, I am in control now.'

ZOYA

Zoya's family know that she told the police her cousin was a terrorist. But how?

She feels sick.

Where is he? And what is he planning to do next? Zoya can't work it out.

She's barely slept.

Back in her car, she lights her third cigarette of the morning.

She turns into the car park near work. She is going to have to talk to her boss, tell him what's been going on and who her cousin is. She knows this probably means the end of her journalism career, but she feels she has no choice. Maybe she should just hand in her notice. Save herself the aggro of explaining.

She's about to turn off the engine when a notification appears on her car display. It's a message from a number she doesn't recognize. She clicks on it and the car reads it out loud.

I have control of your broadcast. Do not cut away from Rose. I have Rose's wife Kate and her son Rory. They will only be safe if you do as I say.

She picks up her phone and reads the message this time. It doesn't make any sense. Who is this and what are they going on about?

She tries to dial the number that the text has come from. It goes straight to voicemail.

There's no point ringing Rose because she'll be on air now.

Shit. Rose is live on air now. This is about her broadcast. But who is this from and why have they sent the message to her?

It doesn't make sense.

This time she phones Kate. It rings.

'Please pick up. Please pick up,' Zoya is saying to herself.

The reality of what this message might mean is now starting to frighten her.

There is no answer.

She dials the number again. Still no answer.

Kate. Oh my God. Someone has kidnapped Kate. And Rory. Someone has kidnapped Rory. No, no, this can't be right.

Her mind is piecing it all together.

Kate had called her yesterday lunchtime and Zoya hadn't picked up. Had the call been about this? Could Zoya have stopped whatever the fuck this is? She had been so obsessed with her own drama she hadn't even considered that Kate might need her help when she called her. Then a thought hit her.

Fuck. What if this is about her? She always knew she was putting Kate in danger by telling her about Abdul.

That must be why Zoya had been sent the message.

This is Abdul.

GARY

'What the fuck is wrong with Rose?'

Gary, the programme editor, has stormed into the gallery. It's a dark room full of screens. And in front of them are a load of control panels. There are seven people in there already – a mix of technical and editorial staff, including the output producer, Danielle, who is chewing her pen as she watches the chancellor interview play out on several of the screens.

Gary continues his rant as he paces up and down behind the team.

'Why the fuck is she not asking more questions? And what the fuck was that weird head nod about? And why didn't she say anything when he stopped speaking?' Gary shouted the last bit.

Danielle swings around on her chair to respond.

'Yeah, she is being a bit weird, like. Do you think she's having a stroke? I read about that happening to someone on telly the other day.'

Before anyone can reply, Rose asks the chancellor a question. The room falls silent again while they listen to what she is saying.

Chancellor, do you think everyone has a right to be heard?

'What the fuck!' Gary shouts.

He leans over Danielle and presses the button that should connect him directly to Rose's earpiece.

'Back to terrorism, Rose, back to terrorism.'

Usually Gary can tell from a presenter's face if they have heard him, but Rose is showing no sign of a reaction.

He presses the button and speaks again.

'ROSE!' He shouts this time, but still sees nothing to suggest she has heard.

'She can't hear me! What the fuck is going on? Call the producer now.'

'There's no producer with them, remember? Zoya is off sick.'

'Shit! Which button do I press to speak to the engineer in the truck?'

Sharif, who is in charge of the technical side of the outside broadcasts, answers from his corner of the gallery.

'This one,' he says, pointing at one of the many buttons in front of him. 'But I've tried it already. I can't get through to them. I've asked our engineering department to find out what's going on.'

'Never mind that, get on the phone to the engineer who is there on the ground. It's Sandy today, isn't it?'

'They don't have their phones on them,' Sharif responds.

'This is getting worse. So what you're saying is that we have no way of contacting our team on the ground even though our reporter has lost her fucking mind LIVE ON FUCKING TELLY.'

Danielle responds this time.

'There's something not right about this, boss. This is not Rose. It's like she's been taken over.'

'Spare me one of your fucking spiritual lectures about higher forces, Danielle.'

'I don't mean in a spiritual way. I mean that someone is controlling her. Telling her what to say. Look at her, she looks scared. And that question she just asked doesn't make sense.'

Gary walks up to the screen and stares at Rose's face.

'Nah, she's fine, she's just lost it. I bet it's the fucking menopause – it sends you women mad.'

At this point, Louisa from the engineering department walks into the gallery, stopping Danielle from responding to Gary's sexist remark.

'I've just been doing some analysis of the lines on their truck,' Louisa says, 'and it looks like there is only one-way travel.'

'Come again?' says Gary.

'We're getting their output, but they're not getting our input.'

'Once more for me, Louisa, and this time imagine you're telling a child.'

'Someone has hijacked the line.'

Everyone in the room gasps.

'Hijacked the fucking line? I'm not having that. Cut the line from them and go back to the presenters in the studio.'

'No, don't!' shouts Danielle, leaping up from her chair with her phone in her hand. 'Look what I've just been sent.' She shows Gary her phone with a message on it from an unknown number.

I have control of your broadcast. Do not cut away from Rose.
I have Rose's wife Kate and her son Rory. They will only be safe if you do as I say.

'Jesus Christ!' exclaims Gary. 'Don't cut away from the interview until I work out what to do.'

'This is fucking batshit. Don't you think we should be calling the police?'

Gary doesn't respond. He pulls his phone from his pocket to ring the network security team. He sees that he has received the same text message as Danielle. It was sent five minutes ago. He reads it again. This is not good. Not good at all. And it is something that, despite his thirty-year career in the media, he has no experience of whatsoever.

'Boss, I've called the police. They're on their way to RAS. But they reckon they're gonna be at least ten minutes,' says Jake, one of the production team.

'Right, get hold of the security team here too. I'm gonna call this bastard who's trying to fuck with us.'

Gary calls the number the message is from. It goes to voicemail. He starts to reply by text.

WHAT DO YOU WANT, YOU PIECE OF SHIT?

Gary deletes the last four words and then presses send. A message comes back straight away.

Let this interview continue uninterrupted and no one will get hurt. This will all be over in a few minutes.

Gary doesn't reply. He goes back into the gallery.

'I do not like this at all. Who the fuck is this prick holding us to ransom?'

Sharif speaks up this time.

'Boss, you don't think this could be about Janet Jacobs' death, do you? She was banging on about everyone having the right to be heard. And there's been all those attacks on the TV studios.'

'Oh, yeah, and didn't Rose have a run-in with Jacobs once? There's history there,' adds Danielle.

Gary doesn't answer. He stares at the screen in silence.

This is starting to freak him out. He can't let his team see that, though, not without risking mass hysteria.

He just wishes now he'd taken the phone call with the security team yesterday more seriously.

HARRIET

7 a.m

Harriet always turns the telly on at 7 a.m. to see what the headlines are.

She closes the document she is reading on her laptop and pushes it to one side, then turns her attention to the familiar voices on the television.

Harriet's partner walks in.

'Please don't tell me you've been here all night, babe?' Nic says.

'No, no, I woke up early so I've been doing a bit of reading. Do you want a cuppa?'

'No, thanks, I'm going to have to go shortly.'

Nic reaches to pick up the earpiece from the fruit bowl but gets distracted by the pile of ring-bound documents filling up their kitchen table.

'Not exactly light reading this, Haz,' Nic says, flicking through one of them.

'It's just charity casework stuff. Leave it, will you − I don't want you mucking about and getting them all muddled up,' Harriet says as she turns the volume up on the telly.

'Here she is,' Nic proudly announces.

They both stop what they are doing to watch Rose Steedman, who has just started talking on the telly.

Good morning, everyone. I'm here in Teesside at the world's biggest money-printing factory . . .

Harriet and Nic look at each other and smile. They always do that when Rose is on. Without Rose's matchmaking skills, they would never have got together.

'Eee, what a gig she's got today. That place looks incredible,' marvels Nic. 'I didn't even know there was anything like that around here.'

'We need to catch up with her, you know. Maybe she could pop in for a bite to eat on her way home?'

'Ah, man, I've got to cover the derby tonight, remember? Besides, she'll just want to get home to Kate and Rory.'

'Ah, yeah. Never mind.'

Harriet knows that life as a reporter means it's impossible to plan things. She's spent many an evening apologizing to friends and family after Nic was called away last minute for a big story.

'I don't know how Kate copes on her own with Rose away so often. I find it hard enough when you disappear, I can't imagine what it would be like with a baby.'

'Yeah, anyway, talking of disappearing, I've got to go.'

Nic kisses Harriet on the head and leaves.

As Harriet heads back to the table with her cuppa, she notices that Nic's earpiece is still in the fruit bowl. She picks it up and runs to the front door, but it's too late. Nic has gone.

GARY

7.16 a.m.

Everyone in the newsroom has abandoned the jobs they would normally be doing. They are now all focused on working out what the hell is going on and who is doing it.

Producer Jake briefs Gary on where they're up to in the couple of minutes that have passed.

'Boss, I've called the Treasury – it's Arabella on the ground with the chancellor. I've tried calling her, but it's gone to voicemail. She might have handed her phone in too.'

'Whether she's got her phone or not, she'll be focused on the interview. What about the people who work at RAS?' Gary snaps back.

'There's no one on reception yet and the out-of-hours press team are not answering,' says another one of the team sitting at the bank of desks outside the studio gallery.

'They're probably not going to be looking at their phones while this interview is happening,' Jake chips in.

'So we can't get through to anyone. This is a fucking joke!' Gary says as he walks back into the gallery with Jake following.

'Where are we at with the interview?'

'She's asked two more questions, boss. But they were both

quite random; they don't seem to have a point,' says Danielle. 'I don't get it. He's getting a free ride. Why would anyone want that?'

Jake pipes up again. He's getting a bit cocky now, which is starting to grate on Gary.

'Can I just say, I don't think this is about Janet Jacobs. They would have stormed the location, not told Rose to ask a few meaningless questions,' he says.

'Maybe they're not meaningless, though,' snaps Gary.

'I agree with Jake – Janet Jacobs' lot would be shouting about it all over social media if it was them, and from what I can see there's nothing,' says another member of the production team.

At that moment the door of the gallery flies opens and Zoya bursts in, in floods of tears.

'What the hell are you doing here?' barks Gary.

Zoya is struggling to answer. Not only is she crying, she is out of breath from running. Everyone is staring at her. Eventually she manages to get the words out.

'I came in to . . . to hand in my resignation' – she takes a breath – 'and then I saw what was going on . . . and well . . . boss.' She starts to sob.

'What the fuck are you trying to say, Zoya?' Gary interjects.

'I think this, all of this – I think it's my fault.'

ROSE

All I can think about is Kate and Rory being held somewhere.

This is unbearable.

None of these questions I am being told to ask even make sense. They're so vague that they're giving the chancellor free rein to say whatever he likes. It's like a party political broadcast.

I feel as if I'm losing my mind.

I could normally tell you, to the second, exactly how long I have been on air for, but this is so surreal I can't work anything out. Am I even here?

The voice in my ear speaks again.

'You're doing well, Rose, just a few more questions. Kate and Rory will be home soon.'

Hearing the voice say my wife and son's names makes me feel sick. I just need to get through these last few questions.

Surely we must be near the end of our eight-minute slot with the chancellor? What's going to happen then? And what if I don't get to ask all the questions the voice wants me to ask? What will he do?

These thoughts are not helping me.

I look at Arabella, who I know will be keeping a close eye on the time. Eight minutes is a strict deadline she will make me stick to.

But Arabella is not tapping her watch to suggest that the time is nearly up. She's just staring at the chancellor. She can't know what's going on, because if she did she would have got the chancellor out of here by now. Wouldn't she? Or maybe she's in on it too? Is the government controlling this interview? Is this some weird political propaganda stunt?

I'm being forced to give a senior politician an easy ride and he is clearly loving it.

GARY

Gary hates people crying in front of him. Not because he feels sorry them, but because he thinks it's a total waste of energy. He definitely doesn't have time for Zoya's tears now.

'Stop crying and start speaking.'

'M'cousin, m'cousin. He's . . .' Zoya says this at such a speed that Gary has to cut in again.

'Slow down, Zoya, you're not making any sense.'

Zoya doesn't slow down, she just starts blurting everything out.

'Abdul Khalid is my cousin and he knows I'm the person who shopped him to the police. I think he is doing this as revenge. I stupidly told my grandmother where we were going to be today and I think she told him. And I think . . .'

Before she can finish, Gary shouts.

'STOP!'

Zoya falls silent and holds her breath. Gary then continues at normal volume.

'Zoya, look at what's on Sky News now.'

Zoya looks up at the row of TV screens showing what's on the other channels. They are there so the team can see what their rivals are doing.

Her mouth falls open when she sees who is on Sky News.

'Abdul.'

'Yes, exactly, unless he has the power to be in two places at once, he can't be hijacking our broadcast and doing a live interview on the telly.'

Zoya is hit by a wave of relief and then confusion.

'Hang on, if it's not Abdul, who has Kate?'

'That's what we're all trying to work out. Now get out of my face – I've got more important things to worry about and you're wasting my time.'

Gary opens the gallery door and ushers Zoya out.

'Oh, and by the way, I don't give a fuck who your cousin, your dad or your dog is. You're a bloody good journalist, that's all I care about. Now piss off.'

Gary turns back to the team, who are watching the screens. The chancellor is still talking.

'How long has this interview been going on for now?' Gary asks.

'Nearly nine minutes, boss,' replies Danielle.

'So why hasn't Lady Macbeth stopped it yet? She never lets anyone run over. This is getting weirder and fucking weirder. I would not be shocked to see Jeremy fucking Beadle walk in here next.'

'He's dead,' Sharif says.

'Who's fucking dead? Oh my God, I can't take this. Please tell me it's not her son!' Danielle screams.

'No, you fucking idiot. Jeremy Beadle is dead,' barks Gary.

'Who the fuck is Jeremy Beadle? Is that the hijacker?' Danielle asks.

'No, he was a nineties TV presenter who used to do hidden camera—' Sharif's explanation is interrupted by Gary.

'For the love of God, please stop. Now, have we heard from the hijacker again?'

'No. The police have the number now and are trying to trace the location,' answers Jake.

'What about the line itself? Any news on how it's been hacked?'

'No, the police are on it, but it's only been about five minutes since we asked them to look into it,' replies Sharif.

A reminder to them all that this whole drama only started nine minutes ago.

Jake jumps in again.

'I think Arabella is letting it run because he's getting such an easy ride. He's managed to land loads of policy points.'

'Hmmm, maybe Lady Macbeth is in on the whole thing,' suggests Danielle.

'Who fucking knows. And where the fuck are the police?'

'Ohh, here we go,' Danielle says, gesturing to the screen. 'It looks like she's about to ask another question.'

The gallery falls silent.

HARRIET

7.18 a.m.

Harriet is totally gripped by Rose's interview. The paperwork she was reading can wait.

Looking at her phone, it would seem the whole nation is watching too.

Nic comes back through the door.

'Can't believe I left my bloody earpiece. Thanks for ringing. I'd be totally stuffed without it.'

'Your mate Rose is doing the weirdest interview with the chancellor. Everyone is talking about it online.'

'What do you mean?'

'I dunno, she's just letting him get away with saying all sorts and is being weirdly silent. Not like her at all. Normally she'd have him squirming like a toad.'

'Do toads squirm?' Nic says with a laugh.

Harriet ignores the comment, too transfixed by what is happening on the TV screen.

'I suppose she could just be having an off day,' says Harriet.

'Rose doesn't have off days. There'll be some other explanation I'm sure. Maybe she's letting him hang himself somehow.'

'No, something's not right. Like, her face and her body language have changed – she looks anxious.'

'What're you on about, Haz?'

'Let me rewind it and show you.' Harriet picks up the remote and points it at the screen. She takes the interview back to the start.

'Look, look at Rose there, her arms and hands, the way she's purposefully holding her pen and gesticulating. Also, her eyes are bright and fixed on the chancellor. She's in control.'

Harriet holds the remote up to the screen again and fast-forwards the interview to catch up with where it's at in real time.

'And look at her now. Her hands are clenched together on her legs and her eyes are darting about.'

'Yeah, I can see what you mean.'

'What do you suppose has happened?'

'I dunno, babe, but I'm sure it's nothing to worry about.'

Nic picks up the earpiece that's next to Harriet and goes to leave. This action prompts another question.

'You don't think someone is telling her to say all this, do you, in her earpiece?' Harriet asks.

'Well, yeah, I suppose they could be. But who? It's career suicide for any of the editorial team to be getting her to give him this much free rein. Normally they'd be pushing all the hard questions, not this easy stuff.'

At that moment Rose asks the chancellor a question that makes them both stop in their tracks.

GARY

'Did you know that children have died because of you?' Rose's question prompts another collective gasp in the gallery.

'Eh?' says Jake, who, like everyone else, is looking confused.

'Shit, man, I know what this is about. It's those Scouse babies,' Danielle says.

'What are you on about?' asks Gary.

'The ones who died at Liverpool Children's Hospital.'

'What? You think a parent has gone rogue? Seems a bit of a stretch. And to what end?'

'To get a confession, maybe? I heard one of the dads on the radio this morning saying that the government have blood on their hands.'

'Yeah I heard that too.' Jake jumps in. 'I'm sure he said something about not letting them forget it. This could be them getting revenge.'

'And look at the chancellor now – his expression has totally changed,' says Danielle.

'Well, it would do – he's just been accused of being a baby murderer!'

Gary moves nearer to one of the big screens with the chancellor's face in close-up.

'Look at his hairline – he's sweating.'

'I think we've got this all wrong, you know. Rose is about to nail him, I can feel it.'

ROSE

'’m not sure where you're going with this,' is the first thing the chancellor says in response to my question. He sounds unsettled.

Why has the hijacker made me ask this? If this is Billy, why mention children? Does he have children? I have no idea. My mind is desperately trying to figure this out so I can work out a way to end it.

Maybe Billy has got kids and they were taken off him when he went to prison. Is that what this is about?

Fuck. Is this why he has taken my child?

I can't cope with this. But I have to.

The chancellor starts speaking again.

'If your question is in relation to the government's handling of the terrible tragedy at Liverpool Children's Hospital, I would just like to start by sending my deepest condolences to the families whose lives have been ripped apart by their terrible loss. Dame Liz Bourne did a very thorough review and the government will be following up on all her recommendations.'

Is this about the kids' hospital? That actually would make sense. But what's Billy got to do with that?

The chancellor looks as much in the dark about this as I am.

Then a fucked-up thought crosses my mind. What if Billy, in his delusion about his relationship with me, thinks that Rory is *his* son? Fuck. That's got to be it. He'll know that Rory has two mams and is a sperm donor kid. Oh, fuck. He wants to be Rory's dad.

The chancellor is still talking, this time about his own kids.

'As you know, Rose, I have two children of my own and I am on the board of governors for my local prep school. The reason I came into politics is to make a better future for all children.'

He looks incredibly uncomfortable. He's shifting around in his seat. He also catches Arabella's eye.

He wants out of this. But what will happen then?

And where is this line of questioning leading?

ZOYA

7.19 a.m.

's Abdul Khalid really your cousin?' asks Jake, who has come out of the gallery to see if the police have arrived.

'Yeah, he is,' Zoya replies.

'You must be buzzing that he got acquitted. Nearly four years for a crime he didn't do, though, that's shit.'

Up until this point, Zoya hadn't let her brain go there. She couldn't bear to think of the damage she had caused. How could she have got it so wrong?

Abdul isn't a terrorist. He never was. Zoya found out yesterday, along with the rest of the world, that he had been the victim of a terrible miscarriage of justice. It came out in court that the police had retrofitted evidence to secure his conviction. There had been some intelligence gathered to suggest a possible attack on Wembley, so, when the police got a tip-off about Abdul, they assumed they'd got their man. The reality was Abdul had nothing to do with it.

Her family were right all along. The police had been racist. And worse, she had contributed to that. She had done the very thing she was trying to stop. She had racially profiled her own cousin.

What she'd overheard that afternoon five years ago in her uncle's garden was the desperate cry of a man who was up to his neck in it – but not in the way she had thought. Abdul was a gambling addict whose debts had spiralled out of control. The snippet she'd heard about a 'blow-up' at Wembley referred to a match-fixing scam Abdul had got caught up in. Her decision to phone the police about it had ruined his life.

And, from what her brother and nana had told her, Abdul knew that.

But this hijack unfolding now was not Abdul getting revenge. So what the hell was it about?

Who has Kate and why?

Zoya turns her attention to a picture of Janet Jacobs being shown on one of the screens in the office. It then cuts to one of a pale man with dark-rimmed glasses.

'Billy Rubin,' Zoya shouts out loud. 'It's Billy Rubin!'

GARY

'The police have arrived. They're on their way up to the studio now,' Jake announces, running back into the gallery.

'Thank fuck for that. Hopefully they can make sense of all this, cos I fucking can't. How long has the interview been going now?' Gary asks, pacing up and down.

'Ten minutes, boss,' replies Danielle.

'Matt's just replied to me and says he doesn't think it's about those kids,' says Jake.

'Who the fuck is Matt?' asks Gary.

The team in the gallery all look at each other. They're trying to work out if the boss is being sarcastic.

'Our reporter – outside Liverpool Children's Hospital covering the inquiry findings,' Jake replies tentatively, concerned he is about to get his head bitten off. 'Anyway, Matt says he's met most of the parents involved in the case and they're angry but not reckless.'

'Right, so where does that leave us? We don't think it's Janet Jacobs' mob, it's unlikely to be about the baby deaths or terrorism,' says Danielle.

'I have no fucking clue. If there's any mention of penguins, I'm gonna throw myself in front of a bus,' Gary replies.

Zoya bursts back through the gallery door. This time without the tears.

'Christ alive, Zoya, what now?'

'What about Billy Rubin? Could it be him? He turned up at the OB yesterday and scared the shit out of Rose.'

'Nope, definitely not him – he's currently in a police cell in Ipswich.'

'How do you know that?'

'Because security texted me about two minutes ago to say he'd been arrested for murdering Janet Jacobs.'

'Holy shit!' shouts Danielle. 'What a fucking day!'

On the bank of monitors, Rose speaks again.

Do you know Oliver Croft, Chancellor?

PART FIVE

CJ

One year before the hijack

The summer CJ left school should have been the best time of his life.

It was the worst.

CJ's best friend Ollie killed himself.

And he would never forgive himself for letting that happen.

CJ loved Ollie like a brother.

Even though they were total opposites, the two lads, who had known each other since nursery, were pretty inseparable. They'd have occasional scraps and sometimes Ollie would do one of his moody disappearing acts, but CJ got it.

Who wouldn't want to disappear if your mam was dead, your dad was an alcky and you'd been left looking after your kid brothers?

CJ could see that Ollie's life was seriously shit.

That was why he didn't properly kick off when the fella they met at Downing Street was messaging Ollie. He knew it was dodgy, but his best mate was loving it, and what harm could a posh bloke on Instagram do anyway?

CJ thought the only thing they had to worry about was getting their heads kicked in by one of the local gangs.

Turns out the real danger was never in their hometown, the crime capital of the North. It was hundreds of miles away in the playground of the rich and powerful.

There was no denying that last year at Newton Banks had been seriously fucked up.

After the politician and TV crew turned up, everything went mental. But CJ had no idea that this was going to be the beginning of the end for Ollie.

What was mad was that it had all started off so well. They'd both been riding high after that first trip to London; CJ with his social media and Ollie with his politics obsession.

CJ had been living out his dreams, and he thought Ollie was too.

Life was amazing.

And then it wasn't.

Two days after their GCSE results came out, Ollie took his own life.

His suicide was nothing to do with the results, like some people thought. Ollie had stopped caring about school long before exams.

It was what happened on that second trip to London that killed him.

CJ knew that, but no one was interested in what he had to say.

Not until three years after Ollie died, when CJ got a call out of the blue.

OLLIE'S DAD

One year before the hijack

Ollie's dad thought things couldn't get any worse after his wife died.

Then his son killed himself.

He'd been in his early thirties when he met Tanya. It wasn't your usual hook-up. He was a regular in A&E and she was a nurse there. His visits always seemed to coincide with her shifts. Each time she patched him up, he'd try to explain away the injuries with some half-baked story about a scuffle with the footie lads. He'd disguise the truth with gags. He didn't want anyone to know how damaged he was.

On his fourth visit, with what turned out to be three broken ribs, Tanya stopped him before he could even start one of his cover-up stories. And with the simplest of gestures she changed their lives forever.

'It doesn't have to be like this,' Tanya had said to him while placing her hand on his shoulder.

Nothing more, nothing less.

Those words and that touch were the secret code to opening up the vault in his brain that he was trapped inside.

She didn't pity him, which he would have hated, or question him about his life. She simply told him what he needed to hear.

She was right. It didn't have to be like this.

The next day he went to the police and told them exactly what his then-wife, Pamela, had been doing to him. She was given a suspended sentence, but more importantly she wasn't allowed to see him or their two-year-old son ever again.

They were given freedom and protection.

It was two years later in a nightclub when he bumped into the nurse again, his angel. And as the old cliché goes . . . the rest is history.

Tanya was everything to him, and she quickly became an incredible mother to Ollie and then to the two kids they went on to have together.

Of course they rowed and got stressed about money, but they were a team. And unlike his last wife, he wasn't scared of her. The arguments never escalated to anything more than one of them going off in a huff.

He felt safe.

The cancer broke them in the end, though, and Tanya's death was the most brutal thing that he had, at that point, ever experienced.

He felt guilty. It should have been him who had died, not her. She wouldn't have fallen apart in the way he had.

Finding himself alone, with their three sons to look after, he'd realized he needed to step up, but didn't know how. His anxiety was off the scale and the only thing that took the edge off was drink.

He tried not to get wasted every night. He'd tell himself he was just going to have one or two to help him sleep, but the fog that came with the third and then the fourth and fifth always drew him in.

It was a cycle he knew he needed to break, for his sons more than anything, especially Ollie, who was always the one left to pick up the pieces.

His relationship with his eldest reached breaking point the morning his son found him on the sofa covered in his own urine.

He tried to compensate for his uselessness by making grand gestures. This included coming home that day with a puppy. One of his mates had a litter to get rid of and he saw it as a chance to bring some joy back to their house.

To begin with, it did lift the mood. For the first time in ages the boys were laughing and smiling. The sadness wasn't gone, but now there was a distraction.

This also prompted him to try to stop drinking. That afternoon, after bringing home the dog and seeing the atmosphere in the house lift, he'd decided to clean up his act. He didn't drink that night and got himself to bed at a reasonable hour.

He could be a good dad. That's what he'd told himself as he turned off the light on what he thought would be his first night of life-long sobriety.

He managed four days.

Every time he came back from working away he just wanted to disappear again; he couldn't even bear to be around the kids.

The house and the boys were a constant reminder that she was gone and he was useless.

He needed the oblivion drinking brought.

This choice was one he would regret for the rest of his life.

The price of his failure was his son's life.

There had been no note.

Nothing to explain why his son had hanged himself.

The school and the police put it down to depression after his mam's death.

But he knew the truth.

He had killed his son.

Not only had Ollie lost his mam to cancer, he'd lost his dad that day too.

If he'd handled things better, if he'd been at home more, if he'd stayed off the booze, if he'd spoken to the boys more, if he'd . . . His mind was tortured by the 'what ifs'.

In the early days of his grief he'd made the decision to pack up Ollie's room. He could see how hard it was for the boys. Each day they would come home from school and rush up there, hoping to find their big brother lounging on the bed.

He knew how they felt, because he did the same thing himself every morning. He'd wake up wondering if it was all just a terrible nightmare, only to be confronted with the agony all over again when he opened Ollie's bedroom door.

So one morning, after dropping the boys at school, he bagged everything up and put it in the loft.

It was nearly three years before he looked at those bags again. He wasn't keen on going through them, but the boys had asked if they could. They wanted to pick some things out to keep. Their therapist, who was making a huge difference to all their lives, had suggested it.

He reluctantly agreed one Saturday morning to get the bags down. It was two bin bags of stuff, which, on reflection, didn't seem nearly enough for a sixteen-year-old boy.

There was no order to the bags; he'd been too upset to pack them in any rational way.

Although he wished now that he'd taken more care.

The boys sifted through the things. They joked about some of Ollie's dodgy fashion choices and then picked out a few bits each that they wanted to keep.

Among the clothes was a notebook. He couldn't remember seeing it before. It was a posh green one that said *House of Commons* on the front in gold lettering.

He started to cry.

The regret of having never asked Ollie about his trip to London smacked him in the face like a sledgehammer.

He flicked through the pages. It was full of notes in Ollie's scrawly handwriting. He smiled, through his tears, at how similar it was to his own.

Then on the inside page he saw a note. It was handwritten in a style much fancier than Ollie's.

You've got this!

That was it. No detail on who had written it or why. He wondered if it was a present from a secret girlfriend.

There was so much he didn't know about his son.

Things he now wished he'd asked.

That night, after the boys were in bed, he read the notebook in more detail. Desperate to find out more about who his son was.

Ollie's notes were all about politics. He wrote about the politicians he admired and compiled lists of the things he would do if he was one.

He cried again at the life his son should be leading. The things he could have done. The person he could have been.

In the background the news was on. He hadn't noticed it until he heard some of the names mentioned in the book being said on the telly. He turned up the volume.

The story was about a cabinet reshuffle that was happening. Normally he wouldn't give a shit about what was going on in the political world, but now it felt like it was bringing him closer to his son.

The reporter was detailing which politician was moving to which role. The first name that caught his attention was the man Ollie had dedicated several pages to in his book: Joe Stephenson. He was being made defence secretary. Ollie had written about him being a trade unionist who turned to politics in later life. It triggered a vague memory of a morning when Ollie had asked him about trade unions. Now he understood why.

As he read through the notes, he could hear Ollie's voice in his head. He imagined Ollie was sitting next to him on the sofa, telling him all about these politicians on the telly.

The next minister to be profiled appeared on screen. He was a tall man with a big belly. Charles Barrow was his name. He was being made Chancellor of the Exchequer. Ollie had written loads about this man in his book; in fact there were endless pages of notes and even a family tree.

Ollie must have really rated this guy, he thought.

The reporter was talking about how both men had once been in the running for party leader. Then it cut to a clip of Charles Barrow giving a speech at a school where he had been that day. He was waffling on about the importance of exams in school.

What a load of shite these people talk, he thought to himself. His lad would have done a better job than all of them.

He was about to turn the TV off when Charles said something that made him stop and question everything.

CJ

CJ never used to bother answering calls from numbers he didn't have saved.

But now he had a proper job, he thought he better had.

He answered, then instantly regretted it.

It wasn't a work call.

'Oh, hey, CJ, it's Ollie's dad.'

CJ didn't say anything for a second. Hearing Ollie's name was a shock.

'CJ? Are you there?'

'Yeah. Yeah, I am.'

'It's Dan Croft. Ollie's dad.'

'Oh, right, erm. Hello.'

CJ still found it hard to talk to his mates' parents. Plus he was freaked out. The last time he'd spoken to Ollie's dad was at his best mate's funeral.

'I were wondering if we could, er, catch up?' Dan said it in a way that made CJ think he wasn't sure he should be calling him.

CJ stayed silent and let him carry on.

'You were Ollie's best friend and, after he died, well . . .' Dan paused again.

CJ assumed it was because he didn't know what to say, but neither did he, so he wasn't going to fill in the gap.

Dan cleared his throat and started to speak again.

'I realize now that I don't know much about our Ollie and, well, I want to. I know you two were very close. You always looked out for him.'

CJ holds in the emotion that's trying to escape. He was good at hiding how he felt. He had to be. Although this call was pushing him to the edge.

'I'd love it if I could talk to you about him, y'know, and find out what . . .' Dan's voice trailed off.

CJ just wanted the call to be over.

Dan wouldn't need to talk to him if he hadn't been half-cut when Ollie was alive. But CJ stopped himself from saying any of that. It wasn't going to change anything.

Instead he mumbled some half-arsed response.

'Yeah, I s'ppose we can talk.'

CJ didn't want to see him. But he reckoned he owed it to his best mate to help his dad. Plus, listening to him now, CJ thought he sounded different. He sounded sober.

'Oh, thank you so much.' Dan's voice was brighter now. 'Maybe we could go for a milkshake or summat?'

CJ couldn't suppress a laugh. *Milkshake?* Dan must have thought he was still a kid. And, to be honest, he wished he was. CJ felt like he'd aged thirty years in the past three.

'Sorry, I don't mean milkshake, I shoulda said pint. It's just I'm clean now, y'know, so don't get much joy out of a pub these days.'

'I don't drink either. Why don't we meet at Mo's Café?'

'Tomorrow?'

'Er, yeah.'

'Great. You could 'ave a protein shake – that's what you young lads are into these days, isn't it?' Dan started to choke up. Then he began banging on again about being a bad dad. 'Listen, I know I fucked up with our Ollie, I really do, and nowt will change that. You lads shoulda never ended up in half the shit ya did.'

Dan was full-on crying now.

CJ just wanted the call to end.

'I'll see you there at ten,' he said, hanging up.

DAN

One year before the hijack

Dan was mad at himself for getting emotional on the call. He hadn't meant to, but hearing CJ's voice, one that used to boom around his house with Ollie's, was a stark reminder of the fact that he would never hear his own son's voice again.

But CJ had agreed to meet him and that was the main thing.

That night he went to bed feeling a pang of excitement. He wasn't sure if it was the right thing to feel, but he was genuinely looking forward to finding out more about his son.

He got to the café early and found a table near the back. He was nervous.

CJ was almost unrecognizable when he walked in. He looked like a man. A big hairy man.

Dan was taken aback. He hadn't prepared himself for the fact that he'd be grown up now.

How stupid of him not to expect CJ to look different. Of course he wasn't going to look like a sixteen-year-old any more.

He felt a sharp pain in his chest. Another reminder of what Ollie would never be: a grown man.

CJ sat down and Dan quickly started speaking to cover the

awkward silence and distract himself from the emotion that was brewing inside him.

'Thank you for meeting me. I know this is weird — it is for me too. It's just, I were going through Ollie's stuff and it made me realize I don't know that much about him.'

'What d'ya wanna know?' CJ said, before Dan could say any more.

'Well, I don't know . . . What were he into?'

CJ shrugged his shoulders.

'All sorts. He loved the dog.'

Dan smiled hearing that, grateful that he had brought at least a bit of joy to his son's life when he got the family puppy.

'So the dog. Owt else, CJ?'

'Well, yeah, but he didn't follow the other kids, y'know. He had his own thing going on.'

'Like what? It weren't owt dodgy, were it? Is that what yer about to tell me?'

'No, no.'

Dan could feel the chat was getting more awkward instead of less. He was hoping the notebook might help.

'Y'know, I found this notebook.'

Dan took it out of his pocket and put it on the table in front of them.

'It's a posh one, look, with *House of Commons* written on the front.'

At this, the colour completely drained from CJ's face.

CJ

One year before the hijack

CJ stared down at the notebook.

Seeing it on the table in front of him took him right back to the day Ollie found it in his locker on his sixteenth birthday.

'I'm guessing yous must've all got one on the trip to London?' Dan asked.

'Erm, no, Ollie got sent it.'

'Ah, OK, right. I don't remember it coming to the house.'

'No, it got sent to school, as a birthday present.'

'Ah, nice. Wonder why they sent it to school. D'ya know who it were from?'

'Er, yeah, I think so.'

CJ could feel his heart beating hard in his chest. He knew that as soon as he told Ollie's dad who it was from, it was all going to kick off. He didn't know whether to risk it. Last time, no one believed him. Why would it be any different now?

'So who? Why you being so cagey?'

'You're probably not gonna believe me if I tell you,' CJ replied. That was the truth.

'Try me,' Dan said with a punchy tone to his voice.

CJ took a deep breath. He was about to open a door that could never be closed again.

'I think it was from a politician that Ollie had been messaging.'

'Eh? What d'ya mean, messaging? Who y'talking about?'

'On Instagram. Ollie met him when we were in Westminster and they started messaging each other. And then . . .' CJ stopped mid-sentence. He was about to say stuff out loud that he hadn't said since Ollie died.

'And then what?' Dan asked, pure alarm on his face.

'And then it got really fucked up . . .' CJ could hear his voice starting to crack.

He realized in that moment he should have told Ollie's dad all this much sooner.

'I'm sorry, I tried to tell the police everything, but they didn't listen to me. I should have told you.'

'I don't understand what yer saying, CJ. Yer not making any sense.'

CJ knew then he had to tell him everything.

OLLIE

Four years before the hijack

After a five-hour journey on the bus, CJ and Ollie arrived at Victoria coach station. From there they walked for ten minutes, carefully following the directions being announced on Ollie's phone. He had been concentrating so hard on getting the logistics of the day right he hadn't had time to think about what was going to happen when they got there.

And then, with a minute to spare on the phone map's ETA, they arrived at a square lined with houses.

'This can't be right,' said CJ.

'This is where the pin is,' Ollie said, showing CJ the moving map on his phone screen that had a red pin in the middle of it.

'So the map says the club is there.' CJ pointed at a terraced house fifty yards in front of them.

They walked over to it and stopped outside.

'There's no sign. How do we know this is the right place?' CJ asked, bemused.

'It just looks like someone's house.' Ollie was equally puzzled by the scene before them.

'D'ya reckon we just knock on the door then?'

'S'ppose. I can't even see a bell to ring.'

Before they'd made a decision on what to do, the door opened and two lads came out. Both of them were wearing suits. Ollie breathed a sigh of relief that he had called it right on the clothing. He knew they'd be in some type of smart suit or blazer at the very least. Ollie hadn't gone for the full suit option, he couldn't afford it. But he reckoned his blazer, shirt and jeans would work; he'd seen others in the pictures with clothes like that on.

The lads were laughing as they came out of the door, then stopped when they saw Ollie and CJ in front of them. Both sets of lads looked each other up and down.

'Are you here for the party?' the taller one of them asked.

'Yeah, we are.'

'You haven't been before, have you?'

'Er, no, why?'

'You're in for a treat. We're just off to get Charlie.'

They both laughed again and carried off down the street.

CJ looked at Ollie.

'Charlie? They're on a fucking drugs run.'

'Nah, they looked too posh to be druggies. They're on about a lad called Charlie.'

'Mate, I'm tellin' ya, this is a fucking crack house.'

'No, it isn't, ya dickhead. As if they're gonna be dishing out drugs!'

'Well, there's only one way to find out,' CJ said as he knocked on the door.

A middle-aged man in a red suit-style uniform opened the door. Inside, Ollie could see that the place looked a lot like Downing Street. Lots of old paintings on the walls and a grandfather clock ticking loudly. The man ushered them in.

'You must be here for the Young People's Politics dinner?'

'Er, yeah,' Ollie replied, assuming that was what the soirée was called. He actually had no idea. He hadn't been given any details beyond the location and timing.

After asking their names, the suited man gestured to the stair-case.

'You're in room eleven, just up the stairs. Drinks will be available in the study from six thirty.'

Ollie took the key and headed up the grand staircase in front of them.

'This is insane,' CJ said as they opened the door to their room and started to look around.

'Whoa, we've got a bed each — and look in here, a huge bath and a separate shower. I wanna live here.'

CJ carried on inspecting the place, opening every cupboard and drawer.

Ollie sat on the bed and looked out of the window. He couldn't believe he was really there. He went to his DMs and sent Phone Man a message to say they'd arrived. He got a reply straight away.

Good, good. You enjoy yourself and I will see you later on.

Ollie smiled. He couldn't believe his luck.

'Look, there's a mini fridge with little drinks in. Want one?' said CJ, lifting out two small bottles of vodka and turning on the telly. The *Six O'Clock News* came on.

Let's go live to Rose Steedman who is on an oil rig in the North Sea.

'Shit, we need to get ready,' Ollie said, jumping up from the bed having realized the time when he saw the news was on. He opened his bag and took out his neatly folded shirt and an iron.

'Ya brought a fucking iron?'

'Yeah, for my shirt.'

'You crack me up.' CJ laughed. 'There's one in the wardrobe.'

'Is there?'

'Yeah. There's an ironing board too,' CJ said as he knocked back one of the bottles of vodka and started to open the second. 'Here, 'ave this,' he said, holding the bottle out to Ollie.

Ollie didn't want to get drunk – he hated the idea – but he knew it would help settle his nerves. He downed it and then started to gag. CJ went back in the fridge and pulled out a mini Coke can.

'Drink that to take the taste away.'

'Fuck, I can't believe I drank that straight and there was a fucking mixer in there.'

'There's whisky and gin in 'ere too – want one?'

'No, come on, we need to get a move on.'

Ollie put on his newly ironed shirt and brand-new blazer, then posed in the mirror. He looked good, he thought. His trainers were showing signs of wear, but he scrubbed them as best he could. He was, however, regretting the hair gel; it was a new one he'd got in the supermarket that was meant to smooth frizzy hair, but all it had done was make his hair look greasy. There was no time to do anything about it now.

CJ was filming a tour of the room when Ollie came out of the bathroom.

'Twit-twoo. Look. At. You. Ollie Boy.'

'Sh'up, CJ. Get ready, will ya.'

'I am ready.'

'I thought you were gonna get a new Boss T-shirt and wear it with jeans.'

'Nah, Keith wasn't there – apparently the police raided the pub last week so he's moved to the Pineapple and there was no way I was going in there.'

'Right, but yer not wearing that.'

'Yup, I am.'

Ollie had been prepared for CJ letting him down on the clothes front, so had bought an extra blazer. It meant spending another tenner, but if it made them stand out less than they already did, he reckoned it was worth it.

'Nah, mate. I'm not wearing that,' CJ said as Ollie lifted the spare blazer out of his bag.

'Oh, shut up, it's decent. And we haven't got time for this. Get it on. D'ya want the free stuff downstairs or not?'

CJ reluctantly put on the ill-fitting jacket over his tracksuit and pulled out the hood. He checked himself in the mirror.

'Y'know what, I actually look boss.'

Ollie agreed. 'You look a bit like a tech entrepreneur.'

'I fucking am.'

They both laughed.

It never ceased to amaze Ollie how good his daft friend was at taking everything in his stride. Oh, how he wished he had the same ability to not give a fuck.

Still, he was happy that they weren't going to stand out as much as they did last time they were in London mixing with posh people.

The lads made their way downstairs. CJ was filming everything again.

'You'll have to hand over your phones, I'm afraid, gentlemen,' said the man who had been at the door when they arrived and was now standing at the bottom of the stairs.

CJ tried to shove his phone down his pants like he had done at Downing Street. But he got clocked by the security guard.

'No point hiding it. Hand over your phone,' he said, holding out his hand.

'What? I'm not givin ya m'phone,' CJ said in a much broader accent than normal.

'Well, then you won't be going into the event. It's strict Chatham House rules. And I'll need to delete what you have already filmed inside the building.'

'Eh? Why?'

'It's a private members' club for a reason. The clue is in the word *private*.'

'Eh, ya fuckin kiddin us! This is worse than school.'

'It's up to you. No phone, no party.'

'Please, CJ, we've come this far,' Ollie pleaded.

'Oh, for fuck's sake! OK.'

CJ reluctantly handed over his phone and unlocked it so the videos and photos he'd taken could be deleted. He wasn't too bothered about doing that, because he knew he could just retrieve them from the deleted album later.

'Thank you. You'll get them back in the morning.'

'The morning? No way. My missus'll be raging if I don't message her.'

Ollie grinned, still finding it funny to hear CJ refer to his first-ever girlfriend as his missus.

The man ignored the lads and walked off to his desk where he put the phones in a drawer, which he then locked.

'Erm, where do we go now?' Ollie asked politely, desperate not to annoy the man, who could undoubtedly have them thrown out.

'Ah, yes, if you would like to make your way through to the study. There's an honesty bar, so do help yourselves and make notes.'

'What the fuck is an honesty bar?'

Ollie pulled CJ away, worried he might start arguing with the doorman again. He did not want to get kicked out at this stage.

'But what is it?' CJ asked Ollie.

'I dunno, maybe it's a bar where the drinks make us more honest or summat.'

'Sounds fucking weird to me, but let's give it a go.'

They walked into the room that they had been directed to. There was no one in there.

The room looked to them like a mix between an old person's front room and a library. There were chairs clustered around small coffee tables and a wall covered in books.

In the far corner there was a drinks cabinet that CJ had already made his way to.

'Well, I'm gonna mainline the voddy tonight if I'm not getting my phone back,' CJ said as he sniffed the liquid inside one of the crystal decanters that had been sitting on the cabinet.

Ollie had wandered over to look at the books. There were huge volumes bound in worn leather of various colours. They looked old, Ollie thought. He brushed his fingers along their spines, wondering how many powerful people had been in this room and read them.

'D'ya reckon if I pull one of these books it will open a secret door?' Ollie said, laughing.

CJ wasn't listening; he was too busy scrunching his eyes and shaking his head after downing his second shot of vodka from the decanter.

It was at that moment the two lads they had met in the street came into the lounge, followed by four other young men. Ollie couldn't work out their ages; they looked a bit older than them, but not by much.

They were smarter-looking than Ollie and CJ, and by the sounds of their voices they were richer too. Some of them were wearing suits, but others were in mismatched blazers and trousers. There was a common theme of sandy-coloured pants and dark jackets, which didn't make sense to Ollie. Surely you'd at least try to match the colours, even if you didn't get it quite right?

Ollie's thoughts were interrupted by the taller lad of the gang, the one who had spoken to them in the street.

'Oh, hello again, you two,' he said in what Ollie thought was one of the nicest voices he had ever heard.

In Ollie's eyes, this was the guy he wanted to be like. He was sophisticated, handsome and effortlessly cool. Turned out he was also a bit of a twat.

'I see you found some jackets then' – he laughed before delivering the killer blow – 'and on a buy-one-get-one-free deal, by the looks of things, gentlemen.'

'Leave them alone, Oliver,' said one of the lads in chinos.

Ollie was amazed that this man in front of him, who was pretty much everything he wanted to be, had the same name as him.

CJ, however, was not impressed at all.

'Listen, bellend, ya might 'ave a posh mummy and daddy who pay for all yer shit, but it doesn't make ya funny. Now piss off and let us finish the voddy.'

Ollie froze, wondering what was going to happen next.

There was an eruption of laughter.

'Well, you just got your arse caned!' said the lad who had spoken up to defend them against Oliver's snippy remark about their clothes.

'Arse-caning – I thought it was only me who enjoyed that!' said the voice of an older man who had come into the room.

Ollie thought this man looked ancient. Like someone's grandad. He was slight in frame and bald apart from a few wispy strands around the edges of his head. He was making his way in with two young lads either side of him. Ollie assumed they were his grandsons.

'He looks like Mr Burns from The Simpsons,' whispered CJ.

A few of the others around CJ overheard and started to chuckle.

'I wonder who he is,' said Ollie.

The lad who had stood up for them leaned over to whisper.

'He's the guy who set up this group. He's in the House of Lords. Used to be an MP for like a hundred years.'

Ollie stared at the old man, wondering about the life he must have led.

'What is this group anyway?' CJ asked, slightly slurring his words after what was possibly now five shots of vodka.

'Well, it's called the Young People's Politics Group. And this is our annual dinner where we hear from a number of senior politicians about their careers.'

'Jesus, that sounds shit!' CJ said, pouring himself another drink.

Ollie thought it sounded amazing.

'So you've been before?' Ollie asked.

'Oh no, I've just heard about it. My name's Louis, by the way.'

Before Ollie could respond, the old man spoke again.

'Right, gentlemen, dinner is served.'

OLLIE

Four years before the hijack

Ollie woke up face down in his own vomit. His head was spinning. He was not planning on getting drunk, but he must have done. He looked around. He wasn't in the room he was supposed to be sharing with CJ. He didn't recognize this room at all.

He quickly sat up, but the blood rushing to his head made him throw up again.

He tried to stand up slowly, but his whole body was aching. His clothes were strewn across the floor. He was completely naked.

Where was he?

He needed to get back to his room.

Ollie slowly put on his clothes and made his way out. Every movement felt horrendous.

He opened the door and saw a number 9 on it. He couldn't remember ever coming into this room. In fact, he couldn't remember anything.

He could see number 11 across the corridor.

As he approached the door he could hear CJ in the shower.

Aside from CJ's clothes on the floor, the room looked tidy and both of the beds looked like they hadn't been slept in. That didn't make sense either. There's no way CJ would have made his bed after sleeping in it, so where had he been?

Ollie had a million questions he wanted to ask, but they could wait. He needed to lie back down.

He closed his eyes. If only he could get a bit more sleep, then everything would become clearer.

'What a banging night,' CJ said, now standing over Ollie with a towel wrapped around his waist.

Ollie could only offer a croak in response.

'Those posh bastards are fucking wild,' CJ continued.

Ollie slowly tried to sit up. CJ carried on talking at Ollie while he got himself ready. He'd seen CJ naked a million times over the years, but there was something about him getting dressed in front of him in the room now that was making him feel sick. Probably just the alcohol again, Ollie thought.

'I fucking told ya Charlie weren't one of the lads.'

'There were drugs?'

'Ha ha, very funny,' CJ said, as if Ollie's question had been sarcastic.

Ollie felt confused. His head was so foggy.

'What time is it anyway?'

'Nine.'

'Shit, we were meant to be on the Megabus at seven,' Ollie said as he fell back into a lying position on the bed.

'Fuck that, I'll do a sob story at the bus station – they'll let us on the next one.' CJ had his clothes on now and was making his way towards the door. 'I'm gonna get our phones off that sad bastard on the door.'

And with that CJ was gone.

Ollie closed his eyes again; his whole body was in pain. Had he taken drugs at the party? Is that why he felt so bad? There were a million other questions swirling around in his head now.

The biggest of all being whether he had made a fool of himself last night.

He was woken from his thoughts by CJ bursting back through the door.

'I've just seen that lad Louis coming out the room opposite. He looked well dodgy.'

Ollie didn't respond. His head was such a mess, he couldn't process anything.

'The fella on the door won't give us the phones until we're actually leaving the building. Also, the bastard told me he's emptied the fucking deleted folder too. No fucking videos! I'm raging. Anyway, he gave me this for you.'

CJ threw an envelope on to Ollie's lap.

Ollie recognized the fancy handwriting on the front. He opened it.

'Bloody hell,' Ollie said as he pulled out a huge wad of cash.

'What the fuck? How much is in that?'

Ollie counted. There were fifty £20 notes.

'A fucking grand.'

'Is there a note with them?'

'No.'

'Well, we don't need to worry about getting the bus home now. We'll be able to get a limo!' CJ said.

Ollie looked down at the money again and then immediately ran into the toilet and threw up.

DAN

One year before the hijack

Dan had got it all wrong.

He could see that now, from everything CJ had told him. All of it – every single thing that had happened to Ollie in the final year of his life – had completely passed Dan by. How could he have been so stupid not to have seen what Ollie was going through?

Dan's heart was breaking all over again. His eldest son, the rock of their entire family, had killed himself because he was tortured by whatever had happened to him at that event he went to in London. A trip hundreds of miles away that Dan didn't know anything about.

What a shit dad he was.

Dan had let Ollie down so badly, he would never forgive himself.

But he had to get to the bottom of this, no matter what.

CJ had mentioned a lad called Louis being there, but they'd had no luck on finding a surname for him.

The only name they had for definite was Charles Barrow. Now the chancellor. One of the most powerful men in the country.

As far as Dan was concerned, Barrow was the only person

who could help them get to the truth of what happened to Ollie at the party.

Dan sat staring at his computer screen, wondering how you were supposed to go about contacting a politician.

A quick search brought up Barrow's website, which included a section with various contact details. He called the telephone number. *Surely it's not going to be this easy*, he thought to himself as someone answered the phone.

'Hello, Charles Barrow's office. How can I help?'

Dan was relieved to find himself talking to a human and not a machine.

'Hello, I'd like to talk to Charles about my son.'

'OK, well, his surgery is open on Friday. Are you a constituent?'

'Erm, sorry?'

'Do you live locally, in Mr Barrow's constituency?'

'I live in Newton Banks. Does it matter? I just need five minutes to ask him about my son.'

'I'm sorry, we won't be able to help you here. Maybe try going through the chancellor's central government office.'

'How do I do that?'

'Just search online for the details. Thanks. Goodbye.'

And with that the person on the other end of the phone had gone. He was back to square one, this time searching gov.uk for an hour for anything that might connect him to Charles.

He rang every number he came across, but each one of them had an automated voice on the other end and a list of options that was nothing to do with what he needed.

He also tried to send Charles a direct message on his social media site, only to be sent a generic reply.

Thank you for your message. We'll respond to your enquiry in due course.

He knew what that meant. He'd never hear from them again.

His last option, the one he least wanted to pursue, was to send an email. He'd found several addresses on the gov.uk website, so he decided he would try the scattergun approach.

In it he detailed all that CJ had told him about the exchanges between Ollie and Charles.

It made for quite an uncomfortable read.

ARABELLA

One year before the hijack

Arabella was used to getting emails from crackpots making all sorts of allegations about the politicians she worked with, but this one, which had been forwarded on from the press team, felt different. She couldn't put her finger on why, but it was enough to prompt her to do a bit of digging.

She knew her boss wouldn't be happy with her for bothering him with it, but she decided to see him anyway.

'So let me get this right: this man Daniel Croft thinks the chancellor is going to know what happened to his sixteen-year-old son who killed himself two years ago?' Harry said, with a whiff of annoyance.

'Yeah, he says his son was friends with Charles.'

'Friends? With a teenager? Well, that's bollocks for a start!' Harry laughed before continuing in his usual patronizing tone: 'Humour me, why on earth does he think they would even know each other?'

'Well, according to the father's email, the boy met Charles at Downing Street when his school was at an event there. And, well, this is where it gets a bit complicated: the school was Newton Banks Academy.'

'Oh dear God, the kid was at THAT event – the one that got the PM sacked?'

'Exactly. Can you see now why I need to do my due diligence on this? I don't think for a second that the chancellor is in any way involved, but given the Newton Banks connection, I should at least reply in a way that makes it look as if we've taken this seriously.'

Harry studied her with scepticism.

She continued regardless. 'I just need to go back with a few facts to prove that some of the things he is saying didn't happen, or at least not in the way he thinks.'

'OK. So to get back to the point, Arabella, the father is saying his son met Barrow at the Number 10 event. Is that true?'

'Well, I've asked Charles and he says he got there after the event finished, so no, it doesn't look as though they did.'

'That's that then. Easily sorted,' Harry said, turning to face the open laptop on his desk.

'Hang on, I haven't finished. They did meet at another event. At the opening of a new theatre in Newton Banks during the leadership contest. I've looked back and the lad's name was on the list that day. And I know Charles did talk to the students there.'

'That's hardly enough to claim that they were friends.'

'No, of course not. As I said, I don't think they were friends, but it does prove that they met.'

'OK, yes, but at a crowded public event where I am sure Charles spoke to several school groups. This is all very flimsy, to say the least, Arabella,' Harry replied, once again turning back to his laptop.

'There's more.'

'Don't tell me: they once passed each other in Fortnum & Mason, where they both picked up the same tea blend and became firm friends?' Harry said, this time without even looking up.

'Do you want to know or not?' Arabella was losing her patience with him now.

'Go on.' Harry rolled his eyes and positioned himself to face her again.

'The dad says Charles and Ollie were messaging each other on social media.'

'What? Well, that is definitely made up!'

'So I've done a deep dive on Charles's official account, which several of us have access to. It looks as though Oliver Croft did send a message, but no one ever replied to it – well, not personally anyway. He got the usual automated message, but nothing more than that. And his dad has since messaged that account too and got the same.'

'Right, so the father is basing the so-called "friendship" on his son sending one message and receiving an automated reply? Is that what you're telling me?'

'Well, that's what I'm trying to work out. The dad said in his email that the messages went on for months. You don't think there could be a chance that Charles has a private account he messages people from? He might have seen the message from the young man in his official account and then contacted him from his personal one. Innocently, no doubt, but still . . . could that be what the dad means?'

'Oh, do listen to yourself, Arabella. Charles can barely turn on his phone without help; he's hardly going to be running a secret account.'

Arabella agreed with that comment. Charles was, for all his success, quite useless, especially with technology. But if these messages were real, who had been sending them? She genuinely didn't believe it was Charles, but it could have been someone else in the office pretending to be him. She decided not to share this theory with Harry, given that he was clearly agitated by the whole matter.

'To be honest, I don't even know why you're still waffling on about this. None of it sounds remotely plausible. And you already have more than enough to go back to the father and allay his concerns about a government cover-up.'

Arabella knew that her boss had a point, but she was determined not to leave until she had told him everything being alleged in the email. She needed to make sure her arse was covered. If this did come out and it looked like she hadn't dealt with it properly, they'd no doubt end up in a political shitstorm. What's more, it had the potential to destroy Charles Barrow's career – and hers. She wasn't about to let that happen, which meant this needed to be taken care of.

Despite Harry's best efforts to shut her down, she continued.

'There is a photo attached to the email, of a House of Commons notebook that the dad says was sent to the teenager by Charles.'

'Why does he think it's from Charles? Anyone can buy them in the gift shop at Westminster.'

'Because it has a note inside with one of Charles's catchphrases.'

'Catchphrase? Since when did Charles Barrow have a catchphrase?'

'"You've got this."'

'I clearly fucking haven't, Arabella. This is all total bollocks.'

'No, his catchphrase is "You've got this". He does say it a lot.'

'So does everyone. Is this some kind of wind-up? Are you and the team making this up for a laugh? Trying to push me to the limit so I'll have a breakdown or something?'

Arabella shook her head and pressed on.

'There's more. The dad is also claiming that his son was invited to London by Charles. To an event at a private members' club. He's saying the boy attended with one of his friends.'

This statement prompted an unexpected burst of laughter from Harry.

'Right, so now you're telling me that a senior politician took two teenage boys to a private members' club? And nobody noticed? Next you'll be saying he drugged them too.'

'I know, it's a mad claim, and obviously not true, but the club named and described by the dad in the email is one that Charles is a member of.'

'Come on, Arabella, any idiot can do a quick search online to find out stuff like that. It doesn't prove anything.' Harry gets up out of his chair and walks towards the door.

'So far you have presented nothing that we need to take seriously, Arabella. Listen, I feel sorry for the father, he's clearly looking for someone to blame, and that's understandable – he's grieving. But our response must be to tell him, in a kind way, that his son must have made this stuff up. He was a fantasist. Now, if you don't mind, I have some real work to get on with.' He opened his office door, gesturing for Arabella to leave.

'I understand what you're saying, Harry. There's just—'

Before Arabella could tell Harry about the father's claim that the teenagers were given £1,000 as they were leaving the private members' club, her boss cut her off. His tone was different now; he lowered his voice menacingly.

'Arabella, stop. You've done your due diligence, but you need to stop. If word gets out that we've been investigating Charles for links to the death of a teenage boy, his reputation will be ruined. And to be honest, Arabella, so will yours.'

Arabella got the message loud and clear. That was that.

Case closed.

DAN

One year before the hijack

Dan stared at the email he'd received from the chancellor's office.

Dear Mr Croft,

Thank you for your email. The chancellor is incredibly sorry to hear about the death of your son and sends his condolences to you and your family.

He was delighted to meet the pupils from Newton Banks Academy at the opening of the new theatre. We understand that this was the only occasion in which your son and Mr Barrow's paths ever crossed.

We're sorry we won't be able to help you any further.

Yours sincerely,

Arabella Pinchinthorpe

Office of the Chancellor of the Exchequer

Dan was furious. Not a single question he'd asked had been answered. It didn't make sense. He wasn't accusing anyone of anything untoward, he just wanted to understand more about what had happened at the party in London.

Why were they not helping?

The email said nothing, but in a way it told Dan everything he needed to know.

There was more to this.

Dan read the email again.

Sends his condolences.

What a load of bollocks.

This Arabella person, whoever she was, hadn't even bothered to write Ollie's name. Why? It was so disrespectful.

Actually, Dan was starting to think that this was a lot more than simply disrespectful.

This was a government cover-up.

And he was going to prove it.

PART SIX

The day of the hijack

ARABELLA

Arabella moves towards Rose, tapping her watch, the universal sign to wrap things up. The chancellor acknowledges this out of the corner of his eye.

He has gone from being in total control in this interview to looking uncomfortable.

It's not a surprise, given the explosive question about killing children that he's just been asked by Rose.

He is sweating. Never a good look in an interview, especially not for a politician.

Arabella whispers to Quentin, the other SPAD who is with them. She needs a plan to get him out of here.

'This interview has taken a bit of a turn. Will you run ahead and get his car ready at the security gate, just in case we need to make an escape? And also can you push back the next interview for half an hour or so, just to give us a bit of time to debrief? I'll meet you with him at the gate.'

Quentin nods and heads off with their chaperone. He isn't happy about leaving them, but has no choice.

Rose completely ignores Arabella's attempt to stop the interview and asks Charles another question.

'Do you know Oliver Croft, Chancellor?'

The chancellor starts and then looks to Arabella, who springs into action. Time to shut this down and get him out now. She steps in front of the camera she had been standing behind and takes Charles by the arm.

'That's time, Rose, you've covered lots of great ground there, but the chancellor has a very busy day so we need to move on. Thank you.' Polite, but direct.

Arabella is very aware that she's on national television right now and, despite her heart feeling like it's going to explode out of her chest, she needs to remain calm so as not to make this exit look as dramatic as it is.

The chancellor is in a state of shock. Arabella manages to get his microphone off him while manhandling him towards the nearest door. She can feel him shaking.

ROSE

She has no idea why she has been asked to put this question to him, and quite frankly she doesn't care. Her role now is simple. Ask whatever questions the hijacker wants, to protect her family. If she doesn't, they are in grave danger. The chancellor stutters as he attempts to reply. His eyes are fully dilated.

'Erm, what, erm, I don't recall knowing an Oliver . . . what did you say the surname was?'

Before Rose can follow up, Arabella interrupts the interview and manhandles the chancellor away from the camera towards the exit.

Rose doesn't let this stop her saying what she has been told to say next. And this time she is told to shout it.

'HIS NAME IS OLIVER CROFT AND YOU KNOW EXACTLY WHO HE IS!'

ARABELLA

Arabella bundles the chancellor into the golf buggy outside. He still hasn't spoken.

'Are you OK?' she asks as she gets in next to him. He has gone very red in the face and the sweat is rolling off him.

What looked like fear now seems to be turning to rage.

'No! I'm not! I've just been ambushed live on national television,' Charles snaps at her, before leaning forward to shout at the driver. 'Will you just bloody drive?'

'No can do, sir, I'm under strict instructions to wait for a security escort out,' the driver replies.

'Oh, for heaven's sake! This is a joke. Give me my phone – I need to call my lawyer.'

'The security team have it,' replies Arabella.

'My phone? Why?'

'I had to give it to our chaperone while you were doing the interview.'

'That's ridiculous. Give me yours, then.'

'They have mine too. We'll get them from the security gate on the way out. Quentin is there now.'

'In that case, get me to that gate NOW!' Charles shouts the last bit.

Arabella can see that this has rattled Charles, so she speaks to the driver.

'I know they said you can't move, but this is a bit of an emergency. Please can you get us to the security gate?'

'I'm ever so sorry, I'm not allowed. The lad who went ahead of you took the security escort with him. He should be back in a jiffy, though.'

'The absolute audacity of that vile woman,' Charles is ranting. 'Mark my words, it won't be long before the only TV she'll be seeing is the one in her prison recreation room.'

'Don't worry, Charles. I will be straight on the phone to fix this as soon as we get out of here.'

Arabella is desperate to calm the chancellor down and show that she is in control of the situation. She has a job to do.

'You know, Charles, it was completely out of order, but I don't think you come out of this badly at all.'

'Really?'

Charles gives her a quizzical look.

'You landed loads of policy points before Rose lost the plot.'

'Hmmm, yes – that's fair, I suppose.'

'So tell me, what is it exactly you're worried about? I need to know if I'm to fix this.'

The chancellor is definitely calmer now.

'That boy whose name was mentioned at the end . . .'

He doesn't quite finish his sentence, so Arabella fills the gap.

'Yes, Oliver Croft. I came to see you about him. I think you're right to be worried; his father must have talked to Rose Steedman, and the press will definitely want to know more. Particularly why you were asked about him. But we can handle that; we just to need reaffirm the facts.'

'Isn't our line simply that a reporter lost the plot and it's nothing to do with us?'

'Well, yes, that's the line we'll follow. But people are still going to be wondering who Oliver Croft is and what the connection is to you.'

'There is no connection.'

'But we both know there is. I don't think this is anything to worry about. We need to go through it all again, work out what is true and what is not, and then suss out what to tell the press.'

'The truth is I know absolutely nothing about his death.'

'Well, yes, obviously, I know that. But we need to unpick the details, go through all the allegations made by his father.'

'They are simply the ramblings of a fantasist, I'm sure. None of it is true.'

'But you did meet him, so we can't say that didn't happen.'

'Yes, but I meet millions of people every day.'

'I know that. You're not going to be in trouble for meeting him, but the media could easily make it sound like there was more to it if we don't handle this properly.'

'Well, I don't think we should be saying anything.'

'Charles, we cannot be blasé about this and just hope it will go away. I made that mistake when I replied to the father originally, and look where it got us: in this mess we're in now.'

'It's complete rubbish, that's all anyone needs to know. I must speak to my lawyer.'

'Well, he's not here and we don't have a phone.'

Charles leans forward again to talk to the driver.

'You must have a phone on you?'

'No, sir, we're not allowed phones on-site.'

Charles throws his arms up in disbelief at the situation he is in.

'Charles, we haven't got long before we'll be back in front of the press – we need to get this sorted. So can we please go through the details and formulate a plan?'

'OK,' the chancellor says, slumping down into the golf buggy seat.

Arabella can now do her job.

'So we know you met him at the Banks Theatre, which you were opening, and Oliver was visiting with his school. And just to remind you, his school is the one where the headteacher ended up in a row with the Killer Quill.'

'Right, whatever – spare me the lengthy context, let's just get on with it.'

'Fine. I'm going to ask you some direct questions. All I need is the truth, no matter what it is, so I can work out what we can and can't say to cover our arses.'

'Yes, I understand.'

'Did you ever message Oliver Croft?'

'Of course not.'

'Did you invite him to a party at your private members' club?'

'NO!' Charles raises his voice to answer that one.

'Do you have parties at your private members' club?'

'Yes, of course I do.'

'And who gets invited?'

'Politician pals, of course.'

'So definitely not young people interested in politics?'

'Where the hell are you going with this?'

The chancellor's defences are back up again, which is not helpful. She needs to get him on side.

'I really need you to answer these questions, Chancellor. At this stage I don't care what did or didn't happen. I'm only trying to help you here – my job is on the line too, you know. And the press will go wild when they get their teeth into this. If you're prepared, you will be fine, but you can't get flustered like you are now. It makes you look as if you are lying.'

Arabella can see from the chancellor's face that he doesn't like being called a liar. She continues before he can respond.

'I am just doing my job.'

'OK, OK, what do you want to know?'

'Is there a chance that this lad, Oliver Croft, who was very interested in politics, could have been at one of your parties?'

'No.'

'How do you know for sure?'

'Because I don't invite teenagers to parties.'

'Are you sure? Because I know that Louis Carmichael was at one, when he was a teenager.'

The chancellor raises his eyebrows.

'Louis Carmichael's grandmother is an old family friend. That's why he was there. Plus I am sure he was older than that.'

'OK, that makes sense. I'm only asking because the original email from the boy's father mentions a Louis being at the party with his son. I assumed if there was going to be a Louis there it would be Louis Carmichael, because you put him forward for work experience.'

'Well, yes, that's right. But that doesn't prove anything.'

Charles is still being defensive.

Arabella makes the same point again.

'Listen, I'm on your side here. The fact that Louis is named by the dad as being someone his son met at the party does suggest that his son was there.'

'It does not. That information could have come from anywhere.'

'I'm going to say this again, Chancellor. The questions from the press will be a lot harder than this. So let's go over it one more time. Is there a chance Oliver Croft could have been to one of your parties?'

'I don't think so.'

'OK. Let's talk about what happens at these parties.'

'Parties is such an exaggeration of what they are. It's an informal get-together of like-minded people.'

'Of all ages.'

'Yes, of all ages – but all adults, obviously.'

'And is there alcohol? If I know the whole picture, I can put together a response that will protect you without too many lies.'

'Yes, some people drink alcohol, but it's certainly not encouraged.'

'And drugs?'

'How would I know? If they're doing anything like that, it has nothing to do with me. You know what young people are like these days, it's like drinking coffee to them.'

'Where do the drugs come from?'

'I have no idea. The gents no doubt source it themselves.'

Arabella feels like she is finally getting somewhere.

Charles is lowering his guard now – he knows he needs to trust her to get him out of this mess.

'And is it all men who go to these parties?'

'Not exclusively.'

'But the one Louis was at, was that all men?

'Could have been. I don't know, I don't draw up the guest list.'

'Is there an official invite list?'

'I have no idea. As I say, I am not in charge of who gets invited.'

'Which means that Oliver could have been there. If the press get evidence he *was* there and you say he wasn't, then you are going to look like you're hiding something.'

'Yes, OK, maybe he was. But as I said before, I really don't think so. You said he was from Newton Banks, yes? Not exactly the usual clientele for one of my soirées.'

'Fair enough, but we have established that there is a chance he was there, so we can't categorically deny it. That's OK, though.

Now, tell me what happens at these get-togethers. There is drink and possibly drugs. Is there sex too?'

'What? NO!'

'Drink- and drug-fuelled young people tend to end up getting it on together. I find it hard to believe that they wouldn't, in the circumstances.'

'Well, they might, I suppose. I don't know.'

'And you never get involved? I mean it sounds like great fun.'

'Listen, I have nothing to do with anything like that. I am a happily married man. I merely attend these parties to encourage young people into politics. It's my way of giving back, doing some good! Whatever they might get up to there is none of my business.'

'Come on, you must enjoy letting your hair down too.'

Charles doesn't respond. She is losing him again.

'Charles, be honest with me: have you ever had sex with any of the people who go to the parties?'

'ABSOLUTELY NOT!' Charles roars.

'Charles, I honestly don't care. I just need to know so I can help you. As I've said several times now, the press are going to look at every minute detail of this and dig as deep as they can. I can only prepare you if I know exactly what I am dealing with. So, I'll ask you again, have you ever had sex with someone at one these parties?'

Charles takes a moment to think before he answers. He draws in a deep breath.

'I am telling you now, my wife must never find out about this. In fact, if you repeat this to anyone, I will destroy your career. Do you understand?'

'Yes, of course, Charles. This is just so we can get you out of this mess. So you have had sex at one of these parties?'

'Yes, I have, but all above board.'

'When you say "above board", you mean consensual?'

'Christ alive, of course it is.'

'OK. But is there a chance, in the haze of drink and drugs, that some people might get carried away and not know what they're doing?'

'I have never got "carried away", as you call it, in my life. I know exactly what I am doing.'

'OK, but the person who you had sex with might not have known what they were doing.'

'Oh, come on, you've had drunken sex before, Arabella. Everyone still knows what they're doing.'

The phrasing of this alarms Arabella. But she still has a job to do. It's now or never to find out the truth.

'So is there a chance that Ollie didn't want to have sex with you that night at your party?'

'No, he was totally up for it,' Charles snaps back.

Arabella's eyes widen with shock. He has just admitted he did it.

His breathing quickens. He pulls at the collar of his shirt to loosen it.

But she needs to know everything.

'Then why did you give him a thousand pounds in cash afterwards?'

Charles starts gasping for air and tries to get out of the buggy.

But something stops him.

HARRIET

7.20 a.m.

'Oh dear God, this is about Ollie.'

Harriet is reeling from hearing Rose say his name live on national television.

She puts her hand on Nic's as if to steady herself.

'Ah, shit, the lad from your school?' Nic replies, knowing how hard Harriet was hit by his death.

'Yes.'

'What's the connection with the chancellor though?' Nic asks as Harriet picks up her phone and starts frantically scrolling back through her messages.

'I don't know exactly, but I have a horrible feeling about this.'

Nic leans over her shoulder to try to see what she is doing.

'What you looking for?'

'The video of me and that Pencil woman arguing.'

'That's all over the internet, you don't need to go back through your messages.'

'No, I want to find the original message. There was something about it that didn't make sense at the time and I want to look at it again.'

Harriet is still scrolling.

'Give it here, will you,' Nics says, taking the phone from her hand. 'There's a simple search function.'

Nic finds the message within seconds and hands it over.

She can now see that there are two messages, each with a video file in.

'That's it, I remember now. CJ sent me the video in two parts. He said it was because the whole thing wouldn't send in one, but the middle bit is missing.'

'I see,' Nic says without actually having a clue what Harriet is going on about. Not that it matters; Harriet is lost in thought.

'I didn't give it much thought at the time,' she continues, 'what with everything that was going on, but actually, now I think about it, I know exactly what they cut out – it was Ollie talking to Charles Barrow.'

'How do you know that?'

'Because Ollie and Charles were in the corridor when I was having the row. I hadn't noticed them until Ollie piped up. I can't remember the exact details, but I do know that Charles said Ollie's name. It stood out to me at the time, the fact that someone as high profile as Charles Barrow knew one our students' names. I'm convinced that must have been caught on camera.'

'So why do you think the kid cut it out before sending it to you?'

'That's what I'm wondering. There must have been more going on.'

'He was probably just protecting his friend.'

'Yes, but from what?'

'Do you think there was something dodgy going on?'

Harriet is up out of her chair now, pacing the room.

'I don't know. Definitely not then, but maybe after. Do you remember we went to that theatre thing when Barrow was running for leader?'

Harriet is back in monologue mode so Nic doesn't bother to answer the question.

She doesn't notice and carries on speaking while pacing to and fro.

'He behaved very oddly around us. Pretending he hadn't met us before. I put it down to him being an arrogant twat – which he is – but something didn't sit right with me. I remember, when I asked him about it, Ollie made out he'd mever met Barrow before, and yet I'd seen how taken Ollie was with him when they first met. That Westminster trip changed Ollie. He wanted to become a politician off the back of it. Yet on the night of the theatre opening, they both lied about having ever met. So that begs the question: why did they lie?'

'Did you ask him?' Nic asks.

'Of course I did. I tried to talk to Ollie about it at the time, but he was so unresponsive. I put it down to all the stress he was going through after losing his mum. But, Nic, what if there was something more sinister going on?'

'You need to find out now. Try ringing that number that kid sent the message from. He might still have the same number.'

CJ

'Er, hello, Miss Waters.'

'You don't need to call me that. CJ, where are you?'

'Erm, well, that's a funny story, actually, you see . . .'

There is crackle, coming from a radio. Harriet hears it.

'What's that noise?' she asks.

'Well, that's also a funny story because, erm, I'm—'

Before he can finish his sentence, his former headteacher speaks again.

'CJ, what is going on?'

CJ, who has instantly reverted to his schoolboy persona, suddenly feels overwhelmed. He doesn't know what to say. And it's clearly too late to lie. She's got him sussed.

'Bloody hell, this is you, isn't it – you've hijacked the broadcast! It's you telling Rose what to say,' Harriet says with some alarm in her voice.

CJ has been so swept up by the whole revenge plan that he hasn't given a thought to the consequences. Until now, at the sound of his headteacher's voice.

He quickly ends the call. And picks up his walkie-talkie.

She calls his phone again. He doesn't know what to do.

He answers.

'What the fuck were you thinking?' shouts Harriet.

'Erm, miss, I dunno. It's just I wanna get justice for Ollie, and this hijack seemed—'

Harriet cuts in. 'No, not the hijack – that was a brilliant idea, although I don't know how you got Rose on board.'

CJ doesn't respond; he is too confused to form a sentence.

'You weren't expecting him to admit anything on telly, were you?' says Harriet. 'He's far too arrogant and self-entitled for that.'

'Well—'

Harriet interrupts again. 'My point is that you have the video. What were you thinking, not releasing that?'

'What video?'

'The one that shows Charles meeting Ollie in the corridor of Downing Street. He said his name. You chopped it up and sent it to me without that bit – I'm assuming, to protect Ollie – but now you need to release the full thing to nail this bastard!'

'Oh, fuck!' CJ says, realizing his old headteacher is right.

'Get that video out there right now. I'll ring every journalist I can to alert them. It's the best evidence you've got, and the only way to finish what you started.'

ARABELLA

7.25 a.m.

'What the hell do you think you are doing?!' Charles shouts as the driver pushes him back into his seat, preventing him climbing out of the golf buggy.

'You don't know who I am, do you?' says the driver as he tightens his grip on the chancellor's arm.

Charles squints to look at him.

'I'm Oliver Croft's dad.'

Charles's mouth drops open.

'You thought you were too powerful to be caught. Too rich to face punishment. Well, I am here to tell ya yer not!' Dan is shaking. 'The world's now gonna know yer a dirty, evil bastard. You killed my son!' He shouts the last bit. Emotion has taken over.

In the distance, there are police sirens.

Charles laughs.

'We both know which way this is going.'

'You confessed!'

'Your word against mine. And who is going to believe the mad ramblings of an alcoholic who neglected his son?'

GARY

'Boss, the chancellor must still be mic'd!' Danielle shouts across the gallery.

'What? But I saw Lady Macbeth take it off when she was getting him out.'

'There must be another microphone.'

They all stare at the screen. The camera is on the floor of the factory. All they can see are various people's feet moving about. But through the speakers they're hearing the voices of Arabella and Charles Barrow.

'Do you want me to mute it, boss?'

'Are you mad? This is TV gold!' Gary replies with a genuine excitement that Danielle hasn't seen in him for years.

'But it's secret recording – OFCOM rules state that the person must be told they are being recorded,' says Sharif in a tone that suggests he isn't someone who would break a rule no matter what the circumstances.

'Unless it is in the public interest,' Jake chips in.

'Fuck that, we must've broken every OFCOM rule already this morning.'

'Also, we're trending worldwide now.' Jake jumps in again.

'The hashtags #WhoIsOliverCroft and #RoseMeltdown are the top two at the moment. And that new video of Charles Barrow and the young lad in the corridor of Downing Street is already at a million views, so God knows how many people are watching us online. This is incredible.'

This time Danielle interrupts Jake: 'Has anyone actually checked on Rose?'

ROSE

7.21 a.m.

'Thank you. Kate and Rory are safe.'

Those are the final words I hear in my earpiece.

My head is spinning.

I pull off my talkback and microphone and throw them on the floor.

I retch.

'Eee, that was a bit of a dramatic exit,' Jonesy says, putting the camera down on the floor. 'I bet that's not the first time he's had to pull out quickly, though,' he adds, laughing.

'GET ME MY PHONE NOW!' I shout.

Jonesy and the chaperones are obviously still unaware of the horror I'm going through.

'We got hijacked!' I roar, bursting into tears.

They quickly scan the room as if there's going to be someone there wearing a sandwich board with the word 'hijacker' written on it.

'MY FUCKING TALKBACK GOT HIJACKED!' I scream at the top of my voice.

Jonesy looks at the sound kit on the floor. 'But how—'

'I don't fucking know, Jonesy!'

I can't bear this.

'JUST GIVE ME MY PHONE! HE HAS MY SON!'

Jonesy grabs the box of sandwich-bagged mobiles being guarded by Russell.

'Oi! You can't have them!' he shouts, trying to grab Jonesy's arm.

'Just you try to stop me, sunshine,' Jonesy growls back.

I scramble to get my phone out of the box. The screen lights up as I rip it out of the bag. There are dozens of messages. I ignore them and call Kate's number.

She doesn't answer. I try again.

Still no answer.

I can't breathe. What have they done to her and Rory?

I keep redialling. On the fourth try, she answers.

'WHAT?!' Kate shouts in my ear.

I gasp. She's alive.

I collapse to the floor, still with the phone attached to my ear.

'Kate, Kate, oh God, Kate!'

'What d'ya want?!' Kate snaps.

'Are you alright? Did he hurt Rory? Did he . . .' I'm rushing to get all my words out.

'What? I can't make out what you're saying?'

'Did he hurt Rory? He said he wouldn't if I did what he said – and I did what he said. Oh, Kate, I am so sorry.'

'I really can't hear you over the noise there. But, if you're asking if Rory is OK, he's fine. We're both fine. I've gotta get back to my meeting.'

Eh? What's she on about? Maybe she's in some type of shock. I don't understand what's happening.

I shout at her slowly: 'WERE YOU KIDNAPPED?'

'Kidnapped, no! I'm at work. Is this because I haven't replied to your messages yet?' Before I can process any of this, Kate speaks again. 'Eee, you're such a drama queen. You knew this morning was gonna be crazy what with this big China meeting and getting Rory around to Lisa's to do the nursery drop. I haven't stopped. Anyway, I've gotta go. We're getting the funding decision any minute.'

Kate hangs up.

What the fuck is going on?

They weren't kidnapped. Kate was in her meeting all along. I'm obviously relieved, but I am also fucking raging.

I've just been totally shafted live on telly. But why?

Before I can make any sense of it all, Sandy runs in from the truck with her chaperone, Marcus, in hot pursuit. 'Guys, they haven't cut from us!' she shouts.

We look at the camera on the floor. Its red light is blinking. We are still on telly.

'Don't panic, your mic is off,' Jonesy replies, knowing exactly what I am thinking.

'No, no, it's not you guys we're listening to. It's the chancellor,' Sandy explains hurriedly.

'The chancellor? But he's gone?' I respond.

'Nope. He's still here, outside by the truck. We need to get the camera on him now.'

'The camera on him?'

I'm now half wondering if we're all unknowingly part of some sick *Squid Games* TV show.

'YES! NOW!' Sandy shouts, beckoning for us to follow her.

I don't need to be told twice.

I run for the fire door. Jonesy follows me with his camera clamped to his shoulder.

'You won't believe what he's admitted to,' Sandy shouts back to us as we all run.

'Something to do with money, I bet,' Jonesy says as we reach the door.

'Nope. Really dodgy stuff with a dead kid.'

Holy fuck. I need to see this.

HARRIET

7.24 a.m.

'He's admitted it! He's admitted it!' Harriet says, staring at the screen, which is still showing a shot of the factory floor.

She puts her head in her hands. Nic grabs her by the arm.

'Look, look! The camera's on the move, heading outside. Looks like they're trying to catch up with that golf buggy in the distance. The chancellor must be in that.' Nic announces all this as if doing a sports commentary.

They both get up and move closer to the screen, squinting to see who is in the buggy.

'I can't make them out, can you?' Nic says to Harriet, whose nose is now touching the screen.

'Well, it's definitely the chancellor – you can see half his arse hanging off the side of the seat. I'm guessing that woman next to him is the one on his team who we can hear grilling him, and then—'

At that moment the driver turns to the chancellor and the camera gets a shot of his face.

'Jesus Christ, it's Dan, driving the buggy – Ollie's dad.'

GARY

'That man is Ollie's dad?! Bloody hell, that's a plot twist I never saw coming,' says Gary, standing in the middle of the gallery with his legs spread and his hands gripped around his bald head.

'I feel like I'm watching a Harlan Coben drama,' cries Jake, who is fist-punching the air unnecessarily every time the driver speaks.

'Looks like the fuzz have arrived at RAS,' says Danielle. 'I'm desperate to see how it's all going to end.'

'I'll tell you how it's going to end,' says the police officer who has just walked into the gallery behind them. 'With you guys cutting from the broadcast – now.'

There's a collective sigh, except from Sharif, who has been desperate to get off the broadcast since the start. But before he can cut the line, Gary raises a hand to stop him.

'You've got to be kidding! The whole world wants to know what's going to happen next,' Gary says. Aware that this won't cut it with the police officer, he adds: 'And we don't yet know that Rose's son and wife are out of danger. So, to be on the safe side, we need to keep it going.'

'We do know they're all right, actually. I've just spoken to Kate on the phone.'

'Oh, thank God,' says Danielle.

'They were never not all right,' adds the officer.

'What do you mean?'

'They weren't kidnapped. Kate is at work and Rory is at nursery. They didn't even know about it until about two minutes ago.'

'Kate was at work all along?'

'Yes.'

Danielle turns to Jake.

'I'm assuming we'd tried calling Kate's phone?'

'Well, erm . . .'

Gary jumps in before Jake can finish.

'Who cares?! We've just got a world exclusive,' says Gary. 'Plus she's clearly alright,' he adds, gesturing to the screen on which Rose has just appeared.

Everyone in the gallery cheers. They continue to whoop as Rose heads out of the fire door. She has a steely look on her face. Nothing like the fear she was showing a few minutes earlier.

'Go get 'em, girl,' Jake shouts, throwing his hands in the air.

'Shut up, you prick,' Danielle shouts back at him.

The police officer steps in front of the screens.

'Will everyone just stop!'

The room falls silent.

'You need to cut this broadcast NOW!'

ROSE

7.23 a.m.

'Eh, that's Dan. Security Dan!' Jonesy says as we get through the fire door.

This is getting weirder and weirder. Why is the security guard from yesterday's broadcast here and in a buggy with the chancellor and Lady Macbeth? This doesn't make sense.

And what the hell are they talking about?

'Go and get a close-up on Barrow, but don't let them see you.'

'On it,' Jonesy whispers as he heads off in stealth mode.

I can see Dan is shaking. And then, as I creep closer, I start to pick up the conversation.

Shit! Dan's son. The chancellor has something to do with it all.

I've heard enough. Time to do what I couldn't do in the interview earlier.

I let the chancellor finish his sentence.

'And who is going to believe the mad ramblings of an alcoholic who neglected his son?' he says.

I step directly into the chancellor's eyeline. He doesn't have time to react before I deliver my line – probably the most important one of my career.

'Well, I believe him and I'm pretty sure everyone watching will too,' I say, motioning to the camera pointing at the chancellor's face.

HARRIET

7.25 a.m.

Nic and Harriet jump and cheer as they watch their mate Rose nail Charles Barrow.

The joy is short-lived.

'Wait, look, the police have arrived,' Nic says, gesturing to the flashing lights now on the screen.

They both stand open-mouthed as an armed convoy surrounds the golf buggy.

'Holy fuck, they've got guns,' Nic exclaims.

'I can't watch,' Harriet moans as she sits down and puts her head on the table. 'Dan is in major trouble.'

Nic watches the police move into position.

They hear the chancellor shout. 'I'm under attack. Help! This mad drunk man is assaulting me.'

One of the officers rushes towards the buggy.

At that exact moment, Nic lets out an involuntarily sneeze. It drowns out the audio from the telly.

The screen fades to a black and goes silent.

Harriet looks back up.

'What are you doing? Turn it back on.'

'I haven't turned it off. They must have cut the broadcast.'

'Rewind it again, will you? I couldn't make out that last bit.'

Nic rewinds the programme feed by ten seconds.

Charles Barrow. I am arresting you on suspicion of . . .

'Wait, they've arrested the chancellor?'

EPILOGUE

'Are you ready to do this, Dan?' Rose asks as they walk into the TV studio together.

Dan looks terrified. 'Yes,' he says.

Dan takes his seat and squints at the studio lights, which are now directed towards him.

'I'm bricking it, mind you.'

'Of course you're nervous, but don't worry, we'll take our time.'

Dan nods and takes a deep breath.

'I want to do this. I need to do this.'

'I'm not going to try to catch you out. I'll just slowly guide you through it, from the beginning. A lot's happened since I first met you at the construction site.'

'You can say that again. Never had to do owt like this in my security guard training,' Dan jokes, trying to lighten the situation he is now in.

The studio floor manager, Tracey, steps into Rose's eyeline behind the camera.

'Coming to us now, Rose,' she says, holding up both hands to signal the start of the ten-second countdown.

'Ten, nine, eight . . .' says the voice in Rose's earpiece. A familiar one this time.

'CUE ROSE,' the voice continues.

Rose looks directly down the camera lens.

'With me now is Daniel Croft. The man at the centre of a brutal story of power, corruption and lies. His son, Oliver Croft, took his own life after being groomed by a predatory ring of men, including one at the heart of government. Today, Daniel is here to tell Ollie's story. I should warn you that some viewers may find this disturbing.'

Rose turns from the camera to look at Dan.

'Dan, thank you for agreeing to do this interview with me. Before we get into the details of what happened, tell me about your son. What was Ollie like?'

As Rose says this, a picture of Ollie appears on the screen behind her. It's a photo of him in his school uniform. He's got a big grin on his face.

Dan takes another deep breath.

'My lad Ollie had a heart of gold. He'd do anything for anyone. He were shy, like most kids his age, but when you got to know him he were dead funny and so clever. Cleverest in the family, I'd say.'

'He sounds lovely, and you were no doubt very proud of him,' Rose says this with a smile.

Dan nods.

She lets her smile drop to say the next bit.

'He'd had a tough start in life, though, hadn't he?'

'Er yeah,' Dan says, looking down.

'We're not going to go into all the details here, but the domestic violence you suffered at the hands of Ollie's biological mother meant you had to leave. That must have been hard for you both.'

'Yeah, but leaving were the right thing to do, for us both.'

Rose can sense that Dan doesn't want to dwell on this, but

she wants to paint a full picture of what the family had been through. Also it is important to explain why Ollie was one of the kids who couldn't be in any of the school photos, which is another part of this crazy story.

'And his biological mother was not allowed to have contact with him,' Rose says, to make the final safeguarding point before moving on.

'No, I wanted to make sure she got nowhere near him.'

'And you did that, Dan. So let's move on to talk more about Ollie. He was a brilliant big brother, wasn't he?'

Rose wants people to know how much Ollie was loved and needed by his family.

'Yeah, he were great with my two younger boys. When I were working away and that, he'd be the one holding the fort, y'know.'

'He wanted to be a politician, didn't he?'

'Yeah, the school got him into it. They went on a trip to London to see Westminster and all that.'

'That sounds exciting.'

'Yeah, it set something off in him. He wanted to do good. He hated injustice and, well, I think he thought he could do something about it if he got into politics. Even though we didn't know anyone in that world.'

'But he met someone in that world, didn't he? Someone very senior – famous, in fact.'

'Yes, on that trip.'

'The Westminster visit. Ollie was fifteen at the time and it was there he met Charles Barrow at an event in Downing Street?'

'Yes, although he . . . that . . . that man denied it, like,' replies Dan.

'I want to come back to that later, because you had some crucial evidence that showed that Charles Barrow was lying. But before that, I want to understand a bit more about what happened after that meeting. Ollie contacted Charles through his social media, didn't he?'

'Yeah, they started messaging each other – which, again, that man denied.'

'Yes, and we know now those messages came from an account connected to the IP address of a device found in Charles Barrow's home.' Rose adds the detail needed to keep this interview water-tight from a legal point of view.

She continues: 'Do you know the nature of the messages?'

'Well, yeah, it were just chit-chat. Ollie were looking for a bit of advice, I think. There were nowt dodgy in those messages.'

'Have you seen them?'

'Well, no, they were recovered during the investigation, but the police gave me the gist of it.' Dan paused for a moment before continuing. 'I don't ever want to see them, not after what he did to my lad.'

'I can totally understand that. So as far as the police were concerned, there was nothing said in those messages to suggest Charles Barrow was going to harm Ollie in any way. However, what they do show is the classic behaviour of a groomer trying to build trust.'

Dan nods with his eyes fixed on the table in front of him.

'Did you know that they were messaging each other?' asks Rose.

'No, I didn't, and I have to say . . .' Dan hesitates, his voice starting to crack. He pushes on to get his words out: 'I have to say, this is where I messed up. There's no excuse, but after Tanya died . . .' He starts to get upset. Rose can see this, so buys him some time by adding context.

'This is your wife, Tanya, who very tragically died of cancer when Ollie was fifteen. She was his stepmum, wasn't she?'

As Rose says this, a family photo of them all appears behind her.

'Yes, yes, she were. An amazing woman who were a proper mam to our Ollie. He loved her, we all did. And y'know . . .' His voice starts to trail off again.

'Dan, I can't begin to imagine what this was like for you all. You and your three boys were put through such a tough time.'

Rose wants to convey to the audience the enormity of what Dan was going through when the grooming started.

'I let myself get in a mess, Rose. I started drinking, y'know, just to get through each day. I weren't a good dad. And I do blame myself for letting this happen. Every day since I lost my boy I've thought about what I could've done to stop it. I should've been there for him. I weren't.'

A single tear rolls down Dan's cheek.

Rose hands him a tissue.

She pauses before she asks him the next question, aware of how powerful this silence and that tear are. She then picks up again.

'I understand they were messaging each other on and off for several months. Then, shortly after Ollie's sixteenth birthday, Charles Barrow invited him to an event in London.'

'Yes. Ollie and his mate CJ went down on the bus. They were a right pair, them two.'

Now a picture of Ollie and CJ appears on the screen in the studio. They're in their PE kit, in a field covered in mud, with their arms draped over each other's shoulders.

Dan had been shown which pictures they were going to use beforehand, though it was still a bit of a gut-punch every time one of them popped up on the screen.

Rose picks up: 'Yes, CJ was a great friend to Ollie, and I want to come back to that. Can I ask, though, Dan, did you know about this trip?'

'No, no, I didn't. The lads just took themselves off without telling any of us.' Dan stops speaking, his emotion getting the better of him again.

Rose pushes on so Dan can't dwell too much on his own failings as a dad. He obviously made mistakes, but he is not on trial here.

'We understand now that this event was held at the Grand Post, a private members' club in Westminster, of which Charles Barrow was a member. The event that evening had been informally billed as a Young People's Politics gathering and there were several teenagers there?'

'Yes, CJ told me that our Ollie thought he were going to meet people and learn more about politics, but it weren't that, it were . . .' Dan stops again and Rose finishes his sentence.

'Something much darker.'

'Yes. It changed him. He kinda just disappeared after that weekend.'

'You mean disappeared metaphorically, rather than literally disappeared?'

'Yeah, he wouldn't come out of his room unless he had to, and he started bunking off school. There were rumours he'd been taking drugs. None of that were my lad.'

'And it was that summer, a few months after this event, that Ollie took his own life.' Rose pauses a beat. 'I won't ask you anything about the specifics of that. But tell me, when did you start to think that Charles Barrow had something to do with it?'

'Well, it kinda came about by accident. I were going through some of Ollie's things and I found this House of Commons notebook, you see. It were packed with all this stuff he'd written about politicians. That man being one of them. And then that night, while I were reading it, I saw a news piece about that man.'

'That man being Charles Barrow.' Rose can understand why Dan doesn't want to say his name, but she needs to keep the audience up to speed with who he is referring to when he says 'that man'.

'Yes. And on the news he said something that jumped out at

me, because it were handwritten on the inside of this book. Of course, I didn't know then that he'd done anything to Ollie, but it got me thinking about my son's life. I knew so little – which were all my fault. So that's when I spoke to CJ and he told me everything he knew.'

Dan looks down at the table again and lets out a sigh of regret.

'That must have been so shocking to hear.'

'It were confusing more than anything. None of it made sense to me. Until I found out the truth.'

'And I've got to ask at this point, why didn't CJ tell anyone what he knew at the time, when Ollie died?'

'He did!' Dan looks up with his eyes wide and his hands gesticulating his frustration. He continues, much more animated than he has been previously in the interview.

'And that's the big problem here! People like us don't get a look-in with the authorities or owt like that.' Dan's anger is coming through loud and clear now. 'It were same with me when I contacted the government and then the police about what I'd found out. No one believes us. And that's how these people get away with it. It's disgusting.'

Rose needs to give a quick right of reply here so she doesn't get into bother with any of the organizations Dan has just slagged off on national television.

'It's worth saying that both the police and the government have apologized for their failure to investigate Ollie's case properly. They are making changes in light of this, but let's come back to that later.' Rose carries straight on so as not to give Dan time to say anything else that may be libellous. 'I just want to come back to the events leading up to Charles Barrow's arrest. So we've established you didn't get anywhere with the authorities. That's when you decided to take matters into your own hands. And that involved hijacking my broadcast?'

'Yeah, that's right. And I just want to say I'm dead sorry about

that. I never wanted to hurt anyone. I just needed the world to
know the truth, and when I found out you were seeing that man,
I just couldn't stop myself from doing something. I'm so sorry.'

Rose is still traumatized by the hijack, but every time she gets
upset about it she asks herself whether she would have done the
same for her son. And every time she comes to the same conclusion. She would.

'As a parent myself, I can understand the need to do something.
But this was quite a dramatic way to get justice for your son.'

'It had to be dramatic — nowt were working and *that* man
were getting away with it scot-free.'

Rose can see that Dan's anger is starting to make him shouty,
so she slows down the pace to give him time to breathe and
relax. She doesn't want the audience to go off him.

'It was quite an incredible thing you pulled off, to hijack a
national broadcaster interviewing a senior politician live on air.
There are lots of us wondering how you did it, myself included.'

Because of the police investigation, Rose only knows snippets
of what happened. Admittedly, she could have asked Dan
everything before now, but given this was such a huge story that
she also plays a leading role in, she wanted her reactions to be
authentic. Her researcher had done a thorough briefing with Dan
beforehand and armed Rose with all the legal stuff she needed to
be across, but there were some bits, involving her and her family,
that she would be hearing for the first time.

This part was going to be hard.

Rose continues her line of questioning.

'Take me back to the day you decided to hijack the interview.
It was four years after your son had died.'

Dan described the day Rose and the TV crew turned up at
his work and how he'd ended up bonding with Jonesy over
their shared love of dogs. He explained to Rose about getting
a puppy for his sons after his wife had died. And how, on

hearing this story, Jonesy had offered to take a professional photo of their dog.

The photo Jonesy took of Dan's Alsatian comes up on screen.

This was Rose's idea. The public are obsessed with pets, and she hopes this will help people warm to him, if they haven't already.

Rose interjects halfway through the story.

'Just to explain to everyone watching at home, Liam Jones – or Jonesy, as we call him – is my cameraman, who also has a business in professional dog photography.'

After that clarification, Rose goes on: 'So, to take these pictures, Jonesy came around to your house. Was getting him to your house part of the hijack plan?'

'No, no, not at first. It were only after he said he'd come over that I found out you were seeing . . .' Dan pauses, he stumbles and Rose picks up for him.

'Charles Barrow. So how did you even find out? Because it was all top secret.'

'It were by chance. I got in my car to go home after you lot were finished doing your broadcast from the site and I saw that the lass working with you were struggling with her car battery. It had died. I had some jump leads in mine, so I went over to help. It were when I were in the driver's seat sorting that out I saw the notes with his name on. And alongside it were details about where he were gonna be the next morning with you lot.'

'So, just to be clear, you saw my producer Zoya's notes about the next day's TV broadcast at RAS?'

'Yes. Seeing his name made my blood boil and then my mind went into overdrive. I wanted to turn up with a shotgun and blow his head off, but I'm not that kind of guy. I know violence ain't the answer.'

'So what made you think of the hijack?'

'Well, on my drive home I were getting more and more angry

about him getting away with everything. I'd worked myself up into a right tizz and told myself I were gonna do summat.'

'Right, so then what?'

'I thought about turning up at the site to confront him. I'd taken a photo of your producer's notes, so I had all the details.' Dan pauses and takes a drink from the glass of water in front of him. Then he resumes: 'But when I googled the business RAS I realized how hard it were gonna be to get inside. And then it dawned on me, I didn't need to get physically near him at all.'

'Ah, so that's when the hijack idea came to you. But how did you know what to do?'

'Well, I didn't know exactly, but I'd been watching your crew that morning and seen you using your earpiece to be told stuff by people who weren't there with you. So I thought there must be a way to control that remotely somehow. I'd done a bit of pirate radio, so had an idea of how the audio might work.'

'You didn't do this all on your own, though, did you?' Rose is now moving them into the next phase of the story.

'No, I rang CJ. He's working in telly himself now. He's an apprentice broadcast engineer.'

This time on the screen behind Rose is a picture of CJ with a beard sitting in a satellite truck in front of Buckingham Palace.

'Yes, you can see him here in one of the broadcast trucks we use in telly. I hear he is doing very well for himself, which is lovely to see.'

'Yes, it is. I'm dead proud of him.'

And Rose can see from Dan's face that he really is.

'So let's go back to this call, Dan. You rang CJ?'

'Yeah and he were up for it, straight off.'

'So what happened next?'

'CJ came to mine and we went through everything we knew about how the audio works. Fortunately, I had some pictures to help us.'

'What pictures?'

'You see, we'd had our photo taken with the team in the truck.'

To coincide with what Dan is saying, the pictures he is talking about pop up in a montage of shots.

'Yeah, those pictures. You can see quite a lot of the equipment in the background. And it just went from there.'

Rose knows that this next bit is going to get complicated, so she tries to summarize each point and break down the story into digestible chunks for the viewers.

'So you've vaguely sussed out the kit from the pictures. And then of course my cameraman coming to your house with the kit in his car gave you the perfect opportunity to tamper with it?'

'Well, yes and no. The beauty of our plan were that we wouldn't need to actually touch the kit or tamper with it in any way in order to hijack it; we could do everything remotely. But, saying that, it were very helpful that Jonesy turned up with it, because it meant we could get a good look at it and check our plan were gonna work.'

'And did you tell Jonesy this plan?'

'Of course not – he might have told someone and stopped the whole thing happening.'

'So how did you get him to show you the kit? In fact, how did you even know he had it with him?'

'To be honest, what with all the drama, I'd forgotten Jonesy were even coming around until he arrived on the doorstep. And then as soon as he walked in he started going on about having to travel with the camera and mics and everything because the truck kept getting broken into. So I just asked him if he'd show me and CJ how it all worked. We didn't tell Jonesy our plan, we just told him we were interested, that's all.'

'And from that you worked out how to hijack my earpiece?'

'Yeah, it's not that different to pirate radio. Talkback—' Before Dan can continue, Rose cuts in.

'Just to remind everyone, "talkback" is the system that allows people to talk to me through my earpiece.' Rose takes her earpiece out and holds it up to the camera, along with the talkback box it's connected to.

'Yeah,' says Dan. 'It works using a radio signal. You use a spectrum analyser to scan the radio frequencies in the area where the talkback is being used, and once you know which frequency it's on, all you have to do is use a high-powered transmitter to override the existing radio frequency. Essentially, you're over-modulating the existing frequency.'

'It sounds like quite a technical operation.' Rose says this to make sure the viewers at home don't feel daft if they can't keep up with it all.

'Not if you know what you're doing,' Dan replies with half a smile.

'Right, but what about all the kit, like the spectrum analyser? Where did you get that from?'

'CJ borrowed it from work.'

'So you'd worked out all the technical stuff and got the right kit, but the other key part of this story is me.'

'Well, yes, and I am so sorry we had to do this, Rose, but I honestly felt it were our only option for this to work.'

'What people watching don't know is that, in order to get me to put your questions to Charles Barrow, you told me you had kidnapped my wife and my son.' Saying this out loud again was hard. She concentrated hard on not letting her voice wobble.

'Yes, sorry.'

'And what made me believe that you had them was the fact you knew their names. You even knew the name of my son's nursery, which he is no longer at, I should add.'

'Yes.'

This is one of the bits of the story where Rose knows she'll be hearing stuff for the first time. She fixes her eyes on Dan and concentrates solely on the questions she needs to ask. She does not want to show any emotion. This is about Ollie, not her.

'How did you find that out? Because, before all this happened, it was not public knowledge.'

'I heard you say them.'

'What do you mean? I have never talked about my son or my partner at work.'

'When I were at the truck, you were on the phone. I don't know where you were standing, but I could hear what you were saying coming through the speaker in the truck. I heard you talking to someone called Kate about getting Rory to nursery. I only remembered the names because Ollie were originally gonna be called Rory. And Kate were my mother's name.'

Rose had left her microphone on when she phoned her wife that morning between the live broadcasts.

'But I don't think I would have mentioned my son's nursery name in that call, because my partner knows the name. So how did you work that out?'

'You'd mentioned to Kate about the best road to park on now the roadworks had started. It were Croft Avenue. Again, with that being my surname, I remembered it. So, when I decided I were going to pretend I had your family, I just googled nurseries in Manchester near or on Croft Avenue.'

It now all makes sense to Rose. It was her own stupid fault he got all the details. What an idiot she had been, leaving her microphone on. Still, it had brought her the best story of her career so far, so she couldn't be too angry.

Rose carries on questioning Dan.

'But how did you know that I would fall for this and believe you actually had them? For all you knew, I could have assumed it was one of my team playing a practical joke on me?'

'Because I had also worked out that you had a stalker . . .'

Rose tries not to show the shock she is now feeling from hearing this new piece of information.

'I knew you'd probably be worried that something might happen to them,' Dan says. 'You were vulnerable.'

'How did you know I had a stalker?' Rose snaps, trying to avoid the fact that the nation has now heard her being called vulnerable, which she hates.

'Because I saw how you reacted that day you were at my work and that weird man turned up at the site to see you. You looked genuinely terrified.'

Rose had to agree with him. She was scared, and it would have been obvious to anyone who saw her when Billy Rubin turned up at the construction site. She was right to be scared too. Later that same day, Billy murdered Janet Jacobs. Another drama Rose had had to deal with in the aftermath of all this. When he was caught, the police found him with a list of names of people who he believed had wronged Rose. A hit list. Janet was the first and thankfully the last name on the list that he managed to get to. Thank God, because Kate's name was on there too.

It made Rose sick when she thought about it. Still, Billy Rubin was locked away now. Hopefully for ever.

Forcing herself back into reporter mode, Rose challenges Dan: 'It's all very convenient that you heard these things accidentally. You must understand why it took the police a while to believe that this wasn't planned months in advance.'

'Yes, and I totally get that. But that's my point. When all those things happened, it were like a sign to me that I had to do it. Like Ollie were sending me all the signals to help me stop that man doing anything like this again.'

'I can see that,' Rose says, and she can. Since having her son, she's been way more sentimental. 'So, having decided how you were going to do it, what next?'

'Once the kit were sorted, we drove up to the RAS site and did a recce.'

'What did that involve?'

'Well, we used a Wisy to work out . . .'

Rose interrupts to explain to the audience that 'Wisy' is short-hand for Wisycom, the wireless kit that is used for remote audio transmissions. She'd used them a few times when she was a radio reporter. It's basically a portable satellite system.

Dan picks up again. 'Yeah, we used that to work out what the signal were like around the site and where the broadcast truck were most likely to park.'

'But how did you do that without getting on to the site?'

'We did go on the site. Well, I say "we", it were actually just me. CJ stayed on the outside and followed me round the perimeter.'

This is the bit Rose has always found hard to believe.

'How on earth did you get into RAS? It's one of the most secure companies in the world.'

'Yeah, it is, and we didn't go fully inside. Like I say, we only needed to do a quick scoot round the perimeter with the kit to see where the doors were with the best signal. We knew one of them, probably a fire door, would be used to give the truck access, so we just needed to work out where that were most likely to be.'

'But I still don't understand how you got in? We needed ID to get past the first gate for a start.'

'We nicked Jonesy's passport out of his coat pocket when he were at mine.'

'You stole my cameraman's passport? But you look nothing like Jonesy. How did you get past the gate when you showed them the passport? And also, we had chaperones when we were at the site, so how did you get away with all that?'

'I've worked in security for twenty years, I know exactly how to get past a gate. Like I say, we didn't need to get fully inside the building, so I rocked up at a time when I knew the lads on the gate would be watching the football. The local derby were on, so I had a bit of banter with them about the game. They had my name – sorry, Jonesy's name – on the list for the next morning and they didn't really look at the passport. I explained I were only doing a quick recce outside of the building, so they let me through.'

'That is incredible. I wasn't even able to go to the toilet without having someone with me. It's mad to think you were just let in.' Rose's genuine surprise is clear for all to see.

'If I'd wanted to go inside the buildings it would have been a different ball game. A quick drive around the perimeter in a car were low risk, plus they thought I were Jonesy, who would have gone through loads of security checks to be put on that list in the first place.'

'But then weren't you worried you'd get found out when Jonesy turned up the next morning?'

'It were a risk, but, like I say, the lads were watching football and it were dark.'

'But weren't you worried Jonesy wasn't going to get in because you had his passport?'

'No, I knew he had a spare.'

'How?'

'He told us.'

'He told you an awful lot in that hour he spent at your house, didn't he?' Rose knows that this is all very likely because Jonesy is one of life's oversharers.

'Well, yeah, he is a bit of a talker, like, but that's cause he is a nice lad. He were telling CJ about his life in the army and how he had two different passports. So, depending on which country he is going to, he'll pick which passport he uses. That's when CJ knew to nick the one he told us were in his coat.'

Rose knows the audience are going to find this story unbelievable, so she wants to acknowledge that.

'This story is one of the craziest things I've ever heard.'

Dan is quick to reply before Rose can say anything else.

'It's also the craziest thing I've ever done. And not summat I
were ever expecting or wanting to do either.'

Rose smiles at Dan. It's a fair point.

'Let's go back to the hijack. You've done the recce and worked
out the nearest place you need to be on the outside of the site.
So then what happens?'

'We set up outside Plumpy's Palace, which we were pretty
sure were gonna be the best spot. Actually, I had a panic that
you'd seen me there. I saw you in a taxi when I got out of my
car to get set up. I thought you looked at me, but fortunately
you drove off.'

Rose recalls the silhouette of the man she saw that morning,
mistaking him for a customer heading into Plumpy's. She keeps
that to herself and lets Dan carry on.

'Once we were set up, it were a waiting game. We did what
we needed to with the spectrum analyser and the transmitter.
Then we did a few test runs to check that we could definitely
take control of the signal and talk to you.'

'What do you mean, test runs? Did you speak to me before
the chancellor interview?'

'Yes, CJ did, when you first went on air.'

'What did he say to me?'

'Oh, I don't know, just something like "testing, testing".'

Rose remembers that exact moment. It was when she stumbled
through her first headline. It was so weird to look back on it all
now and think about what she had thought of as inconsequen-
tial things. They all led up to one of the biggest moments in her
life. That day had brought her the greatest terror she had ever
felt and also given her worldwide fame. The whole thing was

mind-blowing. And yet there was still so much more of the story to tell.

'So you'd proven it worked and then it was just a case of waiting for the chancellor to come on?'

'Yes, we knew that we couldn't go in all guns blazing, it needed to be a slow build. Lull him into a false sense of security.'

'Ah, so that's why the questions you gave me to ask him were easy?'

'Yes, kind of, they were still relevant in some way, but we wanted him to think you were giving him an easy ride.'

'You must have known that my team would have noticed I was asking unusual questions, though?'

'Yeah, we knew early on that your guys would suss that you'd been hijacked, so that's why we then . . .'

Rose finishes Dan's sentence to make it more dramatic than Dan will.

'Blackmailed my colleagues?'

'Well, yeah, I suppose you could put it like that.'

'And you did that by messaging them to tell them that I was being controlled by you and they had to keep the broadcast running or you would harm my wife and son.'

'Well, no, we never said we'd harm them,' Dan corrects Rose.

'But that was the implication from the message?'

'Well, yeah.'

'Did you not think they'd just call my partner and find out she hadn't been kidnapped?'

'Yeah, I did, but I knew she probably wouldn't answer.'

'How could you have possibly known that?'

'Because she were gonna be in an important meeting. You mentioned it on the call I overheard. About the bad timing of it all. Her meeting, your interview.'

Rose knows that Dan is right. Because of the time difference with China, Kate's funding meeting was at 7 a.m. The only call she would have left that meeting to take would have been one from their nursery mam friend Lisa, who had Rory at that time. Even Rose calling didn't get an answer, not until the fourth try, so a random call from anyone else would have had no chance of being answered during that meeting.

Rose feels a pang of sadness at the reminder that she'd always put the needs of her job first. She should have been at home that day, supporting Kate. She also should never have said as much as she did about her private life with a microphone on. Too late now. Plus Rose has learned her lesson. And, more importantly, things have changed at home. The dynamic has shifted. Not least because Kate did get the funding she was working so hard for and Rose couldn't be prouder of her. What a life-changing day it had been for both of them.

'So you've worked out my partner probably won't answer the phone to my team, but how on earth did you even get my team's numbers to blackmail them?'

'They were on that original document I saw in your producer's car.'

That made total sense to Rose. Those documents would have team contact details on, along with the broadcast location address and hotels etc. She realized that they'd accidentally given him a blueprint for the hijack.

'So you messaged the programme producer in the studio, Danielle, and the editor of our show, Gary, and also my producer, Zoya, whose car battery you had fixed the day before. And then what?'

'Well, then we let the interview build until we had everyone's attention.'

'You made me ask easy questions. But why? It kept the chancellor there, because he was enjoying it, but were you not worried people would turn off with boredom?'

'No, because you have a reputation for being a fierce interviewer, so we hoped that the viewers who see you every morning would start to question what were wrong, why you were suddenly giving him a free ride. Plus CJ set up loads of fake accounts and put out stuff on social media to encourage the chatter.

'Yes, I understand he started the hashtag "rosemeltdown"?'

'Yeah, sorry about that. Anyway, the idea were that if it went viral, that would then encourage more people to tune in and see what were happening.' Dan is in his stride now, explaining all this, and any nerves he had at the beginning have gone. He carries on.

'I mean we didn't really know if it would work, but CJ, who knows way more about telly and social media than I do, were confident it would.'

'Yes, it's just worth reminding everyone that CJ was the person who put out the viral TikTok video filmed inside Downing Street, the one that led to the downfall of the previous prime minister.' While Rose says this, a montage of headlines from the time appears in a graphic behind her, along with a shot of CJ's TikTok page.

'But why not just get me to ask straight away about Ollie? That would have got everyone's attention too.'

'I suppose we thought as soon as we − sorry, *you* − confronted him and mentioned Ollie, he would try to leave.'

'And you were right: as soon as I said Ollie's name, he left.'

'Yeah, and it were then we released the video, which showed him, that man, meeting Ollie in Downing Street.'

'Why didn't you release that earlier?'

'We only realized we had it in the middle of the hijack. The lads' old headteacher tipped us off about it.'

While Dan explains this, the video he is talking about plays in the background without sound. It slows down at the point where Ollie can be seen talking to Charles Barrow.

'But it didn't stop there, did it?' says Rose.

Rose has not been looking forward to this bit, but still, it has the wow factor she knows will make this interview even more shocking.

'No, we still wanted that man to say what he'd done. So that's when we brought in our secret weapon.'

'Yes, your secret weapon.'

The floor manager is back in Rose's eyeline to confirm that she does have their next guest on standby ready to walk on to the set.

Rose turns to the camera to say this next bit. She is purposefully taking her time to build the drama. She wants everyone at home to be hanging on her every word, even though it involves giving air time to someone she has always hated.

'Ladies and gentlemen, I would now like to introduce you to Arabella Pinchinthorpe, special adviser to Charles Barrow when he was chancellor.'

Arabella walks in and takes a seat next to Dan.

Rose takes a few seconds before she speaks again. She knows that people watching will all be shocked by this latest revelation so she wants to play on that for a moment.

She imagines everyone at home will be letting out a collective gasp.

Then, once Arabella is settled in her chair and a few seconds have passed, Rose speaks again.

'Arabella, thanks for joining us. Now, you and I go back a long way. You were a journalist here before you went into the civil service. And it was you, described by Dan here as the secret weapon, who helped bring down Charles Barrow, wasn't it?'

Arabella nods and smiles.

'Rose, thank you for having me. First of all, I'd just like to thank Dan for speaking out and getting justice for Ollie. It was a terrible tragedy that should never have happened.'

Rose knew she'd do some worthy speech before she answered the question, but she just lets her get on with it.

'I first met Dan when he contacted the government about Charles. Having just lost his son Ollie a few years earlier, he was desperate to find out what had happened in the months leading up to his death. Dan had emailed one of our generic press email addresses and eventually it got forwarded on to me. What I read was unbelievable.'

'Right, but you believed him?'

'Well, yes and no. I had no reason not to believe that parts of it might be true, but equally it did seem a huge stretch for it all to be true. How wrong I was.'

'So what did you do about it? Surely someone in your position could have got this properly investigated?'

'Well, you say that, but no one wanted to listen and every attempt I made to thoroughly investigate it was stopped.'

'By Charles?'

'Yes, him, but also the senior managers I worked for in the Treasury.'

'So then what happened?'

'Well, I had to email Dan and tell him there was nothing more I could do,' Arabella says. She looks to Dan and lightly touches his arm for a moment before she continues. 'It was a cold, heartless email, and I regret not standing up for Ollie more at the time, but I was getting nowhere and my job was being threatened.'

Before Rose can speak, Dan sits up in his chair and protests: 'Arabella is doing herself down here. You have to remember, we were dealing with some of the most powerful and arrogant men in the country. They intimidate and threaten, and I don't blame Arabella for the email. I were raging with her at the time, cos I thought she were covering it up, but I know now she were just as much in the dark as me. We were both being fobbed off.'

Rose doesn't want everyone feeling too sorry for Arabella.

'But Arabella did have more power than you. She could have gone to the police.'

'It's true,' says Arabella. 'I didn't do enough, and I am incredibly regretful about that.'

Rose is happy Arabella isn't going to emerge from this looking too perfect, so she moves it on. The story is about to get complicated again so she needs to do some more unpicking.

'Right, so let me get this straight . . .' She turns to Dan. 'Arabella went back to you saying she couldn't help, but then obviously she did.' Rose looks between the two of them. 'How did that come about?'

'I'll be honest,' says Arabella, 'I tried to forget all about the email from Dan, but there was something niggling away at me. I started to notice things that unsettled me.'

'Like what?'

'Well, for example, I realized that everyone who came in on work experience was a young lad who was always presented to me as being one of Charles's "family friends". I hadn't thought about it before – nepotism is alive and well in politics, so I had no reason to question it. But after Dan's email, I began to see everything in a new light. Including the time I walked in on him naked.'

'Pardon, what?'

Arabella nodded. 'One morning I was due to brief Charles in his hotel room, but was running late. I'd messaged him to say so and he suggested the work experience boy should get the briefing underway and I could take over when I got there. Unfortunately for Charles, I made it in on time in the end. I didn't bother telling him, I just arrived at his room at the same time as the work experience boy, and when we opened the door he was sitting there naked. He panicked when he saw me. I assumed that was because he was embarrassed about being naked. Obviously I now know the real reason he panicked.'

'Whoa, so there were loads of red flags then?' Rose knows she sounds passive-aggressive, but she can't help herself.

Arabella quickly comes back at her.

'Well, yes, but sometimes you only see red flags if you're looking for them, Rose.'

'So then what happened?'

'Well, by chance, one of the young men who came in for work experience after Dan's email was Louis Carmichael. And I'm sure your viewers will remember me mentioning his name to Charles in the confession broadcast, when I confronted him about what happened to Ollie.'

'Yeah, you mentioned Louis being one of the lads at Charles's parties.'

'That's right. And I knew that because, while he was with us, I asked Louis about these so-called parties. He was very, very cagey about it. To the point where he pretended to need the loo to get away from me when I was asking him about it. I could see that, for whatever reason, he did not want to talk about it. So I left it a couple of days and then approached the subject again, this time under the guise of Charles wanting to arrange another one. Louis then let slip that he had been at one and there had been a lad called Ollie there.'

'Did you ask him what happened?'

'I tried, but he totally shut down. He did not want to talk about it at all. That made me even more suspicious.'

'So you had this information now, which proved that Charles was lying. What did you do with it?'

'Well, nothing to begin with, because it still wasn't solid evidence. I knew Louis would just deny it if he was questioned by anyone investigating it and I didn't want to put him through that. He was vulnerable.'

'Yet in the court case Louis turned out to be a key witness for the prosecution. And chose to waive his anonymity.'

'Yeah he did, and it is amazing he did that, but it took us a long time to get him there. Anyway, coming back to the story . . .'

Rose hated the fact that Arabella was so polished and didn't need her in this interview. She just effortlessly glided from one part of the story to another.

'. . . once I had this new information, I had to think of a way to help. I wanted to message Dan, but knew that I couldn't – it was too risky. So I enlisted the help of Quentin.'

'Quentin, the special adviser who was there at the RAS site with you the day of the broadcast?' Rose enquires, trying to identify all the players in this story for the viewers' benefit.

'Yes, he was also the work experience boy I mentioned who was the intended target for Charles's nakedness a year or so ago.'

'Ah, right. I see. So go on.'

'Well, first I had to establish where his loyalties lay. I didn't want to get myself sacked by telling him about my suspicions and then have him run off and tell Charles. So I just started to drop a few hints now and again about it all and he took the bait and told me he had heard the rumours too from other young men working in the office.'

'Gosh, it sounds like everyone knew.'

'Yes, I know. Hiding in plain sight.'

'So then what?'

'I decided the best thing to do would be to contact Ollie's best friend, CJ. We had his details from the Downing Street debacle, when we had to speak to him as part of the investigation into what happened. So I got Quentin to contact CJ on social media.'

'Why Quentin, not you?'

'I thought it would be too risky for me to do it. Quentin being the same age as CJ would be easier to justify if it ever came out.'

'And what did you get him to say?'

'That we were going to try to help him and Dan get justice for Ollie, but that it might take some time.'

'And, Dan, CJ told you this?'

'Yes, he did, which made me think very differently about Arabella. I could see then there were a chance she were on our side. That were a big deal for me. It were the first time I felt believed, y'know.'

Arabella speaks again before Rose can ask another question.

'So, the night before the hijack, Dan rang me, didn't you?'

'Yes, I did.'

'How did you get her number?' Rose asks, determined to get back in on the interview.

'It were also on that sheet in the car that morning.'

Dan was right. Arabella's number would have been on the list as the contact for the chancellor.

'So you rang Arabella. And what did you think, getting that call, Arabella?'

'Well, I was obviously shocked. Dan's call didn't make a lot of sense to begin with,' she says, placing a hand on his arm.

God, she is good, Rose thinks to herself.

'And, Dan, were you not worried she'd spill the beans?'

'Yeah, course I were, but she were the only chance I had.'

'So what happened?'

'Once I'd got over the initial shock and put the millions of reservations I had to one side, I realized there was a chance that between us we would get him to admit to at least some of it. Charles is an arrogant man who thinks he is untouchable, I knew that there was no way he would ever say it on air, but there was a chance he would say it to me afterwards, if he thought I was helping him and he was in a highly stressful situation, like being humiliated on television and then being stuck with me without his phone.'

'Arabella, were you not worried you'd lose your job?' Rose asks.

'Of course I knew I'd probably lose my job and possibly be arrested. But, no matter how posh you think I am, I still don't believe in the rich and powerful not being accountable. I wanted Ollie to get the justice he deserved after what happened to him.'

'So, coming back to the technicals for a minute, several people saw you take his microphone off as you walked him out of the door.'

'I did – but I attached it to my jacket, discreetly. I knew, given we wouldn't be inside a loud factory any more, the microphone would be able to pick up what he was saying if we sat close enough – and the golf buggy was the perfect place for that.'

'Of course the other twist to this is that Dan was driving the golf buggy. How on earth did you pull that off?'

'Well, that was a bit of a last-minute move, wasn't it, Dan?' Arabella says, raising her eyebrows.

'Yeah,' Dan says sheepishly. 'I think I just wanted to be able to look him in the eye, y'know. The original plan were to have no driver.'

'We needed Charles to think that he was about to be rushed out of there, like I would normally do in my job. I needed him to trust me, but we couldn't move him because then the microphone would go out of range and we'd lose the signal to the truck.'

'In other words, the audience wouldn't be able to hear what you were saying if you moved too far,' Rose adds, to help the audience make sense of all this.

'Yes, so we needed him stationary, but with him thinking he was about to be rushed off. That is why I sent Quentin with the chaperone to prepare his car to leave at the security gate. Obviously that was just to get him and the chaperone out of the way while I got the confession from Charles in the golf buggy.'

'That all makes sense. So now, Dan, tell me, how did you end up in the buggy?'

'Quentin helped, but it were a bit of a snap decision on my part, which I didn't actually tell Arabella about – sorry,' he says, looking at her apologetically.

'It's OK, although it could have compromised the whole thing,' Arabella explains. 'What Dan benefitted from was Charles being an ignorant snob. Anyone doing a job like driving is invisible to him in an intellectual sense. He talked openly in front of Dan because he assumed he was thick.'

'Which I am, to be fair,' Dan says, half laughing.

'Don't do yourself down. You are the cleverest man I've ever met,' Arabella says to Dan with a smile.

Rose nods in agreement, inwardly annoyed that she didn't say it herself.

'So Charles did end up confessing. How did it feel, when you heard those words coming out of his mouth, Dan?'

'I just couldn't believe it. We'd spent so long with no one believing us. And then when he said it — well, like I said, I just couldn't believe it.'

'And yet he had no idea he'd confessed on telly, did he?'

'Nope, not until you turned up. That were the nail in the coffin, that. His face. It were a picture. We'd finally got him.'

'And of course that confession led to a huge investigation, which saw several other victims come forward and ultimately unearthed a powerful grooming ring at the heart of Westminster.'

As Rose says this, a picture appears behind her showing the mugshots, names and convictions of the men she is talking about. In the centre is Charles Barrow.

There is silence for a moment while the graphicized montage of the men fully plays out.

Dan then speaks again.

'It won't bring back our Ollie, but at least we have stopped that man and his disgusting mates from hurting anyone else.'

Rose nods and then picks up again. 'And, of course, off the back of this a new law is being tabled in Parliament. Ollie's Law, which means that any accusations of abuse against senior personnel will always be thoroughly investigated by the police. No matter what.'

Dan smiles. 'You see, Rose, Ollie did change the world for the better in his own way. I hope, wherever he is now, he can see that and be proud of it, because I am so proud of him. My son, Oliver Croft.'

'And I don't doubt Ollie would be proud of you too,' Rose says, tears welling up in her eyes. She needs to hold it together to wrap up the interview.

Rose thanks Dan and Arabella, then turns to the camera to deliver her closing words. All she can think about is her own son. As she says goodbye, the tears start streaming down her face.

The voice in her earpiece speaks to her.

'Thanks, Rose. We're off air.'

ACKNOWLEDGEMENTS

To the readers. Thank you for giving me your time. Hopefully it wasn't a waste of it! There are so many great books out there by lots of talented authors, so thank you for letting me take up a little space in your head to tell you my story.

It's a story I dreamt up from my years working in live telly. So I want to say thanks to all the colourful characters I've met and collaborated with along the way. Especially to my breakfast and lunchtime TV show families. Not only did they make me look and sound better than I actually am, they also inspired me. They are a big part of this story too. I will now, however, stop asking them 'what would you do if this broadcast got hijacked?' while we're in the middle of a show. I really hope, from this book, you get a sense of how hard the people behind the scenes in telly work. They are the real TV 'talent'.

The stories and characters are all made up, obviously. Apart from Jonesy and his dog Murphy – they are very real and I hope you love them as much as I do, although Jonesy will tell you that he is much funnier than I have portrayed. Two other very real and important people from the TV world are the camera and sound experts, who made sure that everything I wanted to happen could technically happen. So thank you, Ollie Riches and Tom Steedman.

This story is also one that comes from the heart and from growing up in a place constantly slagged off. It's northern at its core, but I hope that, wherever you're from, you can see that this is about everyone who has ever been underestimated because of their background.

Now to my book mates.

This novel would never have got off the ground without three formidable women: my good friend and neighbour, Ann Cleeves (you might have heard of her, I believe she has written some decent crime novels); her former publicist, Maura Wilding; and the person who would go on to become my commissioning editor, Francesca Pathak. While everyone was baking banana loaves in lockdown, I was encouraged by these three legends to write a book. I didn't think I could do it, but they convinced me I could.

The process was one of stops and starts. I wrote the first 15,000 words of a story I'd been thinking about for decades. But then, with a new baby, a daily TV show and a crisis of confidence, I stopped. Fran, however, refused to let me. Stalking is probably too strong of a word to describe what she did next, but it's not far off. This included turning up at my house in Tynemouth (she lives a three-hour train ride away) for a chat and a walk along the beach — way before I'd signed a book deal. So thank you, Fran, for believing in me and for making this so much fun. It has never felt like work. This book is also a million times better than it would have been without her. I just bloody love Fran. And our days of listening to the *Bridgerton* soundtrack while editing the book will long stay with me.

I like to surround myself with formidable women (who doesn't?), so there are more I need to thank. Val McDermid, Nicola Sturgeon and Cecelia Ahern — thank you for reading the early drafts of my book and giving me such invaluable notes.

I've mentioned Ann Cleeves – but also many of her team behind the scenes have been a great support to me over the years too, including her publicist Emma Harrow and her former commissioning editor Vicki Mellor.

Next up I want to thank the Theakston Old Peculier Crime Writing Festival in Harrogate. For the past ten years, it's been the highlight of my social calendar. I've always been a big crime fiction fan, but getting to be part of this event every year, whether it's to interview authors or judge the Crime Novel of the Year, has been a massive treat. I was also buzzing when they let me launch my book at the festival, with the help of my mate Richard Osman (you might have heard of him, I believe he's also written some decent crime novels).

Talking of crime authors, can I give a shout-out to some of my faves? Harlan Coben, M. W. Craven, Lisa Jewell, Gillian McAllister, Steve Cavanagh, Adrian McKinty, Jo Callaghan, Fiona Cummins, Liz Nugent, Sarah Vaughan, Araminta Hall – to name a few. Thanks for writing such cracking books that I have learned so much from.

The book world is mad. Steering me through it has been my fabulous literary agent, Millie Hoskins at United Agents, and a crack team at Pan Macmillan, led by two publishing rock stars, Joanna Prior and Lucy Hale. Thanks for taking a chance on me. I've mentioned my commissioning editor, Fran, but also working with her is Emily Sumner. Keeping me right throughout the editing process was the marvellous Melissa Bond. And a big shout-out to the legend that is Anne O'Brien for pointing out that I say 'really' far too often. Really? I love the cover and that is thanks to designer Siobhan Hooper. I also want to give a thank-you hug to publicity queens Laura Sherlock and Poppy North, who are not only brilliant, but great fun too. I just want to hang out with them all the time.

And I would be nowhere without the sales team: Christine

Jones, Stuart Dwyer, Leanne Williams, Rory O'Brien, Ruth Brooks, Richard Green, Andy Belshaw and Jamie Forrest (in marketing). So thank you for all your graft too.

Life would be boring and less rewarding without my talented agent, Matt Nicholls, and his impressive sidekick, Tom Kehoe. Not since Mario and Luigi has there been a more iconic duo. I am very lucky to have them in my life.

And, finally, to my actual family. Thank you for putting up with me. For letting me be me, which means regularly bringing chaos into our world with my random career curveballs. This book has been living with us for years and, at times, it has taken over our holidays and our lives. Thank you for always supporting me. Being loved is the best feeling in the world and I never take that for granted. So thank you, especially to my partner and my daughter – my rocks.

ABOUT THE AUTHOR

Steph McGovern is an award-winning broadcaster who currently presents the podcast *The Rest Is Money* with Robert Peston. Steph has worked in journalism for more than twenty years, eight of those as part of the *BBC Breakfast* family. She went on to present her own BAFTA-nominated live daily show, *Steph's Packed Lunch*, on Channel 4 and is a regular *Have I Got News for You* panellist and host. Steph is an avid crime reader, has interviewed countless authors, including Val McDermid, Ann Cleeves, Hillary Clinton, Harlan Coben, Lee Child and Don Winslow, and has judged the Theakston Old Peculier Crime Novel of the Year Award at the Harrogate Crime Festival since 2019. *Deadline* is her first novel.

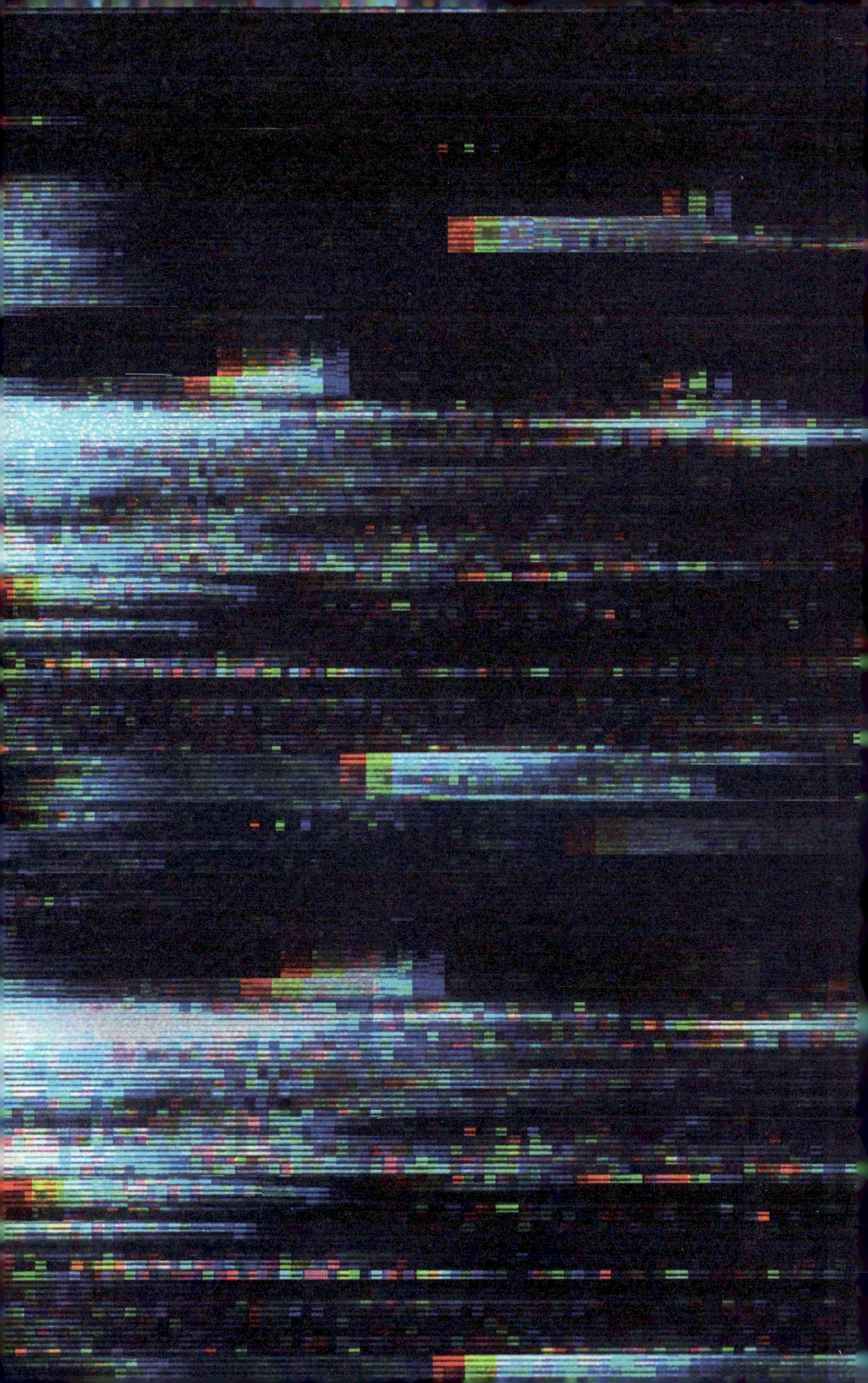